Praise for *Laura's Shadow*

"Allison Pittman is one of those rare a[uthors who writes with bril]-liance no matter the time period she writes. *Laura's Shadow* is the perfect showcase for the gritty nineteenth-century historical on the South Dakota prairie, and the 1970s Twin Cities tale of an utterly lovable newspaper cartoonist on a quest to unlock her great-grandmother's secrets. Pittman breathes life and love, hope and heartache into a minor character first penned by Laura Ingalls Wilder, and then surrounds her with her own world, complete with generations to round her out. I couldn't read this absorbing story fast enough."

– Jocelyn Green, Christy Award-winning
author of *Drawn by the Current*

"It's a daring endeavor to take even a tangential run at another author's famous characters, but rest assured, Dear Reader, the world of our beloved Laura Ingalls Wilder is in more than capable hands in Laura's Shadow. Pittman weaves a wonderful dual timeline story showing how the past reaches out to the present, and how 'no man is truly free in whom a thousand ancestors ride.'"

– Erica Vetsch, author of The Thorndike &
Swann Regency Mysteries

"*Laura's Shadow* is an expertly layered book about generational patterns and stories woven from love and loss. Readers will fall in love with the Gowan women—earnest Trixie, an artist pursuing a career in 1974, and her great-grandmother Mariah who comes of age in late 19th century South Dakota. Both eras are vividly painted and every scene engrossing. It was a challenge to put the book down at bedtime (so I just didn't.) Another gorgeous novel that serves to further Allison Pittman's reputation as a uniquely gifted author."

– Kimberly Duffy, author of *A Tapestry of Light*

"Pittman's novels have the ability to immerse and transport readers to the past, and her latest, *Laura's Shadow*, is no exception. Rich prose, lush descriptions, and astute characterizations combine to weave a story wrought from minor characters in Laura Ingalls Wilder's beloved books, as well as a more modern counterpart. A nostalgic tale told with heart and insight."

– Anna Lee Huber, *USA Today* bestselling author

"Allison Pittman has crafted a stunning book of two women, three generations apart, deftly weaving their stories into an unputdownable tale. Pittman writes gorgeous prose that tugs at the heart even as it fills the reader with hope. This is a book not only for fans of *Little House on the Prairie* but for anyone who enjoys a captivating story. I loved it!"

– Liz Johnson, bestselling author of *The Red Door Inn* and *Beyond the Tides*

LAURA'S *Shadow*

ALLISON PITTMAN

BARBOUR
PUBLISHING

Laura's Shadow © 2022 by Allison Pittman

Print ISBN 978-1-63609-350-5

Adobe Digital Edition (.epub) 978-1-63609-351-2

All scripture quotations, unless otherwise noted, are taken from the King James Version of the Bible.

This book is a work of fiction. Names, characters, places, and incidents are either products of the author's imagination or used fictitiously. Any similarity to actual people, organizations, and/or events is purely coincidental.

Cover Photograph: Magdalena Russocka, Trevillion Images

Published by Barbour Publishing, Inc., 1810 Barbour Drive, Uhrichsville, Ohio 44683, www.barbourbooks.com

See the series lineup and get bonus content at DoorsToThePastSeries.com

Our mission is to inspire the world with the life-changing message of the Bible.

 Member of the
Evangelical Christian
Publishers Association

Printed in the United States of America

A NOTE FROM THE AUTHOR

$\mathscr{I}$ don't remember the first time I read *Little House on the Prairie*, but I have no strong memory of a reading life that doesn't include the Laura Ingalls Wilder books. When I was in third grade, I wrote a letter to Mrs. Watson, our librarian, complaining that they were housed in the Fiction section when, really, shouldn't they be in Biography? She explained, gently, that there was a difference between the two: She said that biography was the story of a person's life and that what Laura Ingalls Wilder did was to put her life into a story.

Over the years, as my interest in Laura Ingalls Wilder grew and matured, I learned that, of course, details were changed, personages recast and reimagined, timelines resequenced. I cannot recommend highly enough the *Pioneer Girl: The Annotated Autobiography* (edited by Pamela Smith Hill) and the Pulitzer Prize–winning *Prairie Fires: The American Dreams of Laura Ingalls Wilder* by Caroline Fraser for a more in-depth look not only into the life of the Ingalls family but a look at their life in the context of American history.

All that said, this novel, dear readers, is a pure work of fiction, woven completely from my imagination, inspired by my lifelong crush on Cap Garland, a minor character in the latter novels of the Little House series. The sole bits of truth: Laura Ingalls was a teacher for a small school (five students) for a brief moment in time. Two of those students were a brother and sister—Charles and Martha (or Marthe, as Wilder spells it in *Pioneer Girl*)—whom I have conscripted for this story, renaming the girl once more—Mariah. The prologue of this novel retells a scene from Wilder's *These Happy Golden Years* from Mariah's point of view. And while I stayed true to the bullet points of Cap Garland's life and death, every word about Mariah and their paths crossing is just my writer's imagination run wild.

My fellow Little House fans will, I hope, run wild with me.

Allison Pittman

PROLOGUE

The schoolhouse was nothing more than a shack, with sunlight and drifting snow blowing through the spaces between the thin, rough-cut slats. The previous owner, terrified of winter on the South Dakota prairie, had hightailed it back east until spring. Mr. Bouchie had taken it upon himself to make four desks out of scrap lumber, paint a black square on one wall, and bring in a fine table with spooled legs for the front of the room.

It took a moment for Mariah Patterson's eyes to adjust to the dimness after walking a mile squinting against the morning sun. Once they did, she turned to her brother, Charles. "Looks like we're the first ones here."

"Yup." It was Charles's favorite word, and without another, he took a long match from the box on the wall behind the small stove in the corner, lit it, and dropped it in. Their pa had come home from the school board meeting (meaning, coffee at Mr. Bouchie's place) declaring that the first students to arrive at the school were responsible for lighting the fire, and the teacher would lay it ready for the next day. This morning Pa had prodded Mariah and Charles out the door, fearful they might be tardy but also wanting them to be early enough to take on this honor and to welcome the young woman who would be their teacher for the short winter term.

Mariah felt no compulsion to remove her coat and hat while she waited for the first tendrils of warmth to enter the room, but she did unwind her muffler and discard her gloves, stretching her hands toward the little stove in anticipation. Any worries about puddles forming as the snow melted from her skirt disappeared along with the tiny streams that ran into the cracks in the floor. Her cheeks were just beginning to thaw when the room filled with light as the door opened and three more students came in.

"I'll beat you here tomorrow." The boy who issued the challenge had the stature and voice of a full-grown man. Clarence, she remembered. Clarence Bouchie, son of Mr. Bouchie, the self-appointed superintendent. At seventeen, he was the oldest student, followed by Charles, sixteen, and Mariah, fourteen. "I would have today, but I had to cut a path for the little ones."

The *little ones* were hardly more than two mobile mounds of wool, but with each layer peeled off in the warming room, she saw a little boy, Tommy, and a tiny girl, Ruby. They'd all met once, gathered in Mr. and Mrs. Bouchie's parlor—the same meeting in which all the rules and procedures for the school had been set. Mariah remembered Mrs. Bouchie saying, "Please, come sit in the parlor," as if it were something more than a bare room with a single sofa and the table that now sat in the front waiting for the teacher.

"You don't think we might be a little too old for school?" Mariah asked. Besides being close in age to Clarence and Charles, she was nearly as tall and felt like a giant next to the younger Bouchie children.

"Maybe," Clarence said. He had a mop of unruly dark curls that poked out from the fringes of his cap. He took it off and combed them back, revealing dark brows that seemed to dance as he spoke. "But sitting around in a dark cabin is the same whether at home or here, and at least at school there's a chance to look at a pretty girl."

Mariah felt a blush rising but cooled when Clarence elbowed Charles in the ribs and said, "I hear the teacher's not but sixteen."

"And how do you know she's pretty?" Mariah asked.

Clarence shrugged. "I don't know that she's not."

Warm now, Mariah took off her coat and left the tight circle to hang it on one of the hooks beside the door. She herself, she knew, would never be pretty enough to prompt a young man to leave his home to spend a day looking at her. She needed no looking glass to affirm this; she need only look at Charles's face to see her own— long, drawn, with a thin nose that had an incongruous bulbous tip, and wide green eyes dusted with sandy-brown lashes. Unlike Clarence's, Charles's hair was straight and fine, and—as in all other features—Mariah's was the same. But Charles had the enviable advantage of wearing his clipped short, while Mariah was forced by some unspoken mandate to wear hers long, even though the silky texture of it defied any attempt at pinning or curling. For her whole life, or at least since the loss of their mother when Mariah was eight years old, she'd worn her hair in one plait down the center of her back, tied at the end with a scrap of ribbon. Or string, or twine—whatever came closest to hand. Little Ruby had the same thick, dark curls as her oldest brother; Tommy was a towhead blond. But then, the Bouchie family was a mishmash of siblings and half siblings and stepsiblings acquired through a series of marriages and death. (This too she learned at the meeting in the parlor where she sat on the floor with a cup of warm, weak tea and a gingerbread cookie.) She envied the chaos of their household, on full display that evening. The Patterson household consisted of only her father, her brother, and herself, with no one inclined to conversation. In fact, most evenings meant a collective sigh of relief when the sun dipped low enough to send them to their narrow beds.

The schoolhouse door opened one last time, bringing a *whoosh* of cold air into the now cozy room, and suddenly the students' silence seemed less comfortable with the arrival of their teacher.

Mariah's first thought was that the woman was small. Not merely short but diminutive. Taller than Tommy, but then he was a little boy. Her little feet barely made a sound as she walked across the room, and as she approached—drawn by the heat of the stove— she unbuttoned her coat to reveal a figure even tinier than Mariah had speculated.

Nobody spoke, not until Teacher said, "My, it is cold, isn't it?" And they murmured in unison agreement that yes, it was. And then the silence fell again while the clock on the front table ticked out five more minutes before Teacher instructed them all to take their seats.

Class was about to begin.

Clarence volunteered to take the last seat in the room, which made sense because he was the oldest and biggest, but that also meant he would be farthest away from the warmth of the stove. The closest would be Ruby, in the front, then Tommy, then Charles and Mariah who would share a seat because they would also have to share a textbook. And a slate.

When Teacher inquired as to what level reader she and Charles shared, Mariah answered, "*McGuffey's Third*," and tried not to flinch at the teacher's facial expression in response. Was it pity? Disdain? She may as well have *tsked* and said, *Poor prairie children. Barely literate, and here I am their age and already teaching.* What Mariah didn't tell her was that the reader had been their mother's last purchase before succumbing to the illness that took her spirit long before it took her life, or that Mariah had devoured the book within days, reading the passages aloud at her mother's bedside, or that Mariah had taken it upon herself to coach her older brother through page after torturous page. She also didn't mention that she owned three novels herself: *Around the World in Eighty Days, Through the Looking Glass*, and *The Adventures of Tom Sawyer*, each of which she had read a dozen times, portioning out the pages by candlelight in her room. Maybe if she had, things would have been different between Mariah and the teacher. They might have become friends, staying inside while the big boys and the little children played at recess, talking about books and literature and favorite authors. But to do so would leave Charles behind, struggling to recall even the most basic details from the simplest stories. Not that Charles was stupid—far from it. There wasn't a piece of machinery he couldn't repair or build outright if given the materials and time. He could measure and calculate with unwritten precision; his hands were never idle, but they were never meant to hold a book. They hadn't been to a school for more than two consecutive terms since Mama died, always moving to board with one relative after another until Papa built this claim. At each school, when asked about their reading, Mariah answered, "*McGuffey's Third*," and they started on page one.

The first day passed pleasantly enough, as did the first week, though Teacher gave Mariah and Charles a tardy demerit when they were five minutes late arriving that Wednesday morning.

Never mind that we had to break a path for over a mile in two feet of new snow, Mariah thought, hoping the flush she felt on her cheeks would be mistaken for the cold.

"It is important to cultivate good habits," Teacher said, and Mariah noticed her tiny feet barely reached the floor beneath her chair, "and factor in unforeseen circumstances."

"We will try to do better next time," Mariah said. Charles was already in their seat, eyes downcast to the desk. His coat hung on the hook, but Mariah kept hers on not only because she could still feel the cold in her bones but she didn't want to take any more time settling into their lesson. Clarence had been smirking since they walked through the door, and he continued to do so as she walked to her place. When she sat down, he leaned forward, close enough that she brushed her glove against his face as she unwound her muffler.

"Teacher herself only got here ten minutes ago," he whispered. "Don't let her shame you like that."

"I'm not ashamed," Mariah whispered. "I'm determined."

Teacher rapped her knuckles on the table and called for silence, saying that quite enough time had been wasted that morning, and they should conserve their speech for recitations.

The morning passed slowly, and only the boys chose to go outside to play in the snow after eating their dinner. Teacher pulled a chair up to sit with Mariah and little Ruby, and as they finished their bread and butter with bits of pleasant conversation, Mariah took a piece of molasses cake from her tin and broke it into thirds, offering to share it all around. Ruby took hers and chomped into it immediately, heedless of the crumbs that gathered in the corners of her mouth.

"When I was a little girl," Teacher said after taking a single small nibble, "my pa would bring sticks of candy home from the store when he went into town. I would eat mine all at once, but my sister could make hers last for days. I would be so envious, almost like she had more than I did because it lasted longer. I used to beg

Ma and Pa to make her share with me."

"Charles is the same," Mariah said, nibbling too. "Well, not exactly the same. He doesn't care for sweets, so I usually end up eating his share." She thought about the precious bits of sugar and eggs she'd used to make this treat. "I put a piece in his lunch pail, and I'll bet you nine buttons it's in there still and he'll offer it to me on our walk home."

"*Charles.* That's my father's name." The teacher smiled, giving Mariah a peek into the girl she might be if her hair wasn't pinned in a fancy twist, or if she didn't have to ensure they all mastered their arithmetic in the afternoon. She seemed softer after that, to the point of joining in a snowball fight to even up the sides—boys against girls. When Clarence hit her square in the face, she laughed, even as the boy held her steady to wipe the snow out of her eyes with the end of her scarf. Teacher laughed in the moment, but afterward redoubled her effort to maintain discipline and control, especially in regard to Clarence. He was, after all, taller, older, and—Mariah guessed—probably smarter than she. Often, when Clarence would misspell a word or come to the wrong answer on a mathematics problem, Mariah suspected he was fooling them all, not wanting to show off. It was as if there was a taut, thin wire strung between Clarence and the teacher—a tension ready to snap at any moment.

When Friday afternoon of the first week of school arrived, the well of patience and good behavior seemed to have run dry. Clarence was unbearable in his restlessness, constantly flicking Mariah's braid and baiting Charles to misbehave. Tommy knew none of his lessons and had to be reprimanded for lack of applying himself, and even sweet little Ruby whined against instruction. The fire burned low in the stove, bringing the temperature of the room down with it, and nothing in any of the books—not the readers, not the math, not even the Bible—could have enticed anyone into the spirit of learning. Even the teacher's sharp reprimands were incomplete and distracted.

Adding to all of this, the windows looked out on a gray, snow-filled sky, and while the clock ticked its slow, monotonous, regular beat, the snow seemed to be falling faster. The only math Mariah cared about was calculating how fast and how deep the snowfall would be by the time they were dismissed to walk home. There didn't seem to be any danger of a blizzard, but a fresh path was hard work, and the sooner they set out, the easier that work would be. She itched to raise her hand to ask if, since nobody was learning anything anyway at the moment, they might dismiss a little early, when a new sound filled in the tiny bits of silence between the ticking of the clock.

Bells.

Sleigh bells.

Suddenly, all of the restless fidgeting came to a stop while everybody listened. Five students stared straight ahead at their teacher, who stared right back.

Clarence was the first to break the spell, leaping from his seat, running to the door, and throwing it open, heedless of the snow that swirled inside.

"Teacher! Come see!"

But their teacher was already on her feet, unceremoniously ducking under Clarence's arm to step outside. Unfrozen from their places, Mariah, Charles, Ruby, and Tommy ran to the window to look. At first there was only a faint silhouette, obscured by the lacy curtain of fast-falling snow. Ruby clapped her hands and chimed in with the bells. Tommy said, "Look at them horses!" Charles muttered something about the sleigh, but Mariah couldn't speak. At first it almost seemed like the sleigh had arrived driverless, by magic, and not until it pulled up to a stop at the schoolhouse did she clearly see the man buried chest-high in warm hides, reins gripped in gloved hands. He was handsome but unremarkably so, and yet at his arrival, something sparked up in Teacher that none of them had seen before.

"Students," she said, her face and neck flushed in a manner that spoke to a racing heart more than a flash of cold, "we will dismiss a bit early today. So we can get—so you can get home before the storm gets any worser. Any worse. Pack up your things. And Charles, smother the fire in the stove." All the while she was winding her muffler around her neck, perching her hat on her head. Something awoke the gentleman in Clarence, because he stepped behind her to help her shrug into her coat, and little Ruby brought the gloves that had been left to warm on the shelf beside the stove. Then, in a swirl of snow, she was gone as Charles closed the door behind her.

Mariah hadn't left the window, nor had Tommy, though his eyes remained glued to the horses, which he described aloud, from the snow on their forelocks to the impatient swishing of their tails. Mariah, however, hadn't made a single sound. The image of them—Miss Ingalls and her beau, because what else could he be—framed in the window, was like looking at an etching on a Christmas card. In that moment, everything about their teacher transformed. The man reached over her to tuck the robe in over her lap. This, the same woman who could rap on the table and bring the boisterous Clarence to order, became someone who couldn't take responsibility for her own warmth. Her face burst into a smile that none of the students could ever have imagined behind her normally controlled, placid expression, and she emitted a *whoop!* when the horses took flight that made her sound closer to Tommy's age.

They disappeared for a moment, driving around the school, then reappeared in a flash, cutting through the snow in the direction of the house where Teacher was boarding. Mariah pressed her forehead against the cold glass and let her breath steam the window. This wasn't a Christmas card, this was a love story—a gallant hero coming to rescue the damsel in distress. Maybe this shack wasn't a tower, but the prairie loomed as wide as the sky. She could imagine the pounding of Miss Ingalls's heart, because hers pounded the same, only Mariah's was fueled by hope. If little, dour, plain Miss Ingalls could inspire such a grand gesture, surely there might be someone out there who would love her too. Someday.

She cut her glance over to Clarence, the only boy within a million miles, who knelt in front of Ruby, wrapping her muffler up to her eyes.

"Hey, slow poke," he said, looking over his sister's fuzzy head, "better get a move on or we're gonna leave you here to be buried alive. Think you can hold out until Monday?"

Sighing, Mariah took her coat from the hook and was buttoning it as Charles dumped the final shovelful of snow on the fire.

CHAPTER 1

TRIXIE

Minneapolis, Minnesota
Friday afternoon, 1974

*O*n sunny days, Trixie Gowan walked to work. Rainy days too, and even snowy ones, as long as the flakes were lazy and fat, floating harmlessly to land, intact, within the looping stitches of her scarf. It was by no means a short walk. Nearly an hour each way—longer if she fell into strolling or pausing at shop windows or ducking in for a coffee. Walking often meant leaving or arriving home in the dark and in the deepest of winter, both.

"You're going to get murdered," her mother said frequently. "I'm going to turn on the news one day, and there'll be a story about Trixie Gowan, twenty-nine, found strangled in an alley. And that awful driver's license picture on the television."

"I'm not going to get murdered," Trixie would say, fully convinced that her mother dreaded the unflattering photograph more than the hypothetical scenario. "Walking keeps me in good shape. If someone tries to strangle me, I'll fight him off and start running." She'd been a track star in high school—more than ten years ago, but she still ran most weekends, enjoying it more without the pressure of competition.

It's not that Trixie didn't have a car. She did, a 1968 Chevelle she'd bought brand-new with her first city paycheck. Two months ago, March 15 to be exact, she'd sent in the final payment. She was responsible for every mile on the odometer. In the five years of ownership, the seat had never been moved, the mirrors never adjusted, the radio station never changed. The passenger and back seats looked like they did the day Trixie drove it off the lot. She'd calculated the difference between driving and walking to work, and after factoring in the complicated maneuvering through busy Minneapolis traffic, the slow climb to an available parking space in the nearest garage (after circling the city blocks surrounding the *Neighborhood Newz* office building), and the walk from said parking space to her tiny desk in the midst of a pool of a dozen other tiny desks, found it to be a mere fifteen minutes. A brisk walk, without stops or a dreamy gait, could easily shave that down to ten, and ten minutes wasn't worth the hassle. She'd been lucky enough to rent an apartment that came with a garage and was happy to leave the Chevelle (secretly nicknamed "Pumpkin") safely ensconced within.

This morning, mid-June, was glorious. Everything about it demanded attention. She chose a dress that was floral, swingy, and sleeveless, and tossed a white cardigan in her bag for the office. She pulled her hair into a single loose braid, leaving soft tendrils free to frame her face. A new pair of pink Keds meant practical, fashionable comfort. In a flash of inspiration before stepping out, she paused at the machine beside her telephone, lifted the receiver, flipped a switch, and spoke: "Greetings, gentle caller. Outside, spring is blossoming into summer, and I am not letting a moment of it go to waste. Tell me of your adventures, and I shall ring you back to tell you of mine." Finished, the tape whirred its rewinding and she pushed PLAY. The machine played her message crisp and clear, but still she shuddered. *Do I really sound like that?* She'd expected something. . .brighter? Maybe something closer to the ray of morning sunshine pouring through her window or the delectable feeling of new shoes. Something that might make the person on the other end smile, infected by such a cheerful message. But there it was, that familiar, flat quality. More like she was announcing the arrival of a train than the arrival of summer. All in all, it sounded silly.

But it was late, and if she stayed home recording outgoing

messages until she was satisfied, she'd miss work, and her new Keds and pretty dress would go to waste.

"Goodbye, House," she said to the fat tabby cat sitting by the door, impatient for her to leave. "Remember, no girls and no parties while I'm gone."

House responded with a disaffected yawn and went to licking one paw—his usual refuge from eye contact and communication.

Outside she switched her glasses-glasses for her sunglasses—each with a hefty prescription—and shouldered her bag. Her apartment was one of three created in a stately home in a historic neighborhood. Two years ago, her job at *Neighborhood Newz* gave her the advantage—seeing the ad before the paper went to print—and after extensively interviewing her colleagues about the ethics of the act, she met the landlord with the deposit and a promise to care for the cat that came with the house. She never bothered to ask the cat's actual name, and she refunded the cost of the ad from her own pocket.

Because the banister was a bit wobbly and two of the steps in disrepair, she gripped the rail as she descended the front porch. No doubt one of her fellow tenants would bring it up with a note tucked into the rent envelope, but Trixie herself would never lodge a complaint. She liked to tell people she'd lucked into a real-life Mary Tyler Moore bachelorette pad, and she worked hard to stay in the landlord's good graces, tending to the pretty garden flowers that lined the front walk and using Saturday mornings after her run to push a mower across the tiny green stamp of a front yard.

"Well, now, don't you have quite the spring in your step." The voice came from the narrow window-box balcony. Trixie looked up to see Mrs. Claxon in her familiar pink, fuzzy robe, coffee mug clasped in both hands.

"More like summer," Trixie said, now fully turned around. "I'd better get all I can before it's gone."

"Before what's gone?"

"Spring."

"What's that?"

Trixie raised her voice to carry. "Tonight's the solstice. The last day of spring. So if I'm going to have spring in my steps, I have to get it today. Tomorrow I'll have summer in my steps. But nobody ever says that, do they?"

"What?" This time, Mrs. Claxon's question had nothing to do with distance and volume, just the usual response Trixie got when introducing a new concept to the universe.

"Never mind," Trixie said, sending up a wave. "Have a lovely day."

Mrs. Claxon offered her coffee in salute, and Trixie set off on her favorite part of her pedestrian commute. House after house, no two remotely the same, lined the streets of her Linden Hills neighborhood. They came to life in the spring—blossoms overflowing window boxes and lining walkways. Paths winding between the stoop and sidewalk filled with tiny stones and cobbled bricks. Everything that spent the winter under anonymous mounds of snow came to life, and Trixie knew behind each door—those too a parade of different colors and styles—lived a family with a story. Generations of stories like her own. But imagine having your legacy locked away mere steps away from another one.

Her great-grandmother, GG Mariah, had sniffed disapprovingly on her first visit. "I couldn't live with my neighbors peeking straight into my windows," she'd said. "Listening to my affairs over the fence."

"Nobody peeks or listens," Trixie had said, though that wasn't exactly true. When the neighbors next door wanted to hide their rancor from their children, they engaged in hotly whispered tirades that Trixie and Mrs. Claxon listened to while drinking hot chocolate on the back porch. "At least, not to me. Not much to see or hear."

She wondered what it would be like to have an entire home to herself. To be upstairs, quiet with a book, then wander down to get a snack or a cup of tea, then decide to resume her reading in an over-stuffed chair by a front window. To have a choice of space, a variety of rooms—all with solitude under a roof made for a family but belonging solely to her. And House, maybe, if he ever came around.

The neighborhood bled into a series of small stores, with enormous golden arches looming over all. This morning deserved a doughnut, and she stepped into the tiny shop at the end of a ribbon of other tiny shops. It was a rare occasion when the temperature outside perfectly matched the temperature inside, with only the comforting smell of sugar and coffee to separate the two. Feeling generous, she skipped the coffee and opted to buy a dozen mixed to bring to the office—a little sweetness for the last day of spring—and a bag of chocolate doughnut holes for herself.

The strip of shops marked the halfway point of her walk, and she quickened her pace, keeping the doughnut box balanced in one hand, hoping the morning sun would be kind to those with chocolate icing. Walking down Lyndale Avenue brought her into a proper metropolis, and she kept the box aloft through sheer momentum while weaving through the throng of her fellow pedestrians. For a moment, she was aware of being the sole floral sundress in a sea of suits, the only woman with a hand-crocheted shoulder bag and doughnuts rather than a leather briefcase. Of everybody on the street, Trixie's hair was the longest, her shoes the softest, her thoughts least attuned to a bottom line. "Prairie Girl" they called her for her first few months at *Neighborhood Newz*, when her cheeks were still red and chapped from the South Dakota wind. Before her first weekend, she'd trimmed her hair to her shoulders, found the right foundation to balance her complexion, and mastered the subtle art of mascara and lip gloss. The nickname abated once she stopped responding to it.

With one exception.

"Good morning, Prairie Girl." Ronald Tumble's booming voice greeted her the moment she stepped off the elevator on the third floor, as it did most mornings. "And what a beautiful sight you are!" There was a moment, a breath, a tiny little blink when Trixie was sure the compliment was meant for her. A flicker of his eyes on her bare shoulders, a steadying of his steps as he took her in. Thankfully, she was still wearing her sunglasses, so she could hide her own delight at such a perusal. But then, with a rubbing of his hands, he was clearly referencing the box of doughnuts, and he took them from her with reverent care. "I'll take these to the break room."

"Well, thank you, Ron, and good morning," she said with her own level of joviality. "And I think I'll follow you to ensure their safe delivery."

Trixie walked behind him, dropping her bag and sunglasses at her desk. The room went immediately from dark and clear to bright and fuzzy, but she could see well enough to function. Following Ron helped her navigate. He was unmissable, a burly giant of a man who looked like he would be a safe bet in an ax-throwing competition and a nightmare in a bar fight but was actually a kind and gentle spirit stretched over six feet and encased in 250 pounds.

"Now, before I open this box," he said, his sonorous voice filling the tiny break room, "I have to know. Will I find a blueberry cake in there? Coconut? Or are these merely glazed for the masses?"

She reached for her Holly Hobbie mug, a gift from the Secret Santa Swap last Christmas, and filled it with coffee along with a generous pour of sugar and a splash of cream from the fridge. "I asked for mixed, so you never know. But I think you'll be pleased." In fact, she *did* know, and she watched over the rim of her cup, a niggle of anticipation bringing her to her toes as she sipped.

His reaction did not disappoint. His brows raised nearly to the curls that dripped down his forehead, and a full smile burst within his beard. "Get outta town."

"The rare and endangered blueberry cake, glazed, with coconut." She made her voice sound like a woman narrating a nature show.

"You've got the endangered part right." He lifted the thing straight from the box to his mouth, devouring half in a single bite.

"You might want to slow down. Savor it a bit. This was the only one in the case, and according to the girl at the counter, the last of a batch of mistakes. I doubt the blueberry coconut combo will take the doughnut world by storm."

"Thus proving that we live in a world of fools."

He finished the doughnut off in two bites.

This was one of those moments when Trixie thought she might

be slightly in love with Ron Tumble, a thought that popped into her mind, unbidden, at unexpected moments. Like the first time she designed an ad for a local salon, Mane Attraction, with a border of flowing locks and nestled it perfectly on the Lonely Hearts page. He'd tugged at her braid like a schoolboy and said, "Good job, Prairie Girl," and she'd nearly swooned.

But the moment that really mattered, the time when she truly felt her heart would burst through her T-shirt and land square in his massive hands, was the day she'd first shown him *Lost Laura*. The comic, born from her own mystifying transition to life in a city, featured a blond, bespectacled, bewildered girl dressed in a nineteenth-century calico dress and apron. She wore her hair in two long braids, drawn to represent her moods: drooped over her shoulder when she was sad, slightly aloft when she was excited, shaped into a subtle question mark when, as happened often, she was completely at a loss with the ways and workings of the modern world. Her name, Laura, was chosen purposefully, a nod to Trixie's home near De Smet, South Dakota, the heart of Laura Ingalls Wilder fandom. But the figure, Lost Laura, came to life completely from Trixie's own tenth-grade school photo.

The first time she summoned Ron to her desk and shyly offered up the debut drawing, she'd held her breath, waiting. In it, over the course of three panels, Lost Laura stood at a busy intersection, cars whizzing by in broad strokes of ink. The next panel featured the signal image changed to the Walking Man, and the third showed Lost Laura, arms and legs akimbo in replicating the pose, but not taking a single step off the curb. Trixie had designed the story around a neighborhood uproar opposed to the change in traffic signal design, and while she thought it was clever, it seemed too much to think anyone else would.

Until Ron Tumble transformed before her very eyes. Brows furrowed at first, then a slow, spreading smile as he connected with the character, the conflict, and the absurd conclusion. True, the laugh had been little more than a chuckle, but it lifted his massive shoulders in response. He looked over the page at her, then back at the comic, then at her again and said, "*Little Lulu* has some competition."

What followed was a thrice-weekly feature: Mondays, Thursdays, and Saturdays, space allotted for one to four panels. What *didn't* follow was a paycheck, at least not one with a raise in salary that reflected Trixie's new contribution to *Neighborhood Newz*. What started as a lark turned into a labor of sometimes love and finally settled into being its own creative reward. Early cartoons poked gentle fun at Minneapolis local oddities, but those with more generalized appeal were apparently clipped and copied and sent to citizens far beyond the fame-proof borders of *Newz* subscribers. To date, *Lost Laura* was featured in fifteen small Midwest publications, and the envelope dropped on her desk right before lunch promised to change that.

She recognized the return-address logo immediately, a prestigious publishing company, owner of countless papers across the country. And the addressee? Lost Laura c/o Trixie Gowan, the name signed at the corner of each final panel.

The envelope landed at the moment she was engulfed in a complicated design, drawing a series of dogs of various breeds leaping through a sea of bubbles for a local doggie salon. She ignored it at first, until Patrick, the *Newz*'s mail clerk and sandwich runner, said, "You might want to look at that, Miss Trixie," before moving on to the next desk.

Trixie set down her pen and took off her glasses, rubbing her eyes in recovery from the close work, and studied the logo, meaningless to anybody not in the newspaper business. To those who were, it was like a ring on an extended hand of royalty. Her hands were perfectly calm as she opened the envelope but were shaking by the time she read the final line of the letter within. The text was more genial than she'd imagined would come from a big name newspaper mogul, but apparently his daughter had been sending him *Lost Laura* comics for the past year, and he wanted to acquire the rights to feature them in his stream of publications. There was a name and a phone number for her to call and arrange a meeting—herself or her agent as might be applicable—and a sincere wish that

Laura might become a new national treasure.

There was a reason she recognized the return address and logo beyond the industry fame of the company. This wasn't the first letter she'd received. There'd been others—from editors, department heads, acquisitions—but this was *the* guy. The owner. The publisher. Over the course of the previous months, all of the other correspondences had gone unanswered on her part. They'd been vague, one-way missives about setting up meetings and talking through possibilities. This seemed serious. And urgent. And personal. This was the guy, who probably wasn't used to being ignored. She'd kept the others as her little secret, tucked away in her desk drawer, waiting for. . .*what?* Luckily there was no one to ask her that question, because she wouldn't have had an answer. For now, *Lost Laura* lived in a world firmly in Trixie's control, peeking out in three or four panels at a time. Success would change that, and Trixie was not overly fond of change. Still, the tone of this letter promised something more. He wasn't just the head of some conglomeration; he was a father. That paternal image of a man working on behalf of his daughter stirred a familiar longing that announced itself with a burning at the back of her throat and a shadow of pain wrapped around her breath.

She looked up after the third reading to see the entire office gathered at her desk. Ron, as managing editor, front and center, flanked by Joanie and Erin, the classifieds girls; Mack, the advertising sales guy; Bernard, the features writer; Emily, the queen of entertainment and reviews; Gale from recipes and cuisine; Dave from accounts; and Patrick, who must have told each one of them about the missive he delivered to Trixie Gowan's desk. Each of them represented one or the other trajectory of a newspaper career—either young, hungry, and itching to move on to something bigger and better or older, tired, satisfied with a small market and smaller paycheck and a workweek that ended at five o'clock each Friday. Trixie herself sat somewhere in the middle, thankful to have a job that catered to her lifelong addiction to doodling, clueless as to how to turn it into a career. And Ron, she thought, was saddled there with her, content to head up a small staff that acknowledged him with equal parts respect and tolerance.

"So," Ron said, hands thrust into his pockets to rattle his mid-morning Coke machine change, "are we going to lose you to the cutthroat world of national news?"

"He wants *Lost Laura*," Trixie said, refolding the letter and running her thumbnail along the crease. "They've been asking about her for a while, but now I'm to contact my agent and arrange to fly out for a meeting to negotiate a contract."

"I didn't know you had an *agent*," Emily said, breathlessly impressed.

"I don't," Trixie said. "I'm supposed to call this guy."

"I could call for you," Joanie said, "and pretend to be your secretary booking the appointment."

"Are they paying for your flight?" Mack asked. "They'd better be paying for your flight. And your accommodations too. They can afford it."

"And they should take you out to lunch," Gale chimed in. "Dinner too probably. I can call around and get you some recommendations."

"Stop," Trixie insisted, rolling away from her desk and standing to meet their eyes. "I promise to keep all of you in mind every step of the way. But now I need to get back to this doggie shampoo or I'll never meet the Saturday layout. Okay?"

They all murmured affectionately and dispersed, all but Ron. "Can I read it?"

"Of course," she said, having no idea if he even had a right to make the request. She handed over the letter and watched him read, pleased to see his reaction mirror the one he'd had at his first glimpse of *Laura*. Right down to the chuckle.

"Who'd a thought? Our own Prairie Girl, the first of this place to get a big national nibble."

"I don't have anything yet."

"A mere formality. Didn't you notice the name at the bottom? The signature? Keep this for your memoir."

"It's really something, isn't it?" She dropped her voice to a whisper, afraid to voice the hope.

"It might be, Trixie. It might be, and I couldn't be happier for you."

"Maybe I'll take myself out to celebrate. Lunch or dinner? That new burger place Gale reviewed last week." She envisioned a path of invitation between them.

"That's a great idea." He lifted to his toes, as if he needed any additional height to assert his presence in the room. He shouted, "Hey, Dave! How much do we have in the budget for a celebratory lunch?" When Dave shouted the figure back, Ron fell to his flat feet. "Deli sandwiches it is! Today, lunch is courtesy of the *Newz*. Give your orders to Patrick, and we'll eat in the park."

By now Trixie had settled back into her seat, pen uncapped, shrinking from the attention and her obvious inability to flirt her way into a date. Then Ron touched a finger to her chin and raised her face to meet his gaze. His eyes were brown and warm and full of an affection she couldn't quite process. Friendly? Fatherly? She felt herself giving a weak smile in response.

"Thanks, Ron."

"No thanks needed. It's far too pretty a day to waste."

Trixie finished the final details on the dog wash ad, cropped it, and sent it to layout for Monday's paper. The clock read a little after four thirty, so she whiled away the time looking busy—straightening her perfectly straightened desk, washing her mug in the break room sink—all the while thinking about the letter now tucked away in her tote bag. She'd decided to take the weekend, at least, before calling. Maybe even Tuesday or Wednesday. This was Emily's advice.

"Think of it like any other man. You don't want to come off as too anxious. It devalues you."

"So it's like giving myself time to think it over without asking for time to think it over."

"That's right," Emily had said. "It's time for women to stop asking and start taking."

Thus emboldened, Trixie popped her head into Ron's office and *told* him she was cutting out thirty minutes early, if that was all right.

"Got big plans for a Friday night?"

"Yep. Frozen pizza and a bunch of *Lost Laura*s to catalog."

"Sounds wild."

"Couldn't be wilder."

The walk home worked the magic it always did. With each block, her shoulders straightened and the stiffness in her neck and back loosened after so many hours hunched at her desk. The air grew sweeter the closer she got to her home. Summer break in full swing, she dodged children on roller skates and interrupted a jump-rope game and stopped a rollaway basketball beneath her sneaker and held it until a boy ran up, breathless, and took it from her, shouting a *thanks* over his shoulder as he resumed his game. By the time she arrived at her front porch, the streets were much more sedate, and she hummed the little girls' jumping song as she fished her keys out of her bag.

"Hello, House," Trixie said to the cat who draped itself across the back of her secondhand sofa. In response, he stood, stretched, and walked out of the room without a backward glance.

The amber light atop her answering machine flickered with waiting messages. She dropped her bag in the chair next to the table and pushed the Play button, readying herself for her mother's voice.

"Trixie, dear, it's Mom. I know you're at work, but call me as soon as you get home."

A beep and then, *"Trixie, dear. It's me again. Mom. It's a little after one o'clock. I'm sure you're still at work, but if you happen to get home a little early, please call us here at home."*

A beep and then, *"Trixie, dear. It's your mother. I worry that the machine might erase messages after a time, so I just wanted to call again and ask you to call as soon as you get home."*

Over the course of the three messages, Trixie went from bemusement to mild irritation to nascent alarm. Her mother's voice remained cool and controlled—as it did in all circumstances—but this was an unprecedented number of messages, and she'd not yet reached the end.

Beep and a new voice. *"Trixie, it's Grandma. Your mother is beside herself. For the love of peace, call her."*

"I've been at *work*," Trixie said to the machine. "Why didn't you—"

"We didn't want to bother you at work," her grandmother continued with eerily precise timing, *"because we all know that's important to you. But there's important things here too. Call us."*

Trixie was poised to rewind the message tape when the single *beep* indicated one more message. Not her mother or her grandmother, or—of course—her great-grandmother, because by now she'd surmised that the urgent request for her to call home had to be connected with GG Mariah. No, this voice was deep and assured and achingly familiar. So familiar that her knees turned to sand and she clutched at the table to stay upright.

"Trix? It's Cam. Well, Doctor Campbell Carter, I guess. . .but, yeah. Cam. And I think you'd better plan on coming home. Sooner the better. I think it might be. . .time."

Two *beeps* indicated the end of messages. Trixie dropped her bag to the floor and sat in the antique straight-back chair, staring at the framed four-generations photograph on the wall. The photographer had arranged them into something like a diamond, with Trixie—tallest—standing behind her great-grandmother sitting stiffly in a wing-backed chair. Trixie's grandmother, Eugenie, GG's daughter-in-law, rested her sturdy hand on one of the chair's wings, and on the other side, Trixie's pretty, petite mother, Alma, looked like she stepped straight off the set of an old black-and-white television series. Not a man in sight. Eugenie was her usual dowdy, uncomfortable self, and Trixie remembered fighting away a blush at her mother's unabashed flirtation with the photographer. She alone looked *posed*, with her hip jutting and her hand placed perfectly to enhance her narrow waist. Of the four women (Trixie was nineteen at the time), only Trixie and her great-grandmother shared any physical feature, both being tall and lean, their expressions set to something less of a smile and more to indulgence. Their faces so similar, yet separated by two generations, as if an artist had taken a break, experimented in different media, and came back to what was easy and familiar.

Trixie stared into GG's eyes, the only ones like her own. The only person in her life not connected to questions and shame. The woman responsible for all the peaceful, quiet moments of her childhood. The one who would let her read at the table, waste a Saturday away with a book, and hide a flashlight under her pillow so stories could last long after bedtime.

"What is it, GG?" she whispered to the photograph. "What's up with you?"

But there was only one way to get an answer to that question. Trixie picked up the phone and dialed.

CHAPTER 2

MARIAH

Silver Meadow, South Dakota
Summer 1891

I pushed a damp mop across the floor. "We need to close up soon or we'll miss the first inning."

My brother, Charles, remained hunched over the clock, his brow furrowed in the same serious expression he always had when working on something delicate and precise. "Relax, Sister." He spoke in such a way that the movement of his lips was nearly undetectable. "I'm playing today, so they can't hardly start without me."

"*You're* playing?" I didn't even try to keep the note of surprise out of my voice. Charles was good at many things—there was nothing he couldn't repair or build, but his mechanical skills did not often bring success on the baseball field. He was dreamy and lost whenever his hands were idle, and nothing brings about idle hands like a summer afternoon in left field. Our entire town of Silver Meadow was planning to shut down for our match against De Smet.

To his credit, Charles was not offended.

"I suppose I can hit and run and throw as well as the next fellow." The clock clicked and whirred beneath his touch, and he set it down with satisfied reverence.

"If we want to win, you have to hit and run and throw *better* than the next fellow."

"Any fellow in particular?" He still wasn't looking at me, but his mouth had loosened up enough to hold a loopy grin.

I flushed and stomped a bit, dragging the mop—nearly dry—to set it in the bucket in the corner. "I don't know what you're talking about."

"But you know *who* I'm talking about."

"As if *he* would ever give me the time of day."

"Oh, I don't know. He's a man. You're a woman."

"I'm not the type—"

"From what I've heard, just about any—"

We hadn't noticed the door opening (the broken little bell above it proved to be one of the few projects Charles never got around to fixing), so we were both taken by surprise when a sweet voice joined in asking, "Who are we talking about?"

The voice belonged to Katrina Rose, and no name had ever so suited a woman. Not much more than a girl, really. Without ever asking directly, I'd worked it out that she must be older than seventeen but younger than twenty. Her hair was a shade of strawberry blond that looked positively pink in certain light, and her cheeks had a pleasant, perpetually matching tint, as did her lips, though darker. If I were her mother or sister or even friend, I might have told her that because she had such a natural rosiness about her, she might steer away from dressing in all shades of pink, because very little of what she wore complemented her coloring.

"Hello, Katrina," I said. "And we were just talking about the baseball game."

"Oh yes!" She clapped her hands, the pink lace muffling the sound. "I'm going there now. Papa said for me to check and see if our clock is ready first. He's an hour late getting the paper printed and says if he misses the evening edition, he's going to blame me and make me hand deliver the thing myself." The Rose family owned a small printing press and published a small weekly paper that carried as much news as possible for a town of fewer than five hundred people to have. It listed births and deaths, weddings and funerals, baseball scores and national news gleaned from larger papers in which Mr. Rose was heavily invested, thus allowing himself to be one of the wealthiest men in town while still working fewer hours than any citizen would think possible.

I knew of course she was joking by the lilt in her voice and the ridiculousness of the claim but feigned shock anyway. "How could it possibly be your fault?"

"Because I'm the one who broke the clock."

Katrina smiled at her joke, I smiled at her, and Charles scowled at the illogic of it all. He placed the intricate piece he'd been repairing on the shelf behind him and took down the smaller, cheaper, happily ticking clock Katrina had come to collect.

"Like I told you the last two times," he said, "be careful not to wind it too tight or you'll break the spring. Lucky I had one around, but if it happens again, you'll have to buy a whole new clock."

"I shall do my level best, sir," Katrina said with a motion that combined a curtsy and a salute. "And how much do I owe you for your labor?"

I bit my inner cheek, knowing he would quote a price that valued neither his time nor expertise, and was proven right when he asked for fifteen cents.

Katrina unsnapped her small pink handbag and extracted two dimes. "Maybe instead of giving me change, you can buy me a lemonade at the baseball game? I haven't even spread my blanket out, and I'm already parched."

The way Katrina Rose said *spread my blanket* offered all manner of invitation, reinforced by the trail of her fingers along her throat at the word *parched*. Charles, of course, saw none of this.

"Can't. We're supposed to keep company with the other players during the game." He held out his oil-stained hand for the money. "I'll be back with your nickel."

"Sorry," I whispered as he ducked under the counter. "When he sets his mind to something. . ."

Katrina sniffed in a disgruntled way and let the forceful click of her purse speak for her irritation before declaring that she'd be back for the clock tomorrow morning. "Early," she said over her shoulder, and I knew she would come with a plate full of sweet breads for her trouble.

"Honestly," I said when it was the two of us alone, "you have the thickest head."

He seemed genuinely bewildered. "What do you mean?"

"I mean, if you don't start to pay a little more attention to her, she's going to find bigger things to break."

I followed him back to the kitchen behind his shop, where he washed his hands and neck before ripping off a chunk of bread from the loaf in the bread box and chewed it thoughtfully. "You think she overwound the clock on purpose?"

"Either that or she's too stupid to wind a clock, and if that's the case, she's no use to us anyway."

"She's pretty enough, I guess."

I wanted to say, *You guess?* My brother who never guessed anything. Who once made a cup-and-ball man at the circus wait a quarter of an hour while Charles retraced the path of the hidden ball and, after much deliberation, successfully unearthed it under the center cup. My brother who had once walked all the way back from the dry goods store because I'd written both cornmeal and flour on the list, but one looked slightly erased, so he wasn't sure which to buy.

"She is pretty," I said, "and you'd make a handsome couple. I think she has her pretty pink hat set on it, so you might have to give in."

He chewed, staring at me, then swallowed. "What about you?"

I looked up. "What about me?"

"Who would take care of you if Katrina got her hooks in me and dragged me away?"

I burst out with a sound that was something like a laugh, only bitter. "Do you think you've been taking care of *me* all these years?"

He gave a little shrug. "I think we've been taking care of each other."

I couldn't argue with that. When we'd come home after a final, disastrous attempt at schooling to find our father dead on the shanty floor, his eyes bulged large with the effort of waiting and watching for our return, we searched all the nooks and crannies to find enough money to send a telegram to our only uncle who, in turn, wired twenty dollars to cover the expenses of a burial plot and our own survival until spring. I'll never forget that morning at the train station in De Smet, all of our worldly belongings packed in a single valise, when Charles said, "We could stay here, you know." Somehow going it alone with my brother seemed a far better plan than dropping ourselves on the doorstep of a man who was nothing more than a name scribbled in the front of our family Bible. We had our clothing, my books, an abandoned claim, and seven dollars—a little bit more once Charles got our tickets refunded. He worked odd jobs, did a host of repairs, and I kept our rented room tidy and prepared our meals. We never lacked for anything, but sometimes when the soup was thin or the fire was low, Charles would remind me, "You could be a teacher, you know. You're smart enough, I guess."

"Maybe," I'd say, always knowing the truest answer was "Never." I knew I could pass the certification, but I also knew my temperament. Nothing could have suited me less than a classroom, being cooped up all day with the smell of wet wool and dry snot and all that awkward, shuffling silence. Being such a lover of books, I tried my hand at writing one, only to find an endless stream of disappointment and wasted ink. Every Christmas when I gathered the coins I faithfully saved over the year and bought the latest novel advertised in the newspaper, I would look at the publishing house depicted on the frontispiece and wonder how it came to be that I had this new book in my hand. Somebody set the type. Somebody bound the pages. Somebody wrapped the package, tied the string, and put it in a postal bag.

I would have done anything to be a part of that process. Any of it.

One winter night when the snow howled outside like a circling wolf, I spun a tale for Charles in which we left the prairie, went to New York City, and commenced working in some horrible factory that meant long, tedious hours but a reliable bit of money at the end of every week.

"We'd be cold and hungry," he'd said.

"We're cold and hungry now," I'd replied. "But there we'd be cold and hungry and alive."

"We aren't alive now?"

"I guess we won't know until somebody digs us out."

Charles reminded me that all of the pioneers had fanned out across the prairie specifically to get away from the city.

"Except for the ones who went back," I said. "The women who went crazy from the never-ending wind and the men who dropped their last dollar on dying wheat."

For all of my dreams about leaving, however, we only made it out of De Smet to the struggling township of Silver Meadow, trading our rented room in Mrs. Garland's boardinghouse for the living quarters—a kitchen and parlor on the first floor and two bedrooms above a workshop. Charles had inherited both the business and the building after months of working for the owner, who was dying of some lingering illness. The place was a veritable mansion in comparison to anything else we'd ever known. Charles built an impressive bookcase to house my growing collection. In the evenings, I did as I'd done since we were children: supper cleaned up, faces washed, and warm bricks at our feet, I read a chapter from whatever novel I'd purchased for my Christmas present. Charles would want one chapter and no more, no matter how exciting, because he wanted to eke out the story. When we finished one book, we started another—one from my growing library, one that we'd read before but enjoyed a second (or third) read, finding moments we'd missed. Knowing the ending, we would recognize a bit of foreshadowing and gasp in unison.

So, yes. We took care of each other.

I made up a basket with the fixings for a quick, cold supper and filled a jug with cool water. I found Charles's battered cap, unused bat, and leather glove. We walked out of the shop, and I waited while he locked the door—always conscious of the fact that we took on the responsibility for other peoples' treasures.

The whole town seemed to be taking advantage of an excuse to close up shops and seek fresh air. We moved in one accord to the shorn field next to the church on the outskirts that hosted all of our community suppers, Independence Day picnics, county fairs, harvest festivals, and, today, a baseball game. The diamond had been clearly marked with chalk, and a slab of black-painted wood rested on an easel with two marked columns: HOME and AWAY. Neither team formalized its existence with a nickname; there were no Tigers or Black Socks. The team visiting from De Smet showed themselves a step above ours, as each man wore a pale yellow shirt with DE SMET in felt block letters stitched to the front and his name on the back. Our men took the field in the same clothes they'd worn all day on their farms or in their shops. Our town banker stripped down to his shirtsleeves, and our blacksmith had to be reminded to take off his leather apron.

This is how we would spend intermittent afternoons in the summer, playing games against whatever town teams would take the train or pile in a wagon and make the journey here to our little corner. We never traveled. Our runs were never tallied under the AWAY column. But over the course of the years, I saw more than one familiar face turn up on a baseball card and remembered the man who stood in far right field where the cornfield met the cemetery.

I found my spot along the first base line and spread out my blanket, nodding greetings to my fellow townsfolk as I did so. No families asked me to join them, and I hardly gave the impression that I was amenable to company. After all, I had a book open on my lap and a straw hat set low, its wide brim contoured to make a narrow tunnel for my vision. When a shadow crossed my page, I looked over its form before lifting my eyes, my heart already pounding.

"You're reading a book? At my game? You have the chance to see the legendary Cap Garland play baseball, and you're keeping your nose buried in some love story?"

"It's a mystery, actually." Somehow, I could always find my voice when I talked about a book. "A man who inherits a castle but must live there for one year before he can fully claim it. Meanwhile, all sorts of sounds and ghostly apparitions."

"And you're not scared?"

"Not much scares me." *Except for you*, I could have said.

How long had I been in love with Oscar—Cap—Garland? Probably as long as I had known how to be in love at all. A smarter girl—or a wiser woman—would have known not to set her sights so high. Oscar Garland was a hero. Years before Charles and Papa and I ever took a claim, the territory was hit with a deadly winter. Blizzard after blizzard, with snow piled so high the trains could not get through. People were starving, and Oscar Garland, along with the same fellow who would end up riding away with my final teacher tucked into his cutter, braved the frozen danger to bring wheat to the starving people. Charles and I heard the story over and over, told around the supper tables in the homes where we rented rooms. I'd thought of him as a figment of the town's collective imagination until he showed up at the dinner table on our first night at a new boardinghouse—his mother's. My reaction to seeing Oscar that first evening was the same as my reaction this afternoon: a chill like someone had placed a cap of ice on top of my head and a certain loosening of my mind as it melted.

That first evening, he'd looked tousled, fresh from washing up after a day's work, and when he sat across the table from me, I could look him straight in the eye and somehow manage to chat about the weather. I'd been no more than eighteen years old at the time. Now he towered over me. When I looked up, the sun glowed behind him, turning his blond hair into a crown of blinding light. Here was the god who saved the town.

I gripped my book to ease my trembling, despite the fact that I'd just told him I was practically impervious to fear.

"Well, I'm glad," he said, "but you might want to be a little afraid. Of us, I mean. Our team's pretty good. We play to win."

"Is there another reason to play?"

He laughed, and there it was, that satisfying feeling in my stomach, like a dog circling into its place.

"Believe it or not, some fellows get out there just for fun."

"Seems it might be ideal to combine the two, wouldn't it?

Anyway, my brother, Charles, is playing today, so be kind. Try not to hit the ball in his general direction."

He tipped his cap. "I'll try. Good to see you, Miss Patterson."

"And you, Mr. Garland."

I know I did not imagine the sound of a dozen female sighs as he walked away, back to where a group of men in De Smet shirts huddled together, turning away occasionally to spit a stream of tobacco into the dirt.

The game proceeded the way all imagined it would, with a rounding defeat for the Silver Meadow team. Still, when our players left the field after the final inning, they found their families and were greeted like soldiers returning from war. I offered my brother a comforting squeeze to his forearm and complimented a play he made in the third inning. Though many were invited to share our picnic suppers, the De Smet men piled into the lumbering farm wagon that brought them and set out on the two-hour-long ride home, their mugs and bellies full of the beer from the keg on the tailgate.

All of our players too had a mug filled from that keg, including Charles, who drank half of it down in three deep gulps.

"It was a good game," I said, watching him wipe his upper lip with his sleeve.

"No, it wasn't. But it was fun. Do you mind I invited Gowan to join us?"

"Charles—"

"He doesn't have anybody here, Mariah. No family. You remember what that feels like."

"No," I said, "I don't. Because I've always had you."

"All the more reason. . ." Whatever else he planned to say trailed off as he nodded a greeting to someone behind me. I turned to see the object of our conversation, Merrill Gowan, approaching. He was a big man, new to town. In time he would take on the lean physique of a South Dakota farmer, but for now he still carried the weight of a man born and raised on a city's diet. His chest was broad, his middle barreled. Not fat but soft, with rounded cheeks above his sparse beard. He was a distant relative of a farmer who died last winter, leaving a widow who sold the house and fields for the price of train fare home, if rumors were to be believed.

"I don't think I have enough food," I said, speaking out of the side of my mouth in order to keep a pleasant expression on my face.

"Yes, you do. Because I've been invited to supper with the Roses."

I spun my head back to him. "You—what?"

"I haven't given an answer. I said I had to check with you. But I've been thinking—"

"You need to *think* about what's good and proper. Do you intend to leave me here? With this—"

"Merrill," Charles said, extending his free hand.

"Patterson," Merrill said, shaking it. Unlike the other players, he had no beer. After shaking my brother's hand, he turned to me and took off his hat, revealing a hairline more suited to a man twenty years older. I did not extend my hand but did offer a pleasant smile when I said that of course he was welcome to join me "*and my brother*" for a picnic supper. I pinned Charles with my eyes and watched him wither.

"If you'll excuse me for a bit," Charles said. Shoulders slumped, he picked his way through the scattered blankets and half-heartedly dodged running children to make his way to where the Rose family—Katrina, her parents, and younger brothers—were spreading out a feast. I watched long enough to see Katrina's pretty lips pout before turning back to Merrill, who had yet to put his hat back on his head.

"I believe we have met before," I said, sitting down and inviting him to do the same.

"Yes," he said. "At church. And at the men's chorale concert."

"Ah, yes. You have a fine tenor voice, Mr. Gowan."

The tips of his ears turned fire red, and I wished beyond anything that he would put his hat back on and relieve me of the sight of them.

I began to unpack the basket, saying, "I'm afraid it's a modest supper. I wasn't prepared for a guest—not that you aren't more than welcome to share. My brother, bachelor that he is, doesn't always think of such things."

"I'm a bachelor too, Miss Patterson." That's when I noticed the bag slung across his back. He brought it forward and took out a jar of what appeared to be pickled carrots along with a small tin of toasted rye bread. "If Charles hadn't invited me, I suppose I would have gone home to a lonely supper. Or I would have had a lonely supper here. Either way, I brought a little something. . ."

"Did you put these up yourself, Mr. Gowan?" I opened the carrots and inhaled their sweet, briny scent.

"No. Found them in the root cellar. My cousin assured me that everything in the house was still good." He patted his belly. "It's a fine thing when a bachelor moves into a house filled with food for a family."

"I'm sure," I said, noting this was the second time he'd mentioned his bachelorhood.

When Charles returned, he had a plate of cookies Katrina had insisted we take, though I suspected they had been prepared specially for him. I waved a thank-you and set out our supper—sliced, soft buttered bread and cold ham and cheese and hard-boiled eggs. Merrill Gowan's pickled carrots lent a nice bite of flavor, and I told him to send his cousin my compliments in his next letter. I was glad for the Roses' cookies, as I hadn't thought to bring a dessert. They were, however, a bit dry, so I wrapped mine in a napkin and declared I would have them later, dipped in a cup of tea.

As for the conversation wrapped around the food, well, what can I say? My brother had never been one for social talk, and our guest and I found no common ground. So once we'd exhausted the weather (warm, pleasant, mild), we went on to speak of crops (corn, wheat, sorghum) until we finally came to the end of the meager repast. Our fellow townsfolk were rising and lighting lamps for the long walks home, and though Charles and I lived in town, I declared I'd like to be in before dark.

"Thank you again," Merrill said, "for letting me join your supper. I'm still getting to know folks, so it was a treat to feel so welcome."

A twinge of guilt prodded my tongue. "It was a pleasure to have your company. Charles and I know what it's like to find a place in a new community."

To my shock, Merrill took my hand and held it between his,

surprising me with the roughness of his skin. "Would it be all right for me to call on you sometime, Miss Patterson? Maybe we could go for a walk? Or a drive?"

I stared in silence. We were nearly the same height, but his eyes were fixed on the darkening sky behind my head.

"Forgive my forwardness. I guess I should ask your brother for his permission?"

That snapped my attention. "You do not need to ask Charles for his permission. Besides the fact that he is standing right there and can chime in with his opinion at any moment." I took my hand back and laced my fingers at my roiling stomach. "Do you have an opinion, Charles?"

Charles stood, blanket folded over one arm, our basket gripped in his other hand, looking at me as if seeing me for the first time in his life. "I think it would be fine," he said. "Maybe some evening after supper."

"Supper!" Merrill exclaimed, his voice just shy of a *whoop*. "I'd surely like that."

"Next Thursday, then," Charles said. Until now, the lengthiest conversation I'd ever heard my brother engage in was with a child's wind-up tin soldier that refused to march.

"Do I have a say in this? After all, I'm the one who will be doing the cooking."

"Aw, Sister, surely you can't object to inviting a neighbor for supper?"

"Of course not, but—" And not another word came to my mind. I turned to Merrill who, by now, had found the courage to look straight at me, and even in the deepening darkness I could see hope in his gaze. "Thursday evening, then. We usually eat around seven."

Without wishing a good night, I turned on my heel and headed home, ignoring Charles's pleas to slow down. Even when he caught up to me, I refused to speak to him, refused to respond to his repeated inquiries about my anger, lest I treat all of our neighbors to a blathering display. I unlocked the door and strode through the shop, not finding the usual comfort in its scent of oil and sound of ticking clocks. I went straight through to our parlor and lit the lamp, bathing the room in soft amber light and drawing strength from the books lining the wall.

"Mariah?" Charles slunk in, empty-handed, and I knew I'd have dishes to clean later. "Are you mad at me?"

"What were you thinking?" I felt the sting of tears at the back of my throat and swallowed. "Bringing that. . .that *man* over and offering me up like some cakewalk prize?"

"That's just it. I was thinking. The whole time during the game, thinking about what you said about Katrina. And then looking over at her, and she was looking at me. . ."

"Maybe less thinking and looking at Katrina and you would have caught a few of those easy pop flies and not let them score seven runs in a single inning."

He ignored me but ventured closer. "I was wondering what it would be like if I went home with Katrina Rose tonight instead of my sister? And it made me think of you being all alone. And there was Merrill Gowan right there on second base."

"Really? Are you sure you could see him? Because you over-threw to him every time."

He grinned, lifting the left side of his mouth. "Sometimes I wish you knew less about baseball."

I grinned, lifting the right side of mine. "Sometimes I wish you knew more about women. I suppose this is my fault, then, for planting ideas about Katrina in your head."

"I think I would have figured it out."

Something in me warmed. "You *do* like her, then?"

"I do."

"Then I'm happy for you, Charles. I truly am." He'd come close enough to me that I could reach out and lay a hand against the evening soft whiskers on his cheek. We were not, by any measure, affectionate with each other, and I took comfort in the fact that he did not flinch away.

"Her family invited me to supper."

"Did they?" I kept my voice at an enthusiastic pitch, despite the niggling trepidation at a suspected parallel. "When?"

"Thursday." He tensed his body to run, just as he did when we were children and he snuck up behind me to leave a toad on my shoulder.

"Charles. . ."

He held his hands up in defense. "It was the first day that came to mind."

"Because you were thinking about your dinner with Katrina?"

His guilty expression confirmed it. My sweet brother could rarely hold more than two thoughts in his head, and with one of them being Katrina Rose, I'm surprised he could think to breathe.

"But you understand the difference, don't you? You'll be at home with Katrina and her whole family. I'll be alone here with Merrill Gowan. What will people say?"

He shrugged. "Maybe they won't say anything."

I opened my mouth to retort that of course they would. My shelves were full of stories devoted to the wagging tongues of gossips. But then, I was no lady of society, and Merrill Gowan was a lonely, homely farmer from three miles out of town. Who would know? Who would care? Unless I whispered my dalliance into the ear of Mrs. Frank who often shared a pew with me on Sundays, chances were the sordid details of my private life would remain just that. Private. And besides, this was nothing more than a charitable act to a pathetic neighbor, unlike Charles and Katrina who might be brewing a true romance.

"I did see you talking with Garland," Charles said, "before the game."

I ran a finger along the spines of my books. "Yes. He was kind enough to come over and say hello."

"Is there anything—" He stopped, cleared his throat, and started again. "Is there something there that I need to know?"

I almost laughed at the preposterousness of the idea. Only my wide-eyed, innocent brother would think there ever could be a romance between Oscar Garland and me, the dowdy spinster Mariah Patterson. Then again, perhaps he wasn't so innocent. After all, he'd managed to lure a hungry bachelor to my table.

"No, Brother. Nothing for you to know."

"That's good. For you, I mean. From what I've heard, he's not one looking to get married."

"Then perhaps we are well suited, because neither am I. You and Katrina, on the other hand. . ." I led Charles out of the parlor into the kitchen where he had abandoned our basket on the table. I found the Rose family plate that had carried the cookies and gave it a good wipe with a dish towel before handing it over to Charles. "Take this to their home. And thank them again for the delicious treat."

Charles looked skeptically out the window. "It's late."

"It's not yet eight o'clock."

"Isn't that too late to call?"

"Not for a good purpose, which is to return the plate. And especially not for the young lady who is still probably put out that you didn't join her for supper. In returning the plate, you will please her mother. In showing up at all, you will please Katrina, for she will recognize the ruse that it is. And leave within fifteen minutes to please her father."

He took the plate but remained dubious. "How do you know all of this?"

"Call it female instinct. And thousands of pages of stories. The ones I read after you are off to sleep," I added.

He shrugged, then left. I made haste tidying up the kitchen and hurried myself to bed, taking my mysterious ghost story with me. I realized then that my brother was going to leave me. I don't think *he* even realized how swiftly our lives were about to change, but as I sat, my eyes skimming the pages while my ear listened for the door, I knew. The shadows of a lonely future loomed larger than my profile on the wall.

CHAPTER 3

TRIXIE

*S*he made two phone calls that Friday night. One to her mother, assuring her that she'd received the message—*all* the messages—and that she'd be home the next day.

"Not tonight?" her mother said in that wheedling voice that usually worked.

"No," Trixie said with finality. "It's late, and I've been working all day. I'm tired. Then I'd sleep late and get up around the same time that I'll arrive if I leave early in the morning."

"But the doctor—"

"You mean Cam?"

"Just because you know his first name doesn't make him less of a doctor."

"I know way more than his first name, Mom." A lot more, in fact. Trixie knew the feel of his hand in hers, the fit of her head in that place where his neck curved into his shoulder. She'd recognized his voice in the first syllable on her answering machine. She knew his handwriting sloped backward, even though she'd never received a letter—not one since the day he left her frozen in grief on her own front porch. Memories of Cam were what drove her to pursue a life as far away from home as she dared venture. All these years, she insisted on only the most essential details of his life. He went to college, good. Pre-med, impressive—but not surprising, as he treated every high school course like future lives depended on his grades. He went to Vietnam—inhale. He came back—exhale. And his visits to his mother, to their church, to dinners at the VFW and homecoming football games had been conveniently sparse.

"Even an ex-boyfriend can be a good doctor, dear," Mom said, interrupting Trixie's memory.

"Well, this isn't the first time a doctor has declared a state of emergency. And God willing, it won't be the last. I'll see you tomorrow. I love you. Goodbye." She spoke the last three sentences without verbal punctuation, using her finger to depress the button on the phone to end the call so she wouldn't hear her mother's final pleas as she returned the headset to its cradle.

Supper was a reheat of the Chinese takeout from earlier in the week: shrimp fried rice, which she warmed up in a shallow skillet on the stove, sprinkling on the extra packets of soy sauce and adding some thinly sliced celery and the last of a can of mushrooms. To save dishes, she dumped it right back into the take-out container and drank a Sprite straight from the bottle. Trixie watched the local news while she ate, *tsking* at the latest reports of crime and violence in her city and the shameful scandal of President Nixon. From the ongoing energy crisis to global unrest, there wasn't a bit of good news for the entire broadcast. Well, there might have been some during the sports and weather segments, but by then she'd finished most of her food, and House's face was peeking around the corner from the kitchen.

"Time for your supper too?" She turned off the television and switched on the radio, and the first bars of her latest favorite song spilled from the speakers. "Come and Get Your Love" by the band Redbone—the lyrics to the first verse eluded her, so she improvised, looking her cat square in the eye and singing, "Hey there! Hey there—what's the matter with you, Housie? Oh yeah!" She moved into the kitchen, engaging her entire body in slow, groovy disco moves, taking a can of Friskies from the cupboard. "Come and get your food! Come and get your foo-oo-ood!"

House sat and watched, choosing a noncommittal spot in the middle of the kitchen floor. He didn't even bother to move his head to follow her movements, only sat, eyes staring past the bowl, patiently waiting for her to leave so he could eat in peace.

"Look here, Housie," she sang with the vocalist on the second verse. "Look, I saved you a shri-imp. A shrimp!"

She dropped the two little shrimp on a napkin and placed it on the floor, knowing he might be offended if she added them to his Friskies, and left the kitchen as the song faded. She'd learned a lot about House in their first days together, and his eating proclivities manifested early. He would not eat if she was in the room. Or in the doorway, or looking on from the other room. Or if he could hear her breathe. Once, when she poked her head in to check his progress, he'd left the bowl immediately and later barfed in her shoe.

Once House was settled into his soft smacking, Trixie made her second phone call of the evening. Ron answered on the third ring, what Trixie always thought of as the crucial ring—every one after that signaled annoyance or inconvenience.

"Sorry to bother you so late," she said, glancing at the clock. Eight forty-five. Was that late? On a Friday night?

"That's okay. I've got at least an hour before my bedtime. Lucky for you I've taken a break from my usual wild lifestyle."

"Oh? Yes, well, terrific. I don't get lucky very often."

The silence stretched beyond awkward until Ron finally said, "Did you. . .need something?"

"Yes. Sorry, Ron. Yes. I'm going to need to take some days off next week. I'm actually caught up, if you can believe that. I don't have anything pressing until—maybe Thursday? And I might be able to pop back in for a day or so later—"

"So, you're going to New York?"

"New York?"

"The big guy. National distribution. Money, remember?"

"Oh." She hadn't given it a thought—well, not much of a thought—since leaving the office. "I guess I've pushed that aside for a bit. No, this is. . . I need some time off to go be with my family."

"Is everything all right?"

"Yes! It's fine, pretty much. As far as I know. It's my great-grandmother. She's, maybe, dying."

"Oh my gosh. Trixie, I'm so sorry."

"No, it's okay. This isn't the first time."

"She's died before?"

"Not completely." Trixie moved the phone's mouthpiece below her chin for a second to gather her thoughts. She hadn't thought the conversation would require notes, but clearly she'd underestimated the eccentricity of her family. "She—my great-grandmother—is one hundred and four years old."

"Wow," Ron said in that way he had of being genuinely interested and impressed with the smallest detail of a person's story. "That's awesome. And still in good health? I mean, up until now?"

"And even now, who knows?" She caught the irreverence in her voice and worried she might be coming across as some uncaring monster. She took a breath and started again. "You know the whole 'Boy Who Cried Wolf' thing? Well, GG—that's what I call her—she's like the Old Woman Who Summoned the Wolf. She's been trying to die for as long as I can remember, and every now and then something will happen—some trigger, if you will—and she'll declare it's time and take herself to her bed. She shuts us out of her room, sometimes for days, and then comes out. And nobody ever says anything, and we just go on until the next time."

"But this time?" he asked, without commentary.

"This time my mother and grandmother have called a doctor. She's not eating or drinking or talking. And as far as they can tell, not really sleeping."

"So, it's a vigil."

Trixie hadn't noticed the tension in her body until that moment when something seemed to crack at the base of her neck and sent a crumbling sensation through her shoulders and down her back. She slumped in her chair. "Yes, I suppose it is. And, so, a few days. One way or the other, I suppose, and it should be. . .over."

"Take as much time as you need, Trixie. We'll be fine."

We? Of course, the office. Which reminded her of the second reason for her call. "One other thing? I'll need someone to come look in on my cat. And I was wondering if you could steer me to who I should ask. Who would be best suited or lives closest?"

"You don't have a neighbor who—"

"The woman in the other apartment is allergic." Trixie remembered the diatribe, complete with threats if that "*mass of feline dander*" ever crossed her threshold. "And the tenant in the third apartment is out of the country."

"I'll do it," Ron said, blissfully interrupting her before she had to admit that outside of the *Newz* and Mrs. Claxon, she didn't know a single soul in the city. At least not anyone close enough not to be inconvenienced by the request. Even sadder? Her coworkers. After working together in close confines for two years, she still couldn't pinpoint who could—and who couldn't—step in for a favor.

"I didn't mean—"

"When are you leaving?"

Trixie curled the phone cord around her finger. "Around nine."

"Tonight?"

She laughed. "No, tomorrow morning. It's not an emergency vigil."

"Is there such a thing as an emergency vigil?"

The way he said it, she could picture his left brow raised in mock consideration, and she laughed again, trying not to think about how her mother might chastise her for giving such a light tone to the discussion of an old woman's death watch.

"I'll come over in the morning so I can meet the little guy and get all the instructions. Or"—his voice took on a softer hesitancy—"I could even come over now. Tonight. If that would be easier."

"That's sweet," she said, wishing she were the kind of girl who would throw together a cheese plate and invite a guy over at a moment's notice on a Friday night. Late Friday night, in fact—midway through *The Six Million Dollar Man*. "But I'll be up late, packing. Laundry—I don't even know if I have a week's clean underwear." She pressed her palm to her forehead. "I probably shouldn't be talking to my boss about my underwear."

"It's all right. I appreciate knowing that you make clean underwear a priority."

"Well, I'm nothing if not professional." Already she was thinking how to depict this conversation in a *Lost Laura* cartoon. Something with pantaloons on a clothesline? Or maybe a scene in a launderette: a handsome man holding out a pair of pantaloons and saying, "I think you left these in the dryer," with Laura's braids folded over her face to hide her embarrassment.

"Trixie?" Ron spoke through the phone line, vying for her attention.

"Yeah."

"I'll see you in the morning."

Packing might have been an easier feat if she'd allowed herself a second piece of luggage, but doing so made the visit seem more like a commitment. Instead, she ditched a third pair of shoes, one pair of jeans, and anything long-sleeved, knowing she had a cache of school sweaters in her bedroom at home if it got chilly. That helped, and she didn't even have to sit on the suitcase to click the latch.

Just after eight o'clock, she was wrapping an elastic around a single, low ponytail when she heard the knock on her screen door and Ron's voice announcing himself.

"Come on in," she shouted, tossing her hairbrush in the train case along with her hot rollers and shampoo. In a last-second decision, she grabbed a length of gingham ribbon and tied it around the elastic, thinking it complemented her white eyelet blouse and denim skirt. Her stomach was doing a strange flip—nerves, probably. She was, after all, about to introduce her cat to her boss. Ron had been here before, having insisted on giving her a ride home on various bitter cold days, but never inside.

And then he was.

Trixie walked into her own living room and found it filled with Ron Tumble in all his glory: Minnesota Twins T-shirt, blue cap, and surprisingly short shorts. From this vantage point, she couldn't see her front door, and her furniture looked ridiculously small. But when he smiled, he showed himself to be the same man she saw in the office every day, and her nerves shook loose.

Ron held up a brown paper bag with a familiar logo. "I brought breakfast."

"From McDonald's?"

"Have you not yet experienced the glory of an Egg McMuffin?"

"I have not." She hadn't planned for anything beyond a granola bar on the road.

"Well, you are in for a treat." He sniffed the air. "Do I smell coffee?"

He was heading straight for the kitchen when she noticed the duffel bag in his other hand.

"What else have you got there?"

He hefted the bag. "Necessities. You know, clean underwear and such."

"You're staying?"

"If you don't mind. For the weekend, at least. My roommate has fallen in love with the world's most annoying woman, so I could use a break. Figured I could get to know this guy."

Trixie followed his eyes to see House working a figure eight around Ron's ankles. A new, unfamiliar sound permeated the room. Purring.

She swallowed her surprise. "He has never done that to me before in his life."

"Yeah?" Ron bent to drop his bag and rubbed House's head. "Maybe if your legs were hairier? Maybe he likes the friction."

"More likely he likes the food." She grabbed the McDonald's sack and took it straight to the little table beneath her kitchen window. "Will we need plates? Knives? Forks?"

"It's a sandwich, Prairie Girl. I plan to use my hands like a barbarian, but you can rely on your more refined manners."

She responded by placing a pile of napkins on the middle of the table and invited him to sit while she poured their coffee. Strange how something so perfunctory in an office workroom seemed so intimate in her cramped kitchen. At least it seemed cramped, given that he was the first man ever to cross the threshold. When her mother and grandmother and great-grandmother visited, the four women navigated the space with ease, barely brushing one another's hips as they sliced and stirred and assembled a meal. But Ron seemed safest tucked away at the table, rustling the sack and extracting the two clamshell Styrofoam boxes. Trixie set down the coffee mugs and took the chair across from him.

"So, the first thing about feeding House—"

As if on command, the cat leapt up on top of the table and pushed his head against Ron's arm.

"I assume it's that he's not allowed on the table?" Ron gathered the cat, made a kissy noise inches away from his face, and set him gently on the floor.

Trixie watched in open-mouthed surprise. "He has never done that either."

"Then you were right. It's all about the food with him."

Ron pushed a box across the table, and she opened it, feeling dubious about the concoction. To be truthful, she was rarely enticed by food advertised on television. Juicy burgers, steaming piles of hotcakes, effervescent fountain sodas. From what she could tell, this celebrity breakfast sandwich boiled down to egg and cheese on an English muffin, and she had two of those three ingredients in her refrigerator. Now, whatever the meat—

"Is this ham?"

"Canadian bacon."

"What makes it Canadian?"

Ron shrugged. "It's round and polite?"

She of course didn't have Canadian bacon in her fridge. Or any, for that matter. Not that she was a vegetarian; she just hated any form of cooking that included the step of draining grease. All forms of bacon were reserved for restaurants and visits home.

"Hey, I'm sorry," Ron said, having devoured nearly half of his sandwich in a single bite.

"For what?"

"I should have asked. You seem freaked out."

"I'm not freaked out." She picked up the sandwich, happy to

find it still warm. "It's unfamiliar territory, you know? I don't want to rush." Suddenly, House's distaste for being watched during mealtime seemed completely reasonable. She took a small bite and found the combination of flavors and the scientifically perfected texture to be. . .delicious and said as much, speaking with a full mouth hidden behind equally full hands.

"Now," Ron said, grinning like Mayor McCheese on Election Day, "tell me everything I need to know about your cat."

Over breakfast (which grew more satisfying with each bite), Trixie talked through the short list of House Cat's demands and restrictions, soon realizing that none would apply. The cat took a small bite of Canadian bacon straight from Ron's fingers and smacked happily while they both looked on. She did point out the stack of cat food tins and the mug full of spoons dedicated to scooping it from the can to the plate, as well as the fact that they were stacked alphabetically, and House would let Ron know if he was served *tuna* before *liver*.

"And how can he possibly know?"

"I can't explain it. But the barf in the shoe doesn't lie."

She walked him to the litter box in the corner of the laundry room, suggesting—strongly—that he scoop it every evening before seven. She'd changed the litter that morning, and the box wouldn't be due for another complete change until the next weekend. There were also nine plants to water and mail to gather, but phone calls could be managed by the machine, so he needn't bother answering the phone to take a message.

"What if it's you?" he asked.

"Just listen," she said. "If you're here, and it's me, then pick up."

"What if it's someone calling me?"

She hadn't thought about this as a possibility, but then for the next few days, at least, this would be his home. An irritating question niggled the back of her brain: *Who would be calling him?* But of course he had friends, maybe even girlfriends. Plural. The fact that he was home on a Friday night could have been a fluke. Or maybe there'd been someone beside him when they talked. Or waiting in the next room, sipping a glass of wine and whispering for him to hurry and get off the phone. Somebody named Lila, or a fun gal named Betty Jo. Forcing the image out of her mind, she pointed toward the bedroom, noting that the sheets were fresh not because she'd been expecting him to stay but because she wanted to come home to fresh sheets.

"Noted," he said, miming a check mark on his hand.

"And there's the bathroom with. . .everything. And you don't have to, but I usually open the curtains in the morning."

"In the bathroom?"

"No, just everywhere—living room, bedroom, kitchen." They were standing in the perfect spot for her to encompass each space with a vague gesture.

"And do you usually close them in the evening?"

"Of course." He was teasing, and the realization of it loosened something within her. The unease of his staying in her cozy bachelorette space didn't diminish, but it switched course, and for a blinking minute, Trixie wished she didn't have to leave. The single chime of the antique clock on her fitted corner shelf meant that she was fifteen minutes past the time she'd promised her family to be on the road.

"You should get going," Ron said, picking up her thoughts as well as her suitcase.

"I really should." They stood in front of her door and for a moment presented a tableau of an inside-out date. Morning instead of evening. Leaving instead of staying. Trixie opened the door, and he followed her out into the blinding sunlight where her car waited in the driveway. She'd moved it earlier in the morning, self-conscious at the idea of backing out of her garage with an audience. She was about to tell him that his car would be welcome to that space too—or even the garage itself—when Mrs. Claxon's voice pierced the stillness of the morning.

"Where are you off to so early on a Saturday?"

Trixie shielded her eyes and looked up. "Mrs. Claxon, this is Ron. He's going to be staying here for a while."

"Oh, you modern couples," the old woman said, holding her coffee cup in salute. "Or did I miss my invitation to the wedding?"

Trixie heard Ron chuckle but jumped to her own defense. "No, Mrs. Claxon. That's not—"

"You don't have to explain yourself to me. I might be old, but I'm keeping up with the world. I watch *Love, American Style*."

Ron laughed out loud at that, so Trixie punched him in the arm—hard—hissing, "Don't encourage her." Then she took a final stab at saving her reputation. "I'm going out of town for a few days. Ron's apartment-sitting. Taking care of the cat."

At the mention of House, Mrs. Claxon sobered, her thin lips twisting. "You tell him to keep that cat away from me."

"She doesn't have to tell me," Ron said. "I can hear you."

"I'm serious, young man. If I get one whiff of that cat dander, they'll find me dead in my chair. If anybody bothers to look for me, which I doubt. With *this one* gone."

This one, of course, was Trixie, as indicated by Mrs. Claxon's burning cigarette pointed down in her direction. She felt Ron bend himself to her, his face close enough to her ear that she could feel his beard brush the back of her neck.

"Why didn't you warn me about your charming neighbor? I would have brought a bottle of wine and my Dean Martin albums."

Trixie smiled but did not turn around. "She's mercurial but harmless." Then, louder, with a wave, "Goodbye, Mrs. Claxon. I'll see you in a few days." When she *did* turn, Ron was there—*right* there—his hand brushing her hip as he opened the car door, then gently gripping her arm, holding her in that open space, justifying all of Mrs. Claxon's assumptions.

"I really do hope everything is all right. Don't worry about a thing here or at the office. Just be there for your family, and call that guy."

Trixie nodded.

"Promise?"

She nodded again, promising, not trusting herself to open her mouth to answer, fearing her breath would draw him in. He was so close, and everything about him—his stance, his eyes, his breath—seemed poised to kiss her. They'd been in this moment before: once in his empty office while the rest of the *Newz* staff engaged in a rollicking Christmas party in the shared space, and once when a ride home ended in a two-hour conversation in this very spot while snow flurried against the fogged-solid windshield of his Mustang. Each time they'd had the presence of mind to back away, and each time Trixie convinced herself that his reluctance matched her own. So she waited, heart pounding, for him to draw back, but he didn't. Instead, the touch to her arm moved to her cheek and he leaned in and whispered, "Drive safe," before she felt his lips on hers so quickly, so softly, she was twenty miles down the highway before she convinced herself that it happened at all.

CHAPTER 4

MARIAH

$\int$omehow Thursday night dinner became an expectation. I say *somehow*, but I know very well how it came to be. Merrill showed up that first Thursday evening, his hair slicked back, his face pink from an evening shave. Charles stayed long enough to engage in polite conversation, then took himself off for his own dinner with the Rose family. An hour later, as Merrill wiped the lingering gravy from the corner of his lips, he complimented my cooking and declared what a treat it was for a bachelor to get a home-cooked meal. For him a typical dinner was to eat a pork chop straight off the fork, standing over the pan. I heard myself saying something like "Well, that's a shame, unless the pork chop is cooked well, of course."

And then we were comparing cooking techniques.

And then I was intrigued by his method of searing.

And then I was offering to try it for myself, and he was offering to judge my success, and we both were committing to a dinner the following Thursday.

The next Sunday at church, he greeted me at the door with a basket of squash from his garden, and I heard myself offering to bake a casserole on Thursday.

And at that meal, I mentioned that I hadn't made dumplings in ages, and he expressed a particular love for them, and so. . .

I wish I could say I developed an affection for him. Any other man and woman, given the domesticity of a shared meal and quiet conversation might have found themselves moving closer in matter of heart and mind. But I did not. I never gave Merrill Gowan another thought from the moment he pushed himself away from my table until I was politely greeting him at church. And from then, not again until he knocked at the kitchen door. One week he brought flowers, and I dutifully put them in a glass jar. Then, days later, when they began to droop and brown, I had to think for a moment to remember where they'd come from. I could not recall a single word of conversation that passed between us over the hour we spent together, save for this:

One week I'd secured a ham hock from the butcher and cooked it with white beans and onion. In commenting on the meal, I told him that for the four years we were homesteading with our father, Charles and I ate nothing but beans. Every meal (though there was often only one) every day. I was ten years old when I cooked my first pot of beans and had perfected the art by the time I was twelve. I could look at a pot of beans and judge their doneness. I could throw the right amount of salt across the room and season them perfectly. I cooked them in a broth hearty enough to be a meal in itself, as it often was for us. I told him I had vowed to myself if I ever had my own kitchen and the power over my own table, I would never cook another pot of beans as long as I lived.

"What changed your mind?" he asked, blowing across his spoon.

"I didn't change my mind," I said. "I missed them, and it seemed a silly vow to keep. Life is too full of meaningless promises."

I think that's the first night he intended to propose. He'd come especially groomed, seemed excessively nervous, and appeared to deflate when I put my fickle nature on full display. For the rest of the meal, he kept his eyes trained on his dish and was gone before the clock chimed the completion of the hour.

I told Charles of my suspicions and pressed him, saying, "You don't think Merrill Gowan has any designs beyond a weekly dinner, do you?"

To which Charles replied, "How should I know? I guess I talk to him as much as you do."

The next week, I begged Charles to stay. "Bring Katrina here for supper. I'll make whatever you like, and after we can have a hand at cards. I'll pop some corn and get a couple of bottles of ginger ale. A real party."

But he declined. He told me that, at this point, he felt obligated to be at the Rose dining room table on a Thursday night, but I suspect his reason had much more to do with the hour he and Katrina were granted alone in the Rose parlor while her mother stayed within earshot doing the dishes. He'd come home well past nine o'clock, dreamy and musing, never able to remember what he'd had for supper hours before. We didn't read together on those nights. He'd go straight to his room and shut the door behind him, sometimes without so much as wishing me a good night.

Of course he was in love, falling deeper and deeper before my eyes, and I've often wondered if he would ever have taken that first step into the crevasse of romance had I not planted the idea in his head. It is something to watch a man fall in love, to see every bit of his mind, body, and spirit succumb. If Katrina so much as walked past our store window, his hands became useless appendages, scattering tools and screws across the counter. I grew accustomed to asking every question three times (*What do you want for dinner, Charles? Charles? For dinner? What do you want?*). I once stumbled upon him sitting at our kitchen table, pencil in hand, staring at an open, blank notebook.

"I want to write her a letter," he said, and handed me a sheet of pretty pink stationery filled with writing in a perfect, delicate hand. "She wrote me one."

I held it, taking in its faint floral scent. I kept my eyes on the script, but unfocused so as not to invade his privacy. The question had to be asked. "Have you—"

"No."

"Darling brother, you have to tell her." I sat across from him and touched the letter to his hand.

"What kind of a husband can I be if I can't read?"

The shock of his words set me back. "I didn't know you were to be any kind of a husband at all."

He looked up, his eyes full of a pain I'd never seen before. Not when either of our parents died, not when we were forced to move from one place to another, not when we were cold and alone and hungry. "I want to be. I'm sorry, Mariah. But that's what I want."

"Then you must be truthful, Charles. There's no shame. You're not stupid. You're smart in so many other ways—"

"Her father runs the town newspaper. There are no other ways."

"Does he love his daughter?"

"Yes."

"And does his daughter love you?"

Finally, a shy smile like something I'd seen before. "I think she does, yes. We haven't declared as much to each other, but. . ." His voice trailed off as a flush bloomed on his cheek. He pointed to the letter. "I've been wondering what that says."

"Do you want me to read it?"

He nodded.

"Even if it is personal? And. . .private?"

"I trust you."

We'd had only each other for so long, even this scrap of paper felt like an invading force. I read it quickly, bracing myself for having to speak aloud things that no sister should ever have to say to her brother, and found myself instead working through a bitter lump in my throat.

"*Dearest Charles*"—I softened my voice not in an attempt to imitate Katrina but to simply differentiate the text from our normal conversation.

> "*Do you know that I count the days—no, the hours—until I will see you again? The other night when you touched my hand, it was the warmest touch I've ever felt. I couldn't help but think of how well our hands fit together. How we know each other's thoughts, and how we anticipate each other's words. I know I am bold to write this, but I could never have the courage to say such.*
>
> "*And so, I am counting. It is the only reason I do not break the clock.*"

When I finished, he made me read it again, laying the letter flat on the table and running my finger beneath each word. Then again, with *his* finger following. After that, he folded it, running that same finger over and over the crease.

"What do I do?" That's when I recognized the odd quality to his voice and manner. Fear. Charles had never cared about anything enough to be afraid. We always had what we had—no more, no less—and his blissful, ignorant contentment tended to balance out my determination to bring us to the point of having *enough*.

I closed his fingers around the letter. "You go to her, right now. And you tell her the truth."

"I'll lose her."

"Any woman who can share her feelings this way, this boldly. . . You won't lose her."

He glanced at the clock. "They'll be at supper," he said, reminding me why I'd come into the kitchen in the first place.

"Knock on the door. She'll know it's you. She'll leave the table and invite you in. Don't come home until you tell her."

As I spoke, I prayed my words would hold true. If not, I might have had to march over to that house and pluck that Rose right off the porch. I kept my words strong and steady, lest Charles sense any doubt, and gave him an encouraging pat on the back as he rose from his seat. I said, "There's a good boy," in a way I'd never said in our entire life together, which he answered with a wan smile.

The minute he left, a shadow of loneliness engulfed me, and I punished that blank sheet of paper by crumpling it in my grip. Folding my arms on top of the table, I buried my face and gave myself over to such body-wracking sobs as I hadn't cried in years. My heart felt like an imposter of a woman reading Katrina's words. I couldn't imagine feeling that way about a man, enough to carve the essence of every other woman's desire into a perfumed confession.

Safety.

Warmth.

Completion.

Everything I had never had. Everything I *would* never have, and she somehow stumbled upon it with a touch of my brother's hand. It was everything he and I had ever been to each other, and now she was stealing it away. Oh, the jealousy. Not that I would deny my brother happiness, but this made it clear that I had none of my own. Nothing natural. Nothing fulfilling.

I could not imagine touching Merrill Gowan's hand. His sentences weren't interesting enough to finish. He had no jokes to anticipate. And what little I suspected of his thoughts set my blood cold.

All of me, cold.

I knew then that I would never have romance other than what I found written on a page. My heart set itself to beating in rhythm with the lovers in the novels I devoured late into the night. The closest I would come to speaking words of love were those I read aloud from Katrina's letter. I shared my table with Merrill Gowan out of a sense of obligation, but I didn't feel duty bound to share any other part of myself. Not my secrets or my hopes; not my soul, not my body.

Despite the hour, I sensed my brother wouldn't be home to take supper with me. I pictured Katrina offering up her pretty, tear-filled eyes and vowing that Charles's illiteracy meant nothing to her. And then, perhaps after a swift, chaste kiss, she would take his arm and walk him into the family dinner, asking sweetly if there wasn't a place for him. And of course there would be.

So, for myself, I cut two thick slices of bread and slathered them with butter and some of Merrill's aunt's plum preserves (which really were quite good) and made myself a weak cup of tea. I set the lamp in the middle of the table and read and ate long into the night. (There may have been more pieces of bread eaten.) It was a story of a man and a woman afraid to openly declare their love, as the woman's father might not approve, but in the end—which I reached at nearly ten o'clock—they were married with his blessing and a little money to begin a life of their own.

The story did nothing to ease my sorrows, and I felt the sting of tears again when Charles came through the kitchen door. His hair was mussed more than usual, his vest askew.

"So?" I said, barely managing the single syllable.

"You were right," he said, "about everything."

"Good." I brushed my crumbs from the table and took up the lamp. "You know how much I love to be right."

"I'm going to ask her to marry me. And I think she'll say yes. You were right about that too."

"Oh? Well. . ." We'd never been physically demonstrative with one another, so I felt no compulsion to hug him. Besides, my hands were full with a book in one and the lamp in the other, so I chose instead to lift my voice to an enthusiastic pitch and said, "I am so happy for you, Brother. I truly am. I've always longed for a sister."

That was a bald lie, but it seemed the thing to say, and the relief that washed across his face justified the sin.

"It's late," he said. "We can talk more in the morning."

"Yes. I'm taking the light up with me now. Are you coming up? Or shall I leave it?"

"Take it. I'll be up in a bit."

I wished him a good night and made a little joke about knowing his dreams would be pleasant, then went upstairs to my room. I turned down the flame and noticed my shadow stretched across the wall, the dark form pantomiming every movement as I changed into my night dress and let down my hair. Somewhere, not three blocks away, Katrina was no doubt performing the same ritual. I pictured her in a sweet, feminine room with a white iron headboard and thick pink quilt on the bed. She no doubt had a dressing table with drawers, its top cluttered with jars of cream and bottles of perfume. Her hairbrush likely had a silver handle, unlike my wooden one, and I imagined if I strained my ear I might hear her humming some lilting tune as she ran the bristles through her curls, carefully wrapping each one while I plaited mine into the two tails I'd worn to bed all my life. Tonight was an ordinary night, just as tomorrow would be an ordinary day. I put out the light and climbed into bed, finding the darkness welcoming and familiar.

The next morning, over coffee and eggs, Charles replayed his conversation with Katrina. At certain points in the story, he blushed red to the top of his ears, and I knew he was skipping over details. The swamp of self-pity in which I'd wallowed for hours into the night slowly dried as my genuine love for my brother took precedence.

"Tell me," I said, "exactly how you proposed."

"Aw, Sister—"

"Don't tell me you don't remember. Your mind is a trap. Tell me."

"I said, 'Do you suppose a man like me could be a good husband?' And she said, 'Yes, Charles, I do.' And I said, 'Do you think you would like to have me as a husband?' And she said, 'Yes, Charles, I would.'"

"That's it?"

He held up his hands. "Didn't know it needed more."

"It doesn't," I said. "It's perfect. Did you speak to her father?"

"That's tonight. I know you like me to be on hand to greet Merrill, but I'd hoped to get over to the Roses' a little early."

"Of course you should." I sopped up the last of my egg with the heel of bread. "Don't give it another thought."

In the midst of so much excitement, I'd forgotten that today was Thursday and that I would be expected to put a smile on my face and a meal on the table for a man who didn't realize he had no right to expect me to do so. When the breakfast dishes were cleared and washed, I butchered a chicken, stewing it with parsnips and carrots, chastising myself every time I thought about how much Merrill would prefer dumplings to biscuits.

After straightening his tie and checking that his trousers were neatly pressed, I gave Charles a kiss on the cheek for love and a slug to the arm for courage.

"Remember," I said at the door, "you are worthy of this woman. You've taken care of me all my life. You're a man of industry and integrity, and most of all you love his daughter with all your heart, and she loves you."

"Are you sure you don't want to go in my place? Talk to Mr. Rose on my behalf?"

"Oh yes! Please. Just let me fetch my hat and you can stay here and listen to Merrill Gowan tell yet another story about wheat blight."

He laughed but let the end of it trail off. "He's a good man, Sister. He's—what did you say?—a man of industry and integrity."

"That he is," I said, thinking that we'd left out the most important part: *I do not love him.*

I closed the door behind my brother and went about making final preparations for my own evening. I made no concerted efforts in my appearance other than running damp fingers to smooth my hair and tying a fresh apron over my dress. The stew bubbled delightfully, and I removed it from the stove to cool on the table, setting two places on either side.

I hated the anticipation that squirmed inside. I resented that ridiculous satisfaction that came when Merrill declared my food delicious and asked for a second or third helping, chalking it up to domestic vanity. I would be as pleased if my brother offered the same compliment. Or a stranger. Though I'd never indulged myself, I knew this was the reason women baked pies in hopes of ribbons at the county fair.

The knock at the shop door was by now familiar, but the sound on the other side of it was not. Conversation. We'd drawn the shades at the windows and the door, but I could see the shuffling presence of two men on the other side. Had Charles lost his nerve? Or had something disastrous happened to send him straight back home? I hastened to slide the bolt and open the door, then held on to it with a grip strong enough to keep me upright when I saw the man standing shoulder to shoulder with Merrill Gowan.

"Oscar Garland," I said, the name a burst of inquiry.

"I hope you don't mind," Merrill said, stepping across the threshold and taking off his hat. "Oscar's staying with me, doing some work, and I mentioned I was coming here for supper—"

"And I finagled myself an invitation," Oscar said, following Merrill inside.

"I know it's not the custom," Merrill said, "a guest bringin' a guest."

"Nonsense," I said, indicating the tree for their hats. "We're all friends, aren't we? No need for formality. I've plenty of food and plenty of dishes. No trouble at all to set another place."

Words were pouring out of my mouth like water from a drain after a storm, and I managed to say all of this without directly looking at either man. I summoned them to follow me through the darkened shop, apologizing for the lack of a formal dining room, but seeing as it was usually my brother and I at the table, it seemed a better use of space to expand the parlor to make room for all of my books.

"I don't believe I've ever seen your parlor," Merrill said.

"Oh, haven't you?" But I made no offer to invite them there now.

In the kitchen, I laid a place for myself at the table's long edge, filled our water glasses from the pewter pitcher, and put two steaming, open biscuits on each plate. We took our seats and, though I'd always deferred to Merrill until tonight, I myself prayed a blessing over our food, hoping that bit of prayer would give me the courage to actually eat it.

The silence was comfortable as we filled our plates, each man holding his steady as I spooned chicken and vegetables and drizzled gravy over the biscuits. We were quiet for the first few bites too, until Oscar let out an appreciative sound and declared there was something familiar about this dish.

"There should be," I said, daring a glance up at him. "It's your mother's recipe."

He slammed his hand on the table in a gesture more symbolic than startling. "That's it!" He speared a turnip, popped it in his mouth, and spoke around it. "Yours is better, though. And if you ever tell her, I'll deny it."

The warmth on my face had nothing to do with the steaming food. Merrill cleared his throat as if reminding us of his presence, and I felt compelled to explain. "Years ago, my brother and I rented a room in Mrs. Garland's boardinghouse. She let me help in the kitchen, so everything I know about cooking I learned from her." I looked over to Oscar. "I'd never seen a kitchen so grand as that. We never had more than a stove and a grate growing up. She was so gracious and patient."

"I should write her a letter of gratitude," Merrill said, slicing his fork through his biscuit.

The proprietary tone in his comment embarrassed me, and I gave it no attention at all. Instead, I mentioned the subtle changes I made to the recipe, adding rosemary and black pepper, then asked Oscar how it came to be that he was staying out on Merrill's farm.

"Oh, you know," he said, shoveling his food in a way that absolutely thrilled me, "I still don't have a place of my own, so I like to go about, hiring on where I can. All the work and none of the worry, I say. Best way to farm. Can't lose what you don't own."

Merrill's brow furrowed in disapproval, but I laughed off the comment. I wanted to say that it must be nice to be a man, to have the freedom to wander hither and fro in this world without a care about the opinions or expectations of others, but there was already an uncomfortable undercurrent flowing between us, and I thought it better to try to build a bridge instead.

"So, Mr. Gowan," I said, addressing him as I always had, "did you know that you have a real, live hero living under your roof?"

He looked over to Oscar. "I did not."

"You don't," Oscar said, an edge to his voice that fell somewhere between humility and caution.

"Of course he does," I said, blowing past his discomfort. "Have you not told him the story?"

"It's a story people tell *about* me more than one I tell myself."

"Well, somebody tell me," Merrill said.

Oscar raised an eyebrow and gestured toward me in a way that made me wish I'd never brought up the subject, but I had, and there was no turning back now, so I launched.

"Years ago—before my brother and I moved into De Smet—it was a horrible winter. Everywhere. Blizzard after blizzard, and the snow piled so high that trains couldn't get through. So everybody in this town—"

"De Smet," Oscar interjected. "Not *this* town."

I didn't miss a beat. "They were effectively starving to death. No food anywhere. So this one"—I pointed my fork at Oscar—"and another man—"

"Almanzo Wilder," Oscar said.

"Almanzo Wilder took it upon themselves to ride out to a farmer who had his seed wheat and convinced him to sell it to them."

Merrill blinked, and somehow the tale seemed so small around my table, told in my voice—nothing like the regaling cadence of the times I'd heard it before, with people fighting over who would get to fill in the details.

"Well now," Merrill said, "that was brave. You must have been quite young at the time. How old were you?"

"Seventeen," Oscar said. "So I'd say more foolish than brave."

"Nonsense," I said. He was sitting to my left, and before I could think of the implication, I reached over and touched his arm, right above his wrist at the edge of his rolled-up sleeve. I can't claim the boldness that moved me, and I don't think Oscar even noticed. But Merrill did. I only moved my hand because I felt the burning of Merrill's glare upon it. "Anyway, legend has it—"

"There's no legend, Miss Patterson. It's something I did out of boredom from sitting around for weeks on end. Nothing more than any man would do, any man who didn't have a family depending on him."

"You're right," I said, feeling chastised. "And I do not mean to imply that you have ever been a braggart." I looked to Merrill. "When Charles and I moved to De Smet, we heard about this from all sorts of townspeople before I even met Oscar."

"And now I've heard it too," Merrill said. "I've never done anything half so brave."

"We had clear skies and good horses. If we'd had a couple of pretty ladies with us, it would have been a typical Sunday afternoon." Oscar winked at me as I took a bite of biscuit, and only the powers of polite company kept me from choking to death.

"I'll bet you had girls swooning all over town," Merrill said, the conspiratorial upturn at the corner of his mouth the first hint of humor I'd ever seen.

"Yeah, well, the only one that mattered ended up running off with the other guy."

Oscar stared into his plate like he wanted to dive in; otherwise

I'd never have the courage to speak.

"You mean Miss Ingalls? Laura Ingalls?"

He looked up, moustache twitching. "*Miss* Ingalls?"

"She was my teacher. For a little while. A little homestead school north of town."

"That was you?" He gave his head a shake and set his spoon on the table. "I mean, you were part of that school?"

I bristled. "I take it she never had much to say about us?"

"Oh, she had a lot to say."

"None of it very good, I take it?" The way he didn't answer my question confirmed my assumption. I'd always known Miss Ingalls wasn't happy with our school. We all knew it. She made no attempt to hide the fact that she found us dull and dim. "You know Almanzo Wilder was her personal hero too, don't you? He came to pick her up in his cutter every Friday. Once on this bitter, snowy day, and she left us all to find our way home."

"I know. Not about her leaving you to find your way home. But the storm, I know. I sent him off to fetch her."

"You sound like you regret it."

"It was a fool's errand. I put my friend in danger. And what's worse. . ."

I picked up his train of thought. "You put her in danger too. But at least she was in a nice cutter under a pile of snug blankets." I did not imagine his wincing at the image of Laura and Almanzo cuddled together against the cold. That's when I realized that, if nothing else, Oscar Garland and I shared one thing: a jealousy that followed those tracks the cutter left in the cold. Oscar, because Laura loved Almanzo, and I because—it was becoming clear to me—Oscar loved Laura. How could the warm, living, flesh-and-blood man sit at my table and obviously pine for that cold, brittle, long-gone girl? "Anyway," I said, digging in, "Charles and I were battling it out on foot. As were the other children."

"Well," Merrill inserted himself into the conversation with the delicacy of plunging a dull knife into hard cheese, "it seems everyone made it home safe and sound, doesn't it?"

Neither Oscar nor I acknowledged that he'd spoken at all but redirected our energy to the food in front of us. After a few beats of silence, Merrill spoke up again, bringing the conversation around to horses and harnesses and a host of other things I cared nothing about. I let the men talk to each other while I made complementary little sounds and contributed what bits of interest I could. I'd never offered Merrill dessert, ready as I was each week to usher him out at the end of our meal, but even though I knew Oscar to be so far removed from my grasp, I could not help wanting to keep him close a little longer. I had a respectable amount of spice cake, which I sliced and arranged on saucers filled with cream. It was a trick I'd learned from Oscar's mother to disguise the dryness of an old cake, but if he recognized it, he said nothing. I even put on a pot of coffee, and the three of us were somehow chatting easily when Charles came into the kitchen, Katrina on his arm.

It was the first I'd seen them together since before their courtship started, and the sight of them took away my breath. My brother was a different man when standing next to this woman. Everything about him—his countenance, his posture, the set of his mouth, the stillness of his hands—he'd been transformed into yet another man beyond my reach. If the kitchen caught fire, he would scoop Katrina up and leave me to burn. If she and I began to speak at the same time, his ear would tune to her voice.

Being gentlemen, both Merrill and Oscar stood upon Katrina's entrance, and I did too, throwing myself into the instinctual duty of fetching coffee, but Charles waved me off.

"I have to get Katrina straight back home, but we wanted you to be the first to know—well, I guess you and these fine fellows. Evening, Cap." His greeting held the smallest hint of surprise.

"Evening," Oscar said.

"Anyhoo," Charles continued, "we wanted you to be the first to celebrate with us. I have asked Katrina to marry me, and she said yes. Moreover, so did her father."

Through all of this, Katrina hung on adoringly, her eyes never straying from Charles until I said, "Welcome, Sister." Then, with reluctance, she pulled herself away and allowed for my quick embrace. Merrill shook Charles's hand as did Oscar, each taking Katrina's hand too as we spoke congratulations and best wishes.

The conversation became a blur behind me as I busied myself with dishes. Charles and Katrina and Oscar spoke over each other, but I didn't hear a word from Merrill. I did, however, sense a movement over my shoulder and turned to see him, standing, looking at me with a new appetite that had nothing to do with the cake plates in his hands.

CHAPTER 5

TRIXIE

*T*rixie always thought of the drive home as a languid time machine. Her neighborhood was the essence of modern America—resplendent with commercial businesses and residents of every color living together in bustling harmony. Then, after a quick zip of freeways and looping exits, the road grew quiet as she sped past one farm after another, each looking like something out of a children's book: red barns, tall silos, cows, corn. Miles of green forest, miles and miles of crops. Tiny white churches with pointy steeples and stained glass. Except for the massive metal machines hurtling down the paved road, her great-grandmother would have recognized all of this at Trixie's age. Take two steps off the highway and the world took on the silence of a century ago.

Normally, by the time she took the first turn (those were the directions: drive until the road ends, then turn left), she had given herself over to the peace that came with an engine humming an undercurrent beneath a steady stream of rock and roll. But then, she'd never been sent off with a kiss before.

She'd inadvertently managed to time her departure with the first hour of the American Top 40 radio broadcast, something she usually listened to while carrying a portable radio from room to room doing her weekend chores. She sang along as she could, pitching her voice to Karen Carpenter with "Won't Last a Day without You" as well as Elton John's "Bennie and the Jets." She wailed with Carly Simon, singing, "I haven't got time for the pain. . ." and commiserated with

Olivia Newton John—"If You Love Me, Let Me Go." By the time she saw her family's three-story ramshackle blue farmhouse poking through the breakfront trees, she was belting out the week's number one song through tears: *Billy, don't be a hero. Come back to me.*

Always a sucker for a tragic tale, Trixie could *see* the lyrics—the young soldier in his blue uniform, his fiancée's head on his shoulder, begging him to come home. And the tragic letter informing her that he never, ever would.

She wiped the last of her ridiculous tears on the back of her hand as the car came crunching to a stop on the gravel drive. Casey Kasem was signing off, making predictions for the next week's countdown, but she cut him off midsentence, killing the car's engine and taking a deep breath. Normally her car would by now be bombarded with three generations of mothers—hers, her grandmother, and her great-grandmother—who would have been tracking the nearly three-hour drive to the minute. Now, there wasn't even a flutter of a window curtain to let her know that anybody was watching at all.

The thought set like a stone in her stomach. They must all be gathered around GG Mariah's bed, waiting, spending the precious final minutes. Unless—no. Surely they would have called if she had passed in the night.

She got out of her car and took her bag from the trunk, swatting away the memory of Ron's kiss with a promise to herself to get back to it later, and walked up the sagging steps to the porch that spanned the front of the house. The screen door was new, but the front door was the same Trixie passed through a million times over the course of her life. Until today. Because it was locked.

In her life, it had never been locked. Not at night, not when the entire family was away for a day in town, not when the entire family was away for a weekend of camping at the lake. She knocked, quietly at first, like this was some sideways mistake, then again, bolder. The knob turned, the door opened, but there was nobody there. Except—

"Hello?"

Trixie looked down at the tentative voice and saw a little girl standing, clutching a book to her chest.

"Hello?" Trixie returned, equally unsure.

"I'm not supposed to let anybody in."

"You can let me in. I live here." Anybody else might have softened their tone or bent to look the girl in the eyes, but Trixie had been around few children in her life and never counted any as a positive experience.

"Are you Trixie?"

"I am." She had the absurd notion that the kid might ask her to show identification, but instead she backed away, opening the door wider with each step. Trixie got herself and her bag through and took the initiative to shut the door.

The light inside was dim, all the curtains closed as if they'd gotten no attention that morning. It took a minute for Trixie's eyes to adjust, and when they did, they fell on the girl again. The *little* girl. Trixie would guess her to be five or six—the number arrived from a lifetime of watching kids on television. Her long brown hair was parted on the side and secured with a barrette, and she wore a pair of pale pink shorts and a T-shirt printed with tiny blue flowers. Her socks were grayish, and since she wasn't wearing shoes, one seemed to have slipped almost to the arch of her little foot. The sight triggered an irrational desire for Trixie to tug it up, but she resisted and instead asked, "Who are you?"

"Samantha," the girl said. Only, because she was missing four teeth across the front of her mouth, the name came out with the same sound on both ends. *Thamantha.* "And you're Trixie."

"We've established that."

"You don't look like a Trixie."

Like I haven't heard that a million times. "You look *exactly* like a Samantha."

Samantha smiled, something Trixie found immediately, and oddly, rewarding.

"Have you heard of Trixie Belden?" Samantha asked.

"I have," Trixie said. "She's a girl detective. Do you read those books?"

Samantha shook her head. "They're too advanced for me. But

my babysitter reads them sometimes, and she likes them. She has a boyfriend."

"Your babysitter has a boyfriend?"

"No. Trixie Belden has a boyfriend. And she's only fourteen years old, so she's not supposed to have a boyfriend. My babysitter is fourteen years old too. And she doesn't have a boyfriend. Do you have a boyfriend?"

"Wait," Trixie said, too late to interrupt the flow of lisping exposition before it reached the final inquiry, which, frankly, was none of the child's business. "Who are you?"

"I'm Samantha."

"Yes. Samantha. But, like, why are you here?"

"I'm here with my dad. He's a doctor."

Then Trixie saw it. The cowlick on the right side that no barrette could restrain. The squareness of her jaw, the sandy color of the lashes fanning above those too-blue eyes.

"Dr. Carter?" Trixie's mouth still had trouble with the unfamiliar title.

"He's my dad."

"You're—you're Cam's daughter?" Apparently there was one link in the chain of gossip that hadn't made it to the kitchen table.

"Oh, I see you two have met." Trixie's mother swept herself into the conversation as if Trixie and the girl were at a swanky cocktail party for which only she—Alma Gowan—was properly dressed. Trixie's mother always looked like something from a midcentury fashion plate. Her dresses were either belted numbers with a fitted top and wide, swinging skirt, or—like now—fitted within an inch of every curve. Her figure was a testament to the power of a good girdle—nipped waist, proportioned hips. Her bust simultaneously impressive and restrained. She wore her blond hair in a perpetual twist and her makeup precise with black, winged eyeliner and matte red lipstick. Trixie always thought her mother looked like a Barbie doll—the very first ones, with eyes flirtatiously downcast and lips pursed, like she was thinking about giving a gentleman a kiss but probably wouldn't.

"Mom," Trixie said, offering her cheek for the kiss that wouldn't quite land on her cheek. "What is going on?"

"Trust me," she said, the words barely eking out of the corner of her mouth, "we were all surprised." Then, in a normal tone, "We're all upstairs, sitting with Gram."

"All right."

Trixie headed for the stairs but stopped at her mother's, "Wait. You've had a long drive. Come with me into the kitchen. I'm putting on some coffee. And making *this one* some lunch. A late lunch, isn't it, honey? I'm sure you're hungry."

"Yes, ma'am," Samantha said, looking at Alma adoringly.

Trixie rolled her eyes. To the rest of the world—meaning, anyone who actually lived outside of this house—Alma appeared to be the perfect mother. She dressed like a cross between Donna Reed and Mrs. Cleaver, perpetually stuck in the world of the 1950s ideal. Growing up, Trixie loved having friends over to show off her pretty mother. She would host slumber parties and beam when Alma came in with trays of Rice Krispies treats and vats of hot chocolate with homemade marshmallows. Other mothers at other slumber parties would order pizza and roam the house in ratty bathrobes with their hair in curlers. Alma did too, of course, but never with guests or visitors of any kind. If the postman came at nine o'clock in the morning needing a signature on a package, he'd wait on the front porch until Alma was dressed, coifed, made-up, and shod. Fortunately, she'd streamlined the process to a matter of minutes.

As Trixie grew older, around ten, she realized the reason behind the ruse. Inevitably, at some time during the sleepover, or a study date with a new friend, or a birthday party with a beautifully piped cake and a spread of tiny sandwiches, somebody would ask, *"Where's your dad?"* And Trixie would have to answer, *"I don't know."* It never occurred to her to make up a story, because her mother had always been truthful with her. When Trixie asked, *"Who's my dad?"* Alma gave the same answer always.

"Best I can offer is a good guess."

Always a fan of classic romantic films, a young Alma had given herself over to the cause of sending soldiers off to Korea with the memory of a girl worth coming home for. Soldiers, plural, gave a wrong impression. There were only two, and as she always said, a possible third. None had written her their promised letters. None ever came back to see what they'd left behind, and what one of them left behind was Trixie.

Now she followed her mother into the kitchen with Samantha trailing behind, and though she had absolutely no genetic connection to the child, couldn't help thinking, *Oh. Look. Another generation.*

Trixie set about making coffee (Alma always made it too strong) while Alma made a peanut butter and honey sandwich for Samantha before commencing to make a stack of sandwiches, which she cut into triangles and arranged on a large plate.

"So, how is GG?" Trixie asked. The silence upstairs was unsettling, given how this—a house full of women—was usually bouncing with chatter and shouts. "Why are you trying to keep me away?"

Alma licked the knife before plunging it back into the jar. "She's very weak. Taken to her bed, and honestly, it's like she's wasting away right in front of us."

"Is she alert?"

"Mostly. She eats very little and won't drink anything but Dr Pepper, which isn't good for her at all."

"Mom, she's one hundred and four years old. She's a Pepper. They should make commercials with her."

"Well, you know what they say. The kidneys are the first to go."

"My dad says she's an amazing woman," Samantha said, reminding Trixie and Alma of her presence. "He says she knew Laura."

Trixie was taking four mugs down from the cabinet, and at the sound of the name, she let them clatter to the counter.

"She doesn't know," Alma whispered, squeezing the upside-down honey bear over a top slice of bread.

Trixie saw the book Samantha had been holding under her arm now sitting beside her plate. How could she not have noticed before? The familiar shade of yellow. The crayon-colored image of a little girl clutching a doll. Bearded Pa looking on. *Little House in the Big Woods* by Laura Ingalls Wilder. GG always told everyone who would listen that she knew the *real* Laura Ingalls, the word *real* wrapped tight in derision.

"Where did you get that book?" Trixie's voice was unnaturally high, because she knew. She'd recognize that fold along the front cover anywhere.

"I found it."

"She was taking a nap in your old room," Alma said, "while Dr. Carter was seeing to Gram."

"Looks like she was doing a little *snooping* in my room," Trixie said not quite under her breath.

"I wasn't snooping," Samantha said indignantly. "Mrs. G said I could look through the box and find a stuffed animal to sleep with, and I found this."

"You had to dig down through a lot of bears to find that," Trixie said. She had the whole series, each title squirreled away in a different part of the house. She knew she should take them home—to *her* home, in Minneapolis, but they seemed to belong here, with other bits of her childhood. The girl was looking at her through squinted eyes, as if daring Trixie to take the argument further. Instead, Trixie poured a glass of milk in her favorite Winnie-the-Pooh glass (a jelly jar when she was Samantha's age) and set it on the table. "Have you read it?" She rethought the question, having no idea of age and reading level. "*Can* you read it?"

Samantha nodded, biting into her sandwich. "Yes, but I haven't finished it. I love Mary. The sister. She's sweet."

"Don't talk with your mouth full, dear," Alma said, though the mouthful of bread and peanut butter had little impact on Samantha's speech. "Why don't you sit here and enjoy your lunch and read while Miss Trixie and I take our snack to the others upstairs?"

"Okay," Samantha said with the tone of a child used to getting instructions before being left alone.

"Just don't get it sticky," Trixie said, holding the tray of sandwiches in one hand and two of the four coffee mugs in the other.

"I won't. I promise. I'll finish my sandwich and wash my hands." To reinforce her vow, Samantha pushed the book a little farther away.

"Isn't she wonderful?" Alma said when they had barely left the kitchen. "Other than you, the best-mannered child I have ever seen. You'd never even know she's here."

"Always an important trait." Trixie trained her eye on her mother's rounded backside, admiring how the woman could climb the stairs carrying a tray of coffee without rattling a single spoon.

It was warmer on the second floor, even with windows open to the breeze, making Trixie wonder if glasses of iced tea might not have been a better idea than coffee, but a cold beverage wouldn't offer the sipping comfort of a hot one. They were looking for ritual more than refreshment. Once they rounded the corner at the landing, Trixie could hear voices—her grandmother's sharp, straightforward and inquisitive, followed by something low, warm, and familiar.

Cam.

She stopped and took in a restorative breath.

"Yes," Alma said without turning around.

"Yes, what?"

"Yes, he's still as handsome as ever."

GG Mariah's room was the first on the left at the top of the stairs, the largest of the four bedrooms, with its own sitting area and bathroom. It had been renovated as such in the early days of World War II to be a room to let for itinerant officers, Mariah fancying herself Wisconsin's answer to Claudette Colbert in *Since You Went Away*. Later, the sort of drifting, single-room-seeking men who answered the advertisement proved to be looking for a send-off, and when Alma spent every morning from Thanksgiving to Christmas puking in the downstairs toilet, the ROOM FOR RENT sign was tossed into the fire and Mariah moved in.

Trixie rounded the corner and braced herself. In retrospect, a good daughter of the home would have politely set the tray of sandwiches on the sideboard by the door and gone to sit at the bedside of her ailing great-grandmother. All of which Trixie eventually did, but first she stood, clutching the plate, staring at the man framed by the sunlit window, gauzy curtains fluttering around him. Tall, trim, wearing a subtly patterned shirt tucked into tan corduroy pants that sat snugly belted on his hips.

He said, "Hey there, Trix," and everything beneath her skin melted and swirled into the consistency of the sandwiches on the plate.

"Hey there, yourself," she said, and nothing else would come.

"Give me those." Trixie's grandmother, Eugenie, rose from her chair beside the bed and took the plate away, grabbing two triangles before holding it out to Cam. "Sandwich, Dr. Carter?"

"Yes, thank you Mrs. Gowan." He plucked a sandwich off the tray and held it aloft. "I mean, Eugenie."

"There ya go," Eugenie said, bustling to put the plate on the dresser top.

Anyone coming into the room would be hard-pressed to match her as Alma's mother—the two were as unalike as two women could be. Where Alma was round, Eugenie was square. Where Alma had meticulously plucked and pruned and cinched, Eugenie had given over to the forces of gravity and nature. Her figure was an undefined series of squares beneath pale slacks and a front-button cotton blouse. Eugenie Gowan, perhaps the only woman on earth for whom polyester would fade, had hair of an undetermined color cropped close in a mass of unstylish waves. Because she had earned the Gowan name by marrying into the family, GG Mariah often called her the "missing link," and not always out of earshot.

"Hi, Grandma," Trixie said, gravitating to the single bit of normalcy in the room. Alma was doling out coffee like the room was a roadside diner, Cam looked like a soap opera star, and she couldn't bring herself to face GG Mariah quite yet. She gave herself over to Eugenie's big, strong hug, taking in the scent of her sensible soap and the Aspercreme she rubbed on the back of her neck faithfully three times a day.

"Look at our big-city girl," Eugenie said, stepping an arm's length away. "Always the prettiest one in the room, I'll bet."

"Save that money for a rainy day," Trixie said, trying not to imagine Cam's eyes on her.

"I saw your last *Little Laura*," Eugenie said, getting the name of the strip wrong as she usually did. *Little Laura. Lots of Laura. Leaving Laura.* She turned to Cam. "Our Trixie has the sweetest cartoon she draws. And Little Laura was standing outside of a bookstore, holding a copy of *All the President's Men*, and she says. . .she says. . . What does she say?"

"She says they must be keeping all the president's women in the back room of the store."

"That's it! Yes, my little Trixie. Picking up the torch of family feminism."

Trixie hazarded a glance at Cam, who was smiling over the rim of his coffee. There were soft lines around his eyes—new since she last saw him. But then, he'd been nineteen years old. A lot could happen to a face in fourteen years.

"Come on now," Eugenie said, softly gripping Trixie's hand. "She's been asking for you."

It was nothing more than a turn, a pivot to the right, but the moment GG Mariah came into view, Trixie felt her strength drop and squeezed her grandmother's hand.

The bed was tall—something Mariah insisted upon after a childhood and youth spent sleeping on pallets and floors—and looked like something that should be draped with animal skins befitting a Viking lord. Instead, barely making a three-dimensional form beneath the sunflower-scattered bedspread, Trixie's beloved great-grandmother, Mariah Gowan, matriarch of generations, lay with her head propped up against the pillow and her hand listlessly at her side.

"Trixie." Her voice sounded like a handful of dried leaves crumpling between the consonants.

"Yeah, GG. I'm here."

"I know you're here. I'm old, not blind."

This was the GG Trixie grew up with, and the familiar sass in her voice gave more comfort than she knew she needed. She moved to the chair recently vacated by Eugenie and propped her elbows on the side of the bed, leaning in to kiss the soft folds of GG's cheek. "Good to see your spirits up."

"Glad to see your skirt so short. You have fabulous legs, my girl. I did too. Probably. But I was fifty years old by the time I could show them, and by then my knees were already wrinkled."

Trixie laughed, burying her face in the mattress, wondering if Cam heard. Secretly *hoping* that Cam heard. The bedding smelled of detergent and sunlight—in fact, the whole room smelled of lemon and bleach. With the conviviality and snacks, the vibe of the room felt more like a family visit than a vigil.

"Are you hungry, Gram?" Trixie's mother spoke with the same tone she'd used with Samantha. "Or would you like some coffee? Let's sit you up a bit more."

"No," Mariah said with surprising strength. "I only want to talk with my great-granddaughter." She beckoned Trixie closer. "Can you get these people to leave so I can tell you a story?"

Trixie looked around apologetically. "Maybe, give us some time to catch up?"

"That'll be fine," Alma said, smoothing the front of her dress. "Mother?"

"I'm coming," Eugenie said, following Alma out the door. "Need to set something out for supper."

Only Cam remained. He came to stand on the other side of Mariah's bed and laid two fingers against the inside of her wrist while checking his watch.

"I'm still going, right, Doc?"

Cam smiled, bent, and kissed the back of her hand. "Stronger than they taught me in medical school, Mrs. Gowan."

"Then you go back and teach them better."

Cam took a white jacket that had been hanging on the back of the door and draped it over his arm. "I'm taking off now, but I'll be back to check in tomorrow. In the meantime, of course, call me if you have any concerns." He put his hand on the doorknob and turned back. "And, good to see you, Trix."

"Good to see you too."

"Maybe we can find time to catch up a bit?"

The amount of catching up seemed a bit lopsided: he had a

daughter; she had a cat that hated her and may have kissed her boss. When she'd sat silent long enough for her great-grandmother to nudge her elbow, she said, "Sure. I'd like that."

And then he left.

"That is one handsome man," GG Mariah said.

"I know."

"He's a doctor."

"I know."

"And, he's single."

That got her attention. "He is? But he has a daughter."

Mariah's knowing smile knocked twenty years off her face. She patted Trixie's hand and said, "My, my girl. We do need to have a talk. But not about him. Not now. Sit me up."

"Okay." Trixie gently slipped her arm behind Mariah's back and eased her into a sitting position, bringing another pillow to brace behind her. She inhaled the familiar smell of her great-grandmother's favorite apple-scented shampoo as she helped gather her long hair and drape it across one bony shoulder. "Better?"

"Bring me a sandwich," Mariah said, and Trixie brought back the half-depleted plate and set it on the bed between them. Her great-grandmother had worn dentures for as long as Trixie could remember but had abandoned them in the past few years in favor of keeping to a diet of foods she could eat with her toughened gums. Looking on, Trixie couldn't help thinking of the little girl downstairs enjoying the same snack as this woman who had been alive for more than a century. She grabbed one for herself before trotting across the room to grab a cup of coffee, now cooled to the perfect temperature.

She washed down the first bite. "What do you want to talk about?"

Mariah went silent, staring at Trixie for one heartbeat after another as tears pooled in her eyes. "You look just like him."

Trixie felt her own tears. Aside from her blond hair, she looked nothing like her mother. "*Him*? My father? Do—do you know who my father is?"

"No. And haven't I always said to put that aside?"

"You have."

"Now I need you to put something else aside."

Trixie leaned forward. "What?"

Mariah's tongue flicked out to capture a drop of honey. "Every-thing." She pointed, her hand steadier and stronger than Trixie would have imagined moments before. "In the dresser. Second drawer, there's a book. Get it."

Trixie obeyed, pawing through stacks of neatly folded blouses before her fingers bumped against the hard cover. She drew it out, not knowing what to expect, then catching her breath when she read the title. It was familiar; the image on the pristine paper jacket, however, was not. The illustration depicted a round-faced, bright-eyed, grown-up Laura Ingalls, her hoop skirt filling the bottom third of the book cover, Almanzo's buggy in the background with an obscure Almanzo himself inside it.

"Is this a first edition?" Trixie asked, running a careful finger over the design, knowing, of course, that it was.

"I bought that the night you were born. Bring it here."

Trixie returned, finding GG sitting up in bed, hands waiting. She took the book, opened it, and after turning a few pages, held it out again.

Trixie studied the illustration on the open page. The style was wildly different from those in the current, modern editions. Less detailed, though the faces of the characters depicted still managed to be distinct from each other and the scene complete, even without the benefit of depth and shading.

"I know this part of the story," Trixie murmured, the memory of reading it long ago seeping back. "This is when Laura first started teaching, right? Her first students? Two sets of siblings—a brother and a sister, and an older boy with *his* younger brother and sister." She began to skim the page. "What were their names?"

"Clarence," GG said, as if reading them from an invisible ros-ter, "Ruby, Tommy. And Charles. And Mariah. Don't let the name *Martha* fool you."

Trixie tore her eyes away and looked at her great-grandmother, the impact of her words sinking in. Then, back to the illustration, to the tall, plain girl standing next to what looked like a freckle-faced boy. She turned the book and pointed. "This is you?"

GG nodded.

"So, when you say you knew Laura Ingalls, you mean—"

"She changed my name. She changed all our names. But, yes. There I am. Not very flattering, is it?"

Trixie made a sound of commiseration. "I don't think that style of illustration lends itself to flattery. Why are you just now showing me this?"

"Because I want someone—I want *you* to know who I am."

"Not Mom? Or Grandma?"

"No. Just you. For now."

Trixie closed the book and set it aside. "GG, did you by any chance exaggerate your. . .*condition*? So that I'd come to visit?"

"Maybe," GG said with a shifty grin. "Are you mad at me?"

"No," Trixie said, thinking of Ron's swift send-off kiss and the rush of memory at the sight of Cam. "Not mad, but definitely intrigued."

CHAPTER 6

MARIAH

*M*y brother, Charles, he who had been known to dither for fifteen minutes deciding whether or not to toast his bread in the morning, seemed more than ready to rush headlong into marriage. To be fair, Katrina was the driving force, declaring she wanted to be fully wed and established in their new home before the full force of winter.

"And by that," she'd said, cupping her hand to the side of her mouth, "I mean I hope to be with child and spend the worst of the winter sitting under a quilt and getting fat."

I'm not sure why she dropped her voice to a whisper and assumed such a conspiratorial air when she told me this. We were alone in my kitchen, drinking tea while Charles fiddled with something or another in the shop. Still, I acted appropriately shocked at her boldness and matched her giggle.

Moments like this made it difficult to remember that she was two years younger than I. She was the essence of what it meant to grow up as someone's treasure—an adoring mother, doting father, and a household designed to be a shelter from any discomfort. I'd bet my soul Katrina Rose had never been hungry or cold or alone. Hers had always been a life of ribbons and silk stockings. New dresses every season. From what I'd noticed this summer, she owned multiple parasols, each with tassels and a bone handle. And though I could rattle off his good qualities at the drop of one of her feathered hats, I could not quite grasp how she had come to fall in love with my brother.

But she had, and the more I tried to cover that tiny grain of jealousy with disingenuous smiles and false enthusiasm, the more it became my own private, bitter pearl.

They chose the last Saturday in August as the date for their wedding—early enough in the harvest that people would sacrifice a day of work to attend the nuptials and far enough away to plan a true social event.

"Don't know who she's trying to impress," Charles told me one night over one of our increasingly rare suppers alone. "Seems to me we could stand up in her folks' parlor and make it official."

Neither of us had ever been to a wedding, but I'd read enough about them in books to know they could be an all-consuming passion for a woman. "I'm sure she has many friends with whom she wants to share the day," I said. "You're the groom. All you have to do is show up." *Or not*, I wanted to add. Increasingly, my sweet brother seemed to have been swept up in a tide, and I wondered more than once if he knew exactly where he would be washed ashore.

As for me, I lived that summer as a captive of courtship.

The week following Charles and Katrina's announced engagement, Merrill Gowan arrived for our Thursday Supper (as I had begrudgingly come to call it) with a fresh shave, a recent haircut, and a shirt that bore faint scorch marks on one sleeve.

"Is Oscar not with you?" I asked, standing to my toes to look over his shoulder.

"He is not," Merrill said, entering my home with more authority than he had a right to assume. "I hired him to help clear the last acres I need for planting and sent him on."

"*Sent him on?*" I didn't mean to mock, but he spoke as if Oscar were some sort of troublesome vagrant, which irritated me.

"He's not a serious man, Mariah. He'd rather play baseball than work. And for all that, he'd rather work for someone else than own his own land and farm it. He's a boy."

I laughed. "He's the same age as you. Or, I think he is. How old are you? I have no idea."

"I'm twenty-five."

To that, I'm ashamed to say, I laughed again. He had the face, physique, and manner of a man ten years older, at least. My mind scrambled for something to say that would belie the rudeness of my response, but finding nothing, I awkwardly reined in my outburst and walked into the kitchen, knowing he would follow.

As we ate, he monopolized the conversation with his accomplishments. His acres and crops and profits. I listened, making sounds of approval where appropriate, resisting the urge to remind him that, save for the clearing of the acreage with the help of Oscar Garland, all of his success came by way of inheritance, not labor. He told me (again) how his house had five bedrooms, plus a parlor and dining room—far too large for a bachelor's rattling.

"All the more places for your hired help to sleep," I said. "Come harvest. Better than making them bunk in the barn."

"I won't be hiring Garland," he said. "I need workers who are more—"

"*Serious?*"

"For lack of a better word."

"Oh Mr. Gowan. There is always a better word."

Other women—silly women like Katrina—might have been flattered at the idea of one man's jealousy of another, but I was not. I might have been if I had any reason to believe that Oscar was off brooding, plotting some way to pay a calling of his own, but surely he knew he need only step onto my porch to be invited in. There were enough girls in De Smet to keep him company, no need for him to travel seven miles to see me.

I changed the topic then, bringing us to talk about the heat and wind and weather—very nearly the same conversation we had every week. I asked if he had ever seen the ocean, and he said he hadn't but that the shores of Lake Michigan were no poor substitute. I told him I'd recently read a novel by Jules Verne about an adventure in a submarine with great sea monsters and a mysterious captain. He said he saw no use for novels and had little time to read, given the work he must do daily on his farm.

And then we finished our meal in silence.

I'd barely cleared our dishes when I turned from the sink to find him directly in front of me, droplets of sweat on his brow that had nothing to do with the long-cold stove.

"Mariah." He pronounced my name as if he'd been practicing it in front of a mirror for an hour. Each syllable heavy with intent. I could not back away, and to dodge to the left or the right seemed. . . comical. I wrapped my hands in the dish towel to ward off his touch. Subconsciously, my breathing synced with his, and for what seemed an eternity, the only sound was the ticking clock and our labored exhalations. His fueled by passion; mine, fear—not for my safety but for my person. He engulfed me, making it impossible not only for me to move but to think—to form any thought other than *No*.

"Mr. Gowan," I said finally, "if you'll step aside, please. I'd like to clean the table."

He only repeated my name and stepped closer. I never had a mother to warn me about such things, but, like most women, I carried with me a keen sense that men moved through this world with the assumption that any and all in it was theirs for the taking. Including women. And, like most women, I found myself squelching the survival instinct that wanted me to stomp on his toes or kick his shin (or higher, if need be) to initiate my escape. One never knew what retribution a physical attack could inspire. All this left me with a woman's greatest weapon: deception.

"Mr. Gowan, I asked Charles to come home early this evening. The handle on the oven door—"

"You don't need to be afraid of me, Mariah."

"Then step back, please?"

He complied but not without taking my rag-wrapped hands in his, creating both more space between us and none at all.

He lowered his eyes, shuffled his feet, then looked up again, fortified. "What I am about to ask will not be a surprise to you."

"Then, please, Mr. Gowan, don't ask."

He plowed on as if I hadn't spoken. "We have shown ourselves to be well-suited."

"We have shared six meals together."

"Which I have enjoyed, both the food and the conversation."

I had to bite my lip to stop myself from thanking him. Or to return the compliment. I would not give him an inch or a word. I didn't need to. He uncovered my hands and brought them within inches of his lips. "I believe you have too."

Do not kiss me. Do not kiss me. The command rolled through my mind like a log let loose down a hill, but I spoke it only with a silent, narrow-eyed glare. Rage at the injustice of this helplessness—knowing he was in my kitchen, my home, at my invitation—brought a flush to my cheeks that I feared he would misinterpret. I could not stay silent.

"I have come to find you an unexpected friend," I said. A peace offering.

"You know I want to be more than that." He bent his head, and with only a fraction of space and time to react, I squeezed his fingers and turned my arms into resistant pillars of stone.

"I am sorry if I gave you the impression that I return those feelings. But I assure you, I do not."

"You might. In time."

The thread of hope in his voice almost tied itself to my resolve, ready to yank it away. This was not a moment for subtlety or even kindness. I owed him nothing. I worked my hands out of his grip, stepped to the side, and said, "That is not how I wish to spend my time."

"How? Living in a fine home? Being a farmer's wife?"

"Being *your* wife. Being anybody's wife whom I do not love. Don't I deserve the same happiness that my brother has?"

"I could make you happy."

"No, Mr. Gowan. I don't think you ever could."

That was the death blow, and I watched him deflate before my eyes. His shoulders rounded, his head drooped, and his lips remained parted as if waiting for the next thing to say. Every womanly instinct within me wanted to reach out, to stroke his cheek and apologize and tell him that he would be fine. He would recover and see—someday—that this was the best thing. I wanted to heap blame for his sadness upon myself, take that burden in the belief that, as a woman, I could carry his weight as well as my own. Oh, I was tempted, but I held firm and resumed my chore, giving wide berth around him as I took the coffee cups from the table and set them on the sideboard, lest he try again to trap me at the sink.

He asked, "What will you do?"

"What will I do when?"

"After Charles and Katrina marry. And they want to make a home together. Who will take care of you?"

I made a dark, bitter sound. "I suppose it would surprise you to know that *I* have been taking care of *him* all these years. It's Katrina who should be worried."

"You'll be alone."

"I'll have my brother, as I always have. Plus, a new sister. I'll be far from alone." But even as I spoke, my confidence waned. I'd already lost my brother. Maybe not his physical presence, but his affection and attention were already divided and not by equal measure. I took a deep, restorative breath. "Goodness, the time. It's late."

Merrill said nothing in direct response but offered a resigned, sad smile and made his shuffling way through the shop to the front door, not stopping until he was at the hook where I'd hung his hat. He took it and turned it over and over in his hands. "I'm going to ask you one more time—"

"Please don't—"

"And then I won't ask you again. Will you marry me, Mariah? Will you come to my home and make it yours? Will you be my wife?"

"No," I said, my hand gripping the handle of the door. "And no. And no." I intended my response to be a bit of a joke, but he had none of it.

"Then I guess I can assume this was my last supper here?"

"I think that would be best."

Merrill leaned forward one more time, in the least menacing way possible, and planted a soft kiss on my cheek. "You know, he doesn't love you either."

I felt my face burst into flame and only wished that I had burned him.

"Oscar, I mean," he said, as if I needed elaboration. "All that time at my house—four days, I think—and he didn't mention you once. If you think he is the better way to spend your time, I'm afraid it's going to be a waste."

If you had asked me earlier that afternoon if Merrill Gowan had the wherewithal to plunge a dagger into my heart and leave me bleeding on the floor, I would have laughed at the notion and deemed it as likely as a horse sprouting wings. But then, for who knows how long, I stood in my brother's dark, empty workshop with no recollection of the moment when I found myself alone. I was too shocked to cry. Too shocked and too practical. I hadn't earned the privilege of being destroyed by what I knew to be the truth. I was a woman divided, half of me mooning with childish infatuation and half of me already withered and alone, with nothing left to knit my two selves together.

I was still standing there when Charles found me. He'd come in through the kitchen, as he always did. Otherwise, he'd be tempted to pick up an abandoned project and work late into the night.

"Mariah? Sister?" His voice was muffled by the ache pounding in my head. I felt too brittle to even turn my face to acknowledge him. He continued saying my name until he was right in front of me. "Are you all right? You look like you've seen a ghost."

"I'm fine," I said, my tone too flat to convince either of us.

"D—Did Gowan do something? Something. . .untoward?"

I knew Merrill's proposal would not fit my brother's definition of *untoward*, and I felt a smile tugging at the corner of my mouth. "No, Brother. Nothing like that."

"Did he. . .*say* anything?"

He looked so flummoxed, so rumpled and uncomfortable, I once again wondered how Katrina Rose, she of the flitting tongue and bouncing curls, claimed him as the love of her life. I looped my arm in his. "Remind me never to tell you a secret. You are incapable of keeping them. Now, since you are here, come help me with the dishes."

He stepped with me but protested, "What secret? What did I say?"

"Tell me, did Merrill Gowan tell you what his intentions were tonight?"

"You mean, did he ask for my blessing?"

By now we were in the kitchen where I tasked him with shaving soap into the basin while I scraped the plates into the bucket by the door. I straightened. "Blessing?"

"He's a good man. He wanted to make sure that I approved."

At that moment, I could have shattered the plate to the floor but chose instead to grip it until my knuckles turned white. I was so *tired* of hearing about what a good man he was. Would Charles have thought him a good man an hour before when, in this very spot, he loomed over me against my wishes? Or later, when he chose the cruelest words to crush my spirit? Was he a good man for seeking my brother's approval before my own?

Of course, I asked him none of these questions. Only, "And do you?"

"He's a g—"

"Don't!" I dropped the plate in the tub, heedless of the splashing water. "Don't tell me again that he is a *good man*. I don't want to hear it. I do not love him, Charles. As well-intentioned as you were to bring him to me, I do not love him."

"But he loves you."

"Really? Did he say so?"

"Not in so many words. Men don't say such things. But I'm sure he does."

"No." I shook my head to double my response. "No, he doesn't love me. Men *do* say such things to women."

"So that's it? You won't marry him?"

"I won't," I said, my voice gentle now but freighted with finality.

We didn't speak for a while as he rolled up his sleeves and plunged his hands into the soapy water. He ran the dishrag over a plate, and when he handed it over to me to rinse and dry, I thanked myself for preserving it from being a scattering of shards on the floor.

"I don't suppose you'll be doing dishes with Katrina Rose once you're married," I said, putting the plate on the shelf.

"Why not? We intend to eat."

"I have a feeling she is going to pride herself on being the perfect wife. She'll dote on you."

"That'll be fun. I've never been doted on before."

I smacked his elbow with the rolled-up towel, thankful for the lighter mood. "Something we haven't talked about, though. Are you planning to live here?"

"Yes. At first. For a while, at least. But then eventually we will want something bigger. Away from the shop, I mean. A house in town but not here. It's not really suitable for a family."

His answer held an unfamiliar quality. These were Katrina's words, not his own. I was glad to have something to busy ourselves so we didn't have to look directly at each other.

"But you," he said, "you're welcome to stay as long as you like. Forever, even, if you're not going to get married. Katrina won't mind."

"Oh, Katrina won't mind if I continue to live in my own home?"

"I didn't mean—"

I laid my hand on his sleeve, stopping him before he could apologize. "It's fine." The look of relief on his face melted me, and I wanted to end the day free of rancor. "Tell you what. How about I put on some tea and we have some bread and butter and jam for dessert and read some more of the Jules Verne novel?"

"The one about the submarine?"

"Yes. I've read on ahead, but I'll gladly go back."

"That sounds fine."

"Good. You put on the water. I'll go fetch the book."

I took a stub of candle, even though I often navigated the house in darkness. Part of me knew Charles was only indulging me, but our nightly reading had been the ritual that bound us together, distracting us from the saddest chapters in our lives. It had always been an escape, and tonight it was no different, only we were escaping all the *good* that had come our way. However begrudging, I had to admit that his upcoming marriage to Katrina was an unexpected miracle, and—in the life of any other girl—Merrill's proposal would be seen as a blessing.

Upstairs I found the book, marked my place, and then skimmed for the chapter where Captain Nemo is introduced. That would be exciting. Back downstairs, the kettle was hissing and a stack of bread sat directly on the table. No plates.

"I didn't want to dirty dishes again," Charles said, "except the cups. And the knife."

"Good idea." I sat down, grabbed a piece of bread, and took the lid off the butter dish. "What do you think happened to all of our belongings?"

He furrowed his brow. "What belongings?"

"From the cabin. On the homestead with Pa. We had dishes, you know. And a good skillet and a big stew pot. And cups and saucers. Do you remember the pattern?"

He shook his head. "I never thought about it."

"Me either. At least not often. But maybe the upcoming wedding is making me nostalgic." *Plus*—I did not say aloud—*I'm sure Katrina will be wanting her own things. What will happen to these?*

"I suppose whoever got the land got the cabin and just. . .used them."

I smeared a bit of jam atop the butter. It was the last of the good plum jam, put up by Merrill's aunt, and if there were an infinite supply, I might have been more easily persuaded to marry him just for that. "I guess men don't tend to get sentimental about plates."

He chuckled. "I guess we don't."

I read the adventures of the *Nautilus* until deep into the night, until we lost count of the number of the clock's chimes. I read for Charles's sake, and he listened for mine. As I closed the book at the end of a chapter, I wondered if it had always been so. Had he always been more capable than I'd assumed? Did he wander through novels of adventure as a mere indulgence?

"It's a good story," he said, as if reading my thoughts and sensing my need for reassurance.

"It is. I only hope we'll be able to finish it before the wedding."

"If not, then after. There'll still be evenings for reading."

"There will," I said. As far as I knew, it was the first lie we ever told each other.

CHAPTER 7

TRIXIE

*T*rixie crept downstairs Sunday morning, lured by the smell of coffee and the promise of pancakes. Such had been the pre-church breakfast in this house all of her life, and nothing had changed, save for the electric griddle instead of the giant cast-iron skillet. Her mother, wearing a full apron over a floral sheath dress, stood at the ready, spatula hovering with intent.

"You're not dressed," she said as she poured batter from the Tupperware pitcher.

Trixie took a mug from the tree and filled it with coffee. "My jeans and T-shirt beg to differ."

"I mean, you're not dressed for *church*. Didn't you bring anything suitable? Maybe you can borrow something of mine."

"When have I *ever* been able to wear one of your dresses? And, no, I didn't pack anything for church because I was under the impression that GG was living her final moments."

"Well, I'm sorry if her resiliency is disappointing. I, for one, see it as an answer to prayer that she has come back to us."

"Mom, she never left."

"We thought she had. We thought she nearly had. That's why we called Dr. Carter. We couldn't get her to respond."

"I don't think there's a woman alive *or* dead who wouldn't respond to Dr. Carter." This from Trixie's grandmother who breezed into the kitchen wearing her own Sunday best: lavender polyester slacks with a matching short-sleeved top. The fabric *swished* as she walked to the coffeepot and poured a cup. "Once he's finished with Mariah, I'm thinking of throwing myself down the stairs to see if I can't break something."

"You'll break your head if you're lucky," Trixie's mother said, flipping the first pancake.

Trixie took a seat at the table. It was one of the few pieces of furniture that could claim to be older than the house itself, brought from "back east" and unloaded from her pioneering ancestor's covered wagon. A smooth groove had been worn into wood from more than a century's worth of resting arms; she nestled hers into that spot and listened to the soft kitchen banter between her mother and grandmother.

Last night GG's revelation caught Trixie off guard, and she'd spent a good hour lying in bed pondering the question. She closed her eyes and tried to recall any moment at this table when all four generations had gathered for meal after meal, filling the room with conversation while one or another cooked or cleared. Had GG's place in literature really never come up? They talked about all kinds of things in Trixie's presence—politics, men, fashion, even sex. Grandma was known for the occasional saucy comment, which would make Alma gasp and say, "Mother! Not in front of Trixie!" to which GG would say, "Shielding a girl won't make her a better woman. The world isn't made up of secrets."

But maybe it was. At least *this* had been. Oddly enough, the revelation did nothing to answer the question that had been plaguing Trixie since she was a little girl. She'd always known that her great-grandmother held a strong antipathy toward Laura Ingalls Wilder. But she still didn't know why. Yesterday she'd been handed her first clue, and she planned to use this morning to investigate.

She tuned back into the conversation as her mother was saying, "I guess it's best Trixie can't go to church with us. She can have some extra time with Grandma. Maybe they can have their own little church. Would you do that, Trixie? Read some scripture with her? Sing a hymn? She'd like that."

"Sure," Trixie said, trying to remember the last time she'd heard

GG quote scripture or hum a hymn. Hum anything, for that matter. She was stoic, old pioneer stock, as Grandma used to say. Tight-lipped most of the time, until some random occurrence would spark a memory, and then it was like a history lesson come to life. What was it like to be a homesteader on the Dakota prairie?

Miserable.

But then she'd elaborate: the wind a constant roar, snow piled deep enough to bury a house, darkness for days. Chunks of ice in the wash water, making your face feel like it was on fire with the stinging cold. And hunger. Bottomless, unfathomable hunger. Hunger like a knotted rope in your stomach, tugging at you all day long. The kind of hunger you could only escape with sleep. Hunger that greeted you in the dark before you opened your eyes with the hope that there was something. . .somewhere. In that ten-foot-square cabin, there must be a heel of bread or a single potato or a pot with the last of the beans stuck to the bottom.

"Kids today," she'd say, "getting their heads filled that it was a bunch of sleigh rides and wild ponies and stick candy. When it really all came down to coping from dark to dark, hoping not to die."

GG was still sleeping when Alma and Eugenie, laden with purses and Bible bags and a tray of fresh muffins for Sunday school, summoned Trixie from upstairs.

"What?" Trixie said, hanging over the banister.

"You need to move your car," Mom said. "You parked at the garage door, and we can't get out."

"Or," Grandma said with a coy smile, "you could let us take it."

"Take my car?" Trixie's head filled with the horrific image of a million muffin crumbs lodging themselves in the seams of her seats, despite the triple layer of Saran Wrap.

"Relax," Grandma said. "It's a ten-minute drive. You know that."

"That car is my baby," Trixie said, cruelly enjoying her mother's pained expression.

"Honestly, Trixie," Mom said, "don't say such things. You'll make it true forever."

"Who's listening, Mom?"

"God. God is listening. And if you want that car to be your baby, he'll make it so."

"I don't think it works that way," Trixie said, "but you're the one going to church. My keys are in my purse. Enjoy."

Grandma lit up, Mom rolled her eyes, and Trixie resumed the task from which she'd been called away. Once upon a time, she'd had a system for hiding (and finding) her *Little House* books. *The Big Woods* was in her toy chest, safe—or so she'd thought—from being found. *Little House on the Prairie* was in the kitchen, up in a cabinet above the refrigerator where they kept the fancy ice cream sundae dishes they never used. She hadn't thought about the books much in years, though every now and then she considered rounding them up and bringing them to her bachelor girl apartment.

But the last one. The last *real* one. *These Happy Golden Years.* Where was it? It had been her first romance, the first thing she ever read that made her cheeks flush and cause her to fling the book away while she squealed in preadolescent delight at the slow-burning love between Almanzo Wilder and Laura Ingalls. She could go up to GG's room, of course, and see if the antique, original edition was still on the cluttered nightstand where Trixie had left it the night before, but she wanted her *own*. The soft, familiar yellow paperback well-worn with a thousand readings.

Trixie stood on the landing, tapping her middle finger to her thumb—her personal ritual for summoning something lost—eyes closed, turning in a slow circle, muttering, "Where is it? Where is it? Where is it? . . ." until it came to her. She stopped, opened her eyes, and screamed. There stood GG, looking every bit like a silent apparition—a pale figure in her white gown, her hair loose and wild.

"I'm not a ghost, but greet me like that and you might kill me."

"I'm sorry GG," Trixie said, heart still pounding. "You startled me."

"What were you doing just then?" GG tilted her head and gave Trixie a suspicious look. "You aren't on drugs, are you? You look like one of those people I saw on TV. Hippies."

Trixie suppressed a laugh. "No, GG. Not even close. Just trying to remember where I put something."

"Wait until you're my age. You'll be trying to remember where you put everything. Did I miss church?"

"I'm afraid so. Mom and Grandma left."

"Good." She rubbed her hands together. "Did I miss pancakes?"

"I can make you some. Let me help you back to bed, and I'll bring you a tray." She put a hand on GG's shoulder, ready to lead her back, and was surprised by the strength that resisted.

"I'm sick of eating in bed. Because I'm not sick. I'm old. It's not the same thing."

"From what I hear, you had a rough couple of days."

"And now I'm having a better one. I want to go downstairs."

"All right," Trixie said, knowing that arguing would be useless. "But let's get you changed first. I don't want you to trip on your gown going down the stairs."

To this, GG agreed and steadied herself on Trixie's arm as they turned back toward her bedroom. She sat on the edge of her bed while Trixie fetched a pajama set with Bermuda-length shorts and a top that buttoned down the front so GG wouldn't have to raise her arms. But between the gown and the pj's, Trixie was faced with the full revelation of GG's body. Wiry, still, and strong. She'd always been tall and thin—somewhat gaunt, as if her years of hunger decided to become her defining feature. Her breasts were small—a feature Trixie was more than happy to have inherited.

GG opted to remain barefoot, a decision that seemed safest for her uneasy steps, and together they made a careful descent. Once in the kitchen, Trixie pulled out a chair and set a cup of coffee cooled with cream in front of her while the skillet warmed. There was enough batter left in the pitcher for two pancakes if she made them small, and she whisked in a spoonful of sour cream to add her favorite bit to the family recipe.

"I was thinking," Trixie said as she pulled a plate down from the cabinet, "that table might be as old as you, since it came with the house."

"It didn't come with the house." GG was running the pads of her fingers along the table's edge.

"Really? Why did I think it did?"

"It's the *oldest* piece here. But I brought it with me. It was mine when I lived with my brother, Charles. It was our kitchen table, the first piece of furniture I ever owned. Bought it brand-new from a local carpenter. I'd wanted scrolled edges, but that doubled the price and Charles wouldn't have it. I brought it with me."

"When you married Great-Grandpa?" Trixie had never met the man, and the term *great-grandpa* never felt comfortable whenever she had reason to use it. GG Mariah's husband was as much a stranger to Trixie as any man in the street; for that matter, any man in a history text.

"I brought this table, my clothes, and all of my books. It was all that I had."

Trixie flipped the pancakes. "What more does a woman need?"

GG's chuckle was soft, almost inaudible under the sound of the batter sizzling in the pan. GG opted for butter and jelly rather than syrup, and Trixie quickly fixed an egg to have on the side. She made herself a second—no, third—cup of coffee and sat at GG's elbow, ready to assist if needed. For light breakfast conversation, she filled GG in on the wonder of the Egg McMuffin and felt the warmth of the memory rival the warmth of the coffee as she spoke.

"Cheese has no place at breakfast," GG said, unimpressed with the idea of a breakfast sandwich.

Trixie pictured sharing that statement with Ron and then decided it might be a fun caption for a *Lost Laura* cartoon. She'd done one a few months ago featuring Laura, barely visible behind a stack of pancakes piled up to her nose, saying, "*As long as I can see over it, it's a short stack.*"

GG ate steadily, quietly, while Trixie rolled Lost Laura and McMuffin punch lines through her mind. Her thoughts were teetering on the edge of something brilliant when a knock rattled the kitchen door and she looked over to see Cam smiling through the screen.

"Well, good morning," she greeted, rising, coffee in hand. She opened the door and took a moment to appreciate the sight of him in a summer-weight suit and calico tie. "Don't we look spiffy."

"Sunday best," he said, leaving a waft of *clean* as he passed by.

"More like Sunday goin' to church," Trixie said.

"That too. I dropped Samantha off at Sunday school and thought I'd come by and check on Mariah. How is she doing?"

"Before I answer, what's the charge for a Sunday morning house call?"

He breathed deep. "One cup of coffee."

"In that case"—Trixie stepped away from the door and swooped her arm like a circus ringmaster—"here she is. Up, dressed, and eating pancakes."

"Don't talk about me like I'm some exhibit," GG said, never cutting her gaze their way.

"And feeling sassy," Trixie whispered.

Cam set his black medical bag on the counter and took the seat lately occupied by Trixie. "Good morning, Mrs. Gowan. You look like a new woman this morning."

"And your words would make the corn grow ten feet tall," GG said, but Trixie could tell she was pleased by the way her eyes crinkled at the corner and her thin lips contorted in an effort to suppress a smile. She was glad she'd taken the time to brush GG's hair and secure it at the nape of her neck. Any woman would want to feel her best sitting at a table with Campbell Carter.

"Can I get you something to eat?" Trixie asked, knowing her mother would chastise her for waiting this long to ask. "Toast? Or oatmeal?" *Oatmeal?* She was so bad at this.

"No, thanks," Cam said. "I've had breakfast. The coffee's great."

"Good, good," Trixie said. "Then, since you're here, would you mind sitting with GG while I check on something upstairs? I won't be a minute."

"We'll be fine," he said, but GG gave a suspicious look over his shoulder.

"What are you looking for?" Her voice not sounding the least bit feeble.

"Who said I was *looking*? I said *checking*, GG. *Checking*."

"Well, I hope you're checking on a bra," GG said before calmly taking her last bite of eggs.

Trixie had never been so thankful to be staring at the back of any man as she was at that moment when she and Cam could pretend the old woman hadn't said what she said. Refusing to rush, she climbed the stairs and went straight to GG's room. A bench had been built beneath the six-pane dormer window, its hinged top upholstered with a soft cushion topped with pillows. For Trixie, this had always been her favorite place to read, overlooking the yard where the seasons changed beyond the glass. GG claimed she could never get comfortable there, and so she was generous in granting Trixie permission to plant herself for hours on end with a book or a sketch pad. Sometimes entire Sunday afternoons would pass with Trixie in the window seat and GG, in her rocker, the room filled with the sound of sighs and turning pages.

And this was where she'd hidden the book.

Trixie went to her knees, unlatched the seat, and lifted it high enough to fit her head and shoulders in the cavernous space. There were layers of blankets and quilts, the smell of moth balls almost a physical touch to her face. She rummaged with one hand, letting her fingers search for the book, remembering the day she'd sat *right here*, reading it within sight of GG, who would have snatched it out of her hand if she'd bothered to take a close look. How old was Trixie then? Twelve? No. Thirteen. A rainy spring Saturday at the end of eighth grade, and here she'd sat, reading about her own beloved GG Mariah at almost the same age.

Beneath the strata of wool, she finally touched the cool, smooth paperback and gingerly drew it out.

"There you are," she whispered.

The cover was just as she remembered. Laura and Almanzo, hand in hand beneath a tree, buggy in the background. They were looking into each other's eyes with a solemnity that—to Trixie's adolescent heart—depicted the life-lasting depth of their love.

She lowered the seat, latched it, stood, and walked to the tall dresser where she had to open three different drawers—starting from the top—before finding GG's first edition copy. Figured the old woman would have hidden it away again. The vast difference in the cover image was startling, but it was the fanning through the pages of her own abandoned copy that made Trixie's breath catch in her throat. She hadn't looked at this book—any of these books—in well over a decade, but the impact of the Garth Williams illustrations on her own artistic style was undeniable. The soft edges and shading. The details rendered with pleasing precision. And yet her *Lost Laura* strips were much cleaner. Stark, almost, like the originals by Helen Sewell.

Mindful of the passing time, she turned the pages and felt her knees give out when she found the page depicting Laura Ingalls's first five students huddled around a stove on that first wintry morning of school. She knew for a fact that the illustrator had never met GG Mariah, and yet, there she was. Somehow she was captured as precisely as if she'd sat for a portrait. Her long face, her lank hair, her perpetually distant and dour expression.

Had GG ever seen this?

The sound of voices coming up the stairs spurred her into action, returning the first edition of the novel to the drawer in which she'd found it and casually slipping her own edition under one of the window seat pillows. She was in the hall just in time to see Cam walking up the stairs, his steps matched to GG's beside him, his hand resting on the small of her back. Trixie met them at the top step and took GG's arm and resisted asking, *Do you want to lie down?*, knowing she'd never be able to disguise her eagerness at having an afternoon alone to indulge in a little disobedience. Instead, she asked, "What do you want to do now, GG?"

"Need a pit stop," GG said, "which I can still manage by myself, thank you."

"Alrighty." Trixie kept a careful eye on GG's slow but stable steps until she was on the other side of the bathroom door. Then she turned to Cam. "Thanks for stopping by. I'll get in trouble if I don't invite you to come to dinner after church."

"Thank you, but I promised Samantha a picnic."

"That sounds like much more fun."

"She took a shine to you, Trix. I'll get in trouble if I don't ask *you* to join *us*."

"Trixie?"

GG's voice sounded thin and reedy behind the half-closed door, and Trixie immediately ran into the bathroom to find her in need of assistance with the elastic-waist shorts that had dropped to the ground. Trixie helped GG dress and wash her hands before bringing her out into the bedroom, glad to see that Cam had made a discreet exit, but hoping he was waiting somewhere in the house.

"I think I will take a little rest," GG said, showing her age and fatigue for the first time that day.

"Of course," Trixie said. She propped and fluffed pillows, arranged GG's comfort, and—for no reason other than ornery bravado—took an afghan from the storage space in the window seat and laid it across GG's already snoozing form. "Can we talk more, later?" she asked, wanting to capture the final moments before a sleep that might last all day. "About what you showed me yesterday? About being in the book?"

But GG's lips were already muttering the kind of words that narrated a drift between worlds—"She. . .she. . .stupid. . .stupid. . ."—before her breathing became steady and silent, her body motionless with sleep. Trixie bent to give a kiss to the wrinkled brow, grabbed her book from its shallow hiding place, and ran downstairs, arriving in the kitchen as Cam was lifting his medical bag and heading for the door.

"Hey." She leaned against the doorframe, book cradled to her chest, hoping she looked cooler than she felt.

"I've got to get to church. Samantha will be sitting with my mom, and they'll both be mad at me if I'm late. Invitation is open to join us later. Washington Park around one o'clock. We'll be the ones with a kite and pimiento cheese sandwiches."

"That sounds great, actually. I'll find you. Can I bring anything?"

"Yourself. We can catch up."

She saw him to the door and closed it behind him, trying to conjure the feeling she had every time they enacted this ritual in high school after an evening of studying (or some other ruse to justify a few hours spent together at the table or on the couch). On those nights, there'd always been a kiss at the door, then another in the mudroom, then another on the back porch, and if the night was warm enough, another at his car. If it was cold and her mother was already in bed, a few more *in* his car until the windows were steamed as solid as blackout drapes. She remembered living in a perpetual state of churning, waiting for the moment she'd see him at school the next day or on their date the next night. The longing always kicked in the moment he left her presence, taking on a deeper quality whenever he was close enough to touch. There had never been enough of him. Enough of his voice, his touch. She'd been thrillingly unfulfilled. Off-balance.

But there was none of that now.

Yes, he was still devastatingly handsome, pleasant to look at, to talk to. Yes, she looked forward to a Sunday afternoon sprawled on a blanket under the summer sun, but if she was truly honest with herself, what she really wanted was the story. All the stories from the time he drove away to college, leaving her a crumpled mass of tears, until the day she walked in to find him stalwart in the midst of her family's death watch. In between, besides a sprinkling of awkward conversations during visits home, there'd been a war and a baby girl named Samantha. For the sake of their lingering, long-snuffed love, Trixie wanted to share Cam's experience with both.

Until then, she calculated having about an hour—maybe ninety minutes if the sermon proved soul-searching—to read and discover why her great-grandmother might be the only person on the planet to hold a slow-burning grudge against America's pioneer sweetheart, Laura Ingalls Wilder. She considered reading here in the kitchen, slowly filling with the scent of the chicken roasting in the oven, but decided to go back upstairs where she wouldn't be tempted to snack her way from meal to meal. She grabbed two glasses of water (one for GG should she wake up), tucked the book under her arm, and went back upstairs.

This is how people stayed thin in the old days, she thought, feeling the slightest burn by the time she got to the last step.

She could have gone to her own room, but a sense of responsibility tinged with an air of mystery brought her into GG's. She took a sip of water before setting both glasses on the dresser, then went to the window seat. The sense of nostalgia for her old reading spot could not compete with the decided lack of comfort for her older body. The cushion that had once seemed so lush now felt thin, and the pillows refused to hold any shape or support. Channeling her inner Goldilocks, Trixie moved to what seemed to be the next most comfortable spot: GG's bed. She piled pillows at the footboard and climbed up, careful not to disturb the sleeping woman, if indeed she *could* be disturbed at all. Once settled, she opened the book and began.

Sunday afternoon was clear, and the snow-covered prairie sparkled in the sunshine. A little wind blew gently. . .[1]

Trixie found herself drawn into the simple, image-specific prose just as she had been when she read the books as a child. Even more so, perhaps, now that she had an overarching purpose. Soon she was absorbed in this tale of the blizzard-defiant courtship of Almanzo Wilder, braving the dangerous, bone-chilling cold to rescue Laura from the equally dangerous Brewster family each Friday afternoon. She tried to imagine the tedium of those school days—the silence of study and the timid voices of recitation. The soft-key romance thrilled her as much today as it had when she read it as an adolescent, wondering what it would be like to have a beau who would risk so much for a girl's happiness. (Also, wishing the word *beau* was still a common term, as *boyfriend* lacked an air of commitment.)

In all of her reading, Trixie never lost track of her purpose: to find the seed of GG's lifelong antipathy. Was it because Wilder had changed her name? But she'd changed everybody's, GG said. Except Charles's. She pondered a moment when, having to break a path for over a mile in knee-deep snow, Charles and Martha were marked tardy after being only minutes late to school. Pages later, and the insufferable schoolmate Clarence had pinned one of Martha's (Mariah's) braids to the desk; the illustration showed Laura Ingalls with a stern expression, grasping the hilt of the knife to pull it out. What followed were long, listless days, the students not knowing

1 Laura Ingalls Wilder, *These Happy Golden Years* (New York: Harper & Brothers, 1943).

their lessons, not spelling their words correctly, not knowing their history details. Putting that together with what she knew of GG's childhood, the reason for their lackluster academic performance was perfectly clear. They were cold. They were hungry. They'd been cold and hungry the night before and faced yet another evening of cold and hunger. With no mother in the house to provide maternal warmth and a father disinclined to do so, GG and her brother's basic physical and emotional needs simply weren't met.

Plus, at every given opportunity when Laura Ingalls was asked if she enjoyed teaching school, the answer was "No." She was homesick, ill-prepared, and uncomfortable with the authority of leading a classroom, even if the classroom held only five pupils. Trixie read the scene where, in the middle of the night in the home where she lodged during her teaching, Laura was faced with a delusional, knife-wielding Mrs. Brewster. The accompanying illustration gave her the same chills now as it ever did, but it also sparked an empathy for Laura that Trixie could only imagine came with reading that scene as an adult.

GG would not have known any of this as Laura Ingalls's student. True, Laura may have done a poor job of hiding her unhappiness and distaste, but who hadn't had a bad teacher in life? Trixie could think of a few who had stayed in the job too long after retirement age and others who had no business in the profession at all. Laura Ingalls was fifteen years old, younger than two of her students, certified by a single test that she barely passed, and miles away from home sharing a claim shanty with a homicidal woman who hated her. GG was a full-grown woman when she first read any of this—a woman on the verge of becoming a great-grandmother. A woman who knew the love of a good man and the joy of a beautiful son and the satisfaction of years of good health. So what if her teacher marked her tardy on a snowy day or didn't fully appreciate her innate intelligence?

All these thoughts intertwined with the words on the page, Trixie's subconscious roaming freely until—

Almanzo's second-to-last trip to bring Laura home for the weekend had been particularly treacherous; so much so, he'd considered not going at all until his buddy Cap Garland pushed him by saying, "God hates a coward."

"God hates a coward."

If Trixie had heard GG Mariah say this once, she'd heard it a thousand times, and every time the phrase earned the ire of Trixie's mother.

"Stop saying that," she'd chastise. "God doesn't hate anybody."

But GG would counter with a sermon she'd heard once about how the phrase *Fear not* was the most repeated sentiment in the Bible, so being a coward was going completely against God's command. What followed was a recurring, unresolved theological debate into which Grandma would insert herself, saying, "It's just a holdover from the old days, Alma. What God really hates is rancor."

"A holdover from the old days."

But Trixie had never heard the phrase outside of this book and her great-grandmother's mouth. Not in any of the nineteenth-century American literature she'd read in her high school and college courses. Not in any of the authentic pioneer journals and diaries she'd obsessively consumed of her own choice. This was not a common idiom. This was no religious cliché.

This was something particular to Cap Garland, the rapscallion of Laura Ingalls Wilder's teenage crowd.

And so, it seemed, GG not only knew Laura Ingalls, but she must somehow have known Cap Garland too. To understand that connection, though, she'd have to ask, because in a few more pages, Martha would give Miss Ingalls a shiny red apple and disappear from the book forever.

Trixie closed the book and rested one hand on GG's foot, feeling its bony thinness through the quilt. She imagined it cold, perhaps working its circulation by stamping the floor of the tiny schoolroom. These now ancient feet had walked thousands of miles through snow and mud and hard-packed dirt plains. The foot twitched, and Trixie lifted her hand, drawn by slight sounds of wakefulness coming from the pillow at the opposite end of the bed.

"You're reading it, aren't you?"

"Yes," Trixie said. No reason for subterfuge anymore. "I read about your last day of school with her."

"Let me tell you something." By now, GG's eyes were open, and she'd boosted herself up a bit. "I never gave that girl an apple. Where would I have found a shiny red apple?"

Trixie couldn't help but laugh at GG's precise remembering of the text. "So, you're saying Wilder exercised some poetic license?"

Before GG could answer, Trixie heard the sound of a car in the drive, but given the affection of her ownership, knew immediately the car wasn't hers. She went to the window, drew the curtain aside, and peered out to see a comfortable, reliable Ford. Something a doctor would drive, and indeed, there was Cam piling out. Along with her mother. And her grandmother. And Samantha. Leaving one question: If they were all spilling from his car, where was hers?

CHAPTER 8

MARIAH

The wedding of Charles Patterson and Katrina Rose gave the entire town a distraction from its usual August malaise. While Charles maintained that he would as soon stand up in her family's parlor and sign his name, Katrina had been ardently wooing her father into footing the bill to put on an event that would make her wedding a showcase for the entire town. While the reception after the ceremony was largely open to all, the ceremony itself in our little white church was limited to invited guests. Charles and I often joked that if we weren't crucial members of the bridal party, we probably wouldn't have been invited. Food and drink arrived in ice- and straw-packed crates from as far away as New York City, along with glassware and china from her family in Chicago. Gifts poured in from friends and relatives from all over the country—*her* friends and relatives, of course. Charles and I were, ostensibly, the only of both to each other, and every day he came home befuddled by the newest parcel.

The latest was a glazed statuette of two dogs engaged in playful combat.

"Don't much see the use for this," Charles said, eyeing the thing with suspicion.

"It's art," I told him. "Art doesn't need to be useful."

Most of the gifts were kept on a long table in the Rose parlor, as was—I assume—tradition. But the more crowded it became, the more things were shuttled to our home: the dog statuette, a set of cut-glass candlesticks along with a box of beautiful white tapered candles, a tea set painted with a detailed bird pattern, a set of mouse-shaped nesting dolls, a side table with thin spindled legs carved in a design of intertwining vines. Day after day, Katrina skipped breathlessly through the door with some new treasure in her grip, saying, "We'll have to find the perfect spot for this."

But there was no perfect spot. Charles and I had never had a taste for frippery, and all the space in our home was filled with the practicality of life. His tools and my books were the only things on any kind of display, and with each new trinket, I imagined my books would soon be stuffed into boxes and hidden away. Given the opportunity, I supposed Katrina would like to see *me* hidden away as well, but I had no intention of ceding my place in the home I built with my brother.

Not that Katrina was, in any way, unkind to me. In fact, she invited me to stand up with her at the wedding, which meant getting a new dress—at her expense. And her taste. I'd never worn anything other than a serviceable calico, and that ready-made, as I had no talent with a needle and no means to sew a dress. My clothing came from the dry goods store when I had money for something new, and from charity barrels when I didn't. But somehow, through Katrina's design and her father's money, I found myself standing on a stool in Mrs. Bradshaw's dress shop one week before the wedding, wearing the kind of dress I'd never before let myself dream about. Pale green—an impractical color for a woman constantly exposed to grease in her brother's repair shop, never mind all the splatters and stains that came with running a house. The sleeves were full, then narrowed at the elbow with a time-consuming row of buttons. The collar was high, the waist nipped, and for the wedding the skirt had a netting overlay stitched with tiny pink rosebuds that served no purpose at all. The first time I wore it, I dared not breathe for fear one of the thousands of pins would pierce me and my blood would create tiny drops of ruin. Later, through all the fittings, I found myself equally breathless, for fear my exhalation would break the spell. In it, I felt beautiful. No one had ever given me any cause to attach that adjective to myself. I couldn't begin to imagine the loveliness that would be Katrina Rose. Even on the wedding day, I was not invited to her home to dress with the other attendants—a mutual decision between the bride and myself, as someone needed to be here to make Charles presentable. I did what I could, but Charles could rumple a suit of armor. Even clean and freshly pressed, his suit looked like he'd been wearing it for a week. I'd slicked his hair with water (it was too fine for pomade) and checked that he'd washed behind his ears. Grown man or not, he was absentminded with his hygiene. I gave him a final going-over and said, "Ma and Pa would be so proud," but the sentiment didn't earn a single tear. If we told each other the truth, neither of us could claim much thought of Ma and Pa over the past few years. Life had been too long and hard a fight after their deaths. They'd both managed to slip in with all the other memories.

Shortly after he left, somebody (a distant Rose family cousin) arrived at our kitchen door to ensure that I too was buttoned and fastened correctly.

Katrina had requested we all (myself, a cousin, and the daughter of a family friend) wear our hair in a braided crown, which I did, though my hair had always been too fine to hold any style. I held it in place with the ivory combs she'd given as a gift for this occasion.

My instructions were to be on the church lawn at three o'clock, to stand as an adornment—a preview of the bridal party for the arriving guests. I thought the notion silly, but the cousin and the friend (it was a while before I would learn which was which) took the job seriously and offered smiles and greetings to each person as they walked by. I stood under that blazing sun while neighbors passed, expressions alternating between scrutiny and surprise. I transferred my bouquet of silk flowers to one hand and temporarily blocked my vision as I brought my sleeve up to pat the sweat from my brow. When I lowered it, I was standing in front of Oscar Garland.

He arrived with a breeze that carried the smell of his soap. His suit was the color of a pale gray dove, his shirt bleached white.

"Good afternoon, Mariah." To my astonishment, he took my

hand, bowed, and kissed it. The cousin and the friend made a parenthesis of approving giggles. When Oscar stood upright, he offered each a nod of greeting.

I took my hand back and clutched my bouquet. "Hello, Oscar."

"It's a lovely day for a wedding, isn't it?"

"It's a bit warm," I said, feeling sweat trickle down my back and pool at my cinched waist.

A voice piped up beside me. "Whoever heard of a wedding in August?" This must have been the cousin, because no friend would have spoken with such derision.

"It's as good a day as any," I said, fighting the sudden dryness in my mouth. "I don't think any of the three of us standing out here on the lawn are in any position to judge."

At this, Oscar's moustache twitched in approval, and I offered a small smile back. I leaned forward and lowered my voice. "I'm so glad you're here. Charles will be looking for a friendly face."

He leaned even closer and spoke even lower. "Doesn't the bride have a friendly face?"

I brought my bouquet up to cover my laugh but offered no response.

"Ladies," he said as he backed away before turning to enter the church.

"Who was that?" This had to have been the friend, because only a friend would have such hunger in her voice on the day of being a bridesmaid.

"Oscar Garland," I said with as much nonchalance as I could muster. "He and my brother and I have known each other for ages."

"He's very handsome," said the cousin in a way that made it clear that she would bowl both of us over if she sensed the first opportunity to give him her hand.

"He is," I replied, and would have expounded, but the sound of horses' hooves and the soft jingle of bells called our attention.

Our church was set within a small grove a bit off the main road, the trees planted in hopes of protecting the stained glass windows from the relentless South Dakota weather. At that moment, Katrina

Rose, driven by her father in a well-equipped, drop front phaeton rounded the corner. The single horse was a beautiful jet black, as if chosen to match the high gloss of the carriage.

She looked like a swirled mass of silk ribbon and lace. Like she had been plucked out of the summer sky and brought to earth to be a cloud of beauty floating among us. Her father, moving at some silent command, got down and placed a small set of stairs at the side of the carriage, then held his daughter's hand as she descended. The volume of her skirt made it impossible to know if her feet touched the ground in the same way as those of the rest of us mortals as she glided across the lawn of clipped grass. A veil covered her face, but no amount of netting could obscure the pinkness of her lips or her brown-button eyes.

"You go first," she said to me, bringing a sense of relief that, behind all of that beauty, the same bossiness survived. "Stand at the door and signal to the reverend that I'm here. It's time."

I obeyed, as did the cousin and the friend, lining up behind me.

The pews were full, squeaking as people shifted trying to find comfort in the heat. I caught the reverend's eye and nodded. He, in turn, motioned for my brother to come stand before him, and that's when the fullness of the ninety-degree day threatened to take my legs from beneath me. It hadn't occurred to me (*Why hadn't it occurred to me?*) and Charles had never mentioned (*Why hadn't he mentioned?*) that he too would have attendants standing up with him at the top of the aisle. Katrina had three, but my brother only had one. At the first few notes of the bridal march, I took one step, and then another, and then another, flanked by a breeze created by women fanning themselves in a desperate search for relief. A new heat blazed under my hair, and I wanted to claw the collar of my dress away from my neck. I knew all eyes were turned to see the bride, all but those belonging to the man at the front of the church beside my brother.

The best man, Merrill Gowan.

Each step that brought me closer threatened a hitch of bile, and if Katrina could see the expression on my face, she would be furious.

I would have turned, run out of the church, clambered over the friend and the cousin and the bride herself to escape if not for the fact that from his aisle seat in the third pew, Oscar Garland caught my eye and winked at me.

Nobody else, I'm sure, saw this bit of attention, and the nerve of it refreshed me. Buoyed me. As leader of the bridal procession, it was my duty to smile, so I did—first at Oscar and then to the room at large. I took my place standing across from Merrill and held Katrina's bouquet as she took her vows and offered her hand for the wide gold band my brother had crafted for her. Blood rushed in my ears with such great, crashing waves that I heard none of the words. In time Charles lifted Katrina's veil and placed a swift, soft kiss on her perfect pink lips, and soon after, Merrill and I were marching out side by side behind them. Neither of us spoke, and Oscar certainly didn't wink.

Never in my life had the relentless prairie wind been so welcome.

Long tables had been set out on the lawn on the east side of the church, taking advantage of the stretch of afternoon shade and shadow. The table abutted to the church wall, reserved for the bridal party and Katrina's parents, was laid with finery too beautiful to be spoiled by the slices of meat and colorful vegetables that would soon adorn it. The rest of the guests would enjoy something more akin to a church social, with various bits of potluck strewn about. Few were friends of Katrina's, but many had brought work to Charles over the years, and what better way to pass a late-summer evening than with food and conversation? Plus, there would be music. And dancing. Never before had we thrown a party to celebrate the onset of harvest. This wedding proved the perfect excuse.

Given how I'd felt during the ceremony, I didn't think I'd be able to swallow a single bite of food, but the delicacies placed before me transcended my discomfort. Chicken roasted with unfamiliar herbs, cabbage somehow both warm and crisp, soft bread made with flour as white as Katrina's gown—I ate all of it without a trace of self-consciousness, wishing only I knew a protocol to ask for more. When given a glass of champagne to toast the newlyweds, I raised it with a shaking hand, hardly able to contain my excitement for the first taste.

And, oh. How it tasted. The glass was cool against my lips, the bubbles jumping like early raindrops against my nose. The first tiny sip was merely an introduction, but the second (and the third, and the fourth) went down my throat with the ease of a kind word. Fortunately, the protocol for getting more champagne was simply to set the empty glass down on the table. Again. And again. Four people—Katrina's parents, Katrina and Charles—sat between Merrill and me, blocking my view of him completely. Charles sat to my right, the cousin to my left, and neither one seemed interested in talking to me at all, so I dug into my supper with relish and kept my champagne glass filled. After the third, I worked up the courage to look out and seek Oscar, finally finding him sharing a table with a half dozen rough-looking men.

I allowed that moment of public anonymity to gaze at him, his suit jacket abandoned, his shirtsleeves rolled to his elbows, his hair mussed in the wind. The rushing in my head had become something more like a murmuring brook, and I imagined my blood flowing as such—loose and cheerful, smoothing away the earlier tension. Bits and pieces of conversation—all of it amusing—splashed at the edge of my hearing, and I smiled down into my glass. I must have giggled, because the cousin asked me what was so funny, and for the life of me I didn't have an answer. Her annoyed expression was even *more* amusing, so I let out a *bigger* laugh, which I made no attempt to hide. Fortunately, everyone ignored me. Everyone but Oscar. His smile reached across the tables, across the lawn, across the empty plate in front of me. Even from this distance, I sensed a conspiratorial air to his smile, and then I saw the small silver flask that he tipped quickly to his lips.

The shadows stretched, the air cooled. A dozen or more lanterns were lit, and the tables were moved back to create a makeshift dance floor on the church lawn. Three men—our town banker, his son, and a man with an unruly beard and standing-straight shock of hair—took to a makeshift stage with a hand organ, snare drum, and violin, respectively. The man with the violin was vaguely familiar from our days in De Smet, but my mind was too bubbled to give him a name. They struck up a waltz, and by some unspoken cue, Katrina and Charles came up from their place at the table and began a turn that brought muted applause from all the guests.

I watched my brother dance. When had he learned to dance? His movements were as smooth as could be expected, his suit a shameful sight after a long day, though Katrina looked none the worse for wear. Their eyes never strayed from each other; their smiles intermittently sweet and shy. The rich supper roiled in my stomach as I remembered days from our childhood sitting at a dark table while he pointed out phantoms in the window so he could sneak food from his plate and put it on mine. I thought of the frigid night we spent with our father's cold, dead body, distracting ourselves with selections from our shared McGuffey reader. I wondered if Katrina would know when to leave him to his thoughts and when to gently nudge him to speak. If she would know how to read for him without shaming him, if she would let his coffee cool before serving it to him, if she would walk out in the dead of night to look at a star, or if she would listen to see if a clock's ticking was just right.

Midway through the song, Katrina's parents took to the lawn and showed what it looked like to marry well and live long. Their steps were confident enough to allow them to speak small bits to one another—words lost to all of us looking on but understandable all the same. At some point they changed partners, Katrina moving lovingly into her father's arms while her mother made little attempt to hide her dissatisfaction with her new partner. Charles soldiered on, though, and a movement to my left caught my attention. Merrill was standing. He was walking my way. I was a capable dancer, my feet even then shuffling in time to the song. I took a final, bracing sip of champagne and waited for some sort of touch to my arm, my shoulder. But there was nothing. I kept my face forward but slid my eyes to see him take the hand of the cousin and lead her away from the table. The onset of twilight hid the burn of shame on my face. As Merrill and the cousin took their first steps, a host of other couples joined them while the friend and I looked on.

But that was only the first song of the evening. I did dance at my brother's wedding—twice with Oscar Garland. The first was a square dance wherein we did more stumbling and laughing over missed steps than actual dancing. The second, though, was a drawn-out waltz. I felt his hand through the structure of the dress; with the other, he held the back of my hand against his palm. His shirt was of fine quality, and I'd managed somehow to slip my fingers beneath his suspenders and wondered how I would ever get them out without him noticing.

"I'm afraid I don't have much experience dancing," I said as a means to excuse the weakness I felt in every muscle in my body.

"That's all right. I reckon I have experience enough for both of us."

And then he led me, tiny pressure points against my waist, directing me front and back. Left and right. My feet responded, but my mind refused to budge from this moment. Oscar's face framed by a star-filled sky. The rumble in his chest as he hummed the tune. I remembered how Mr. and Mrs. Rose talked to each other as they danced, how it made them look so comfortable and aligned.

"The man playing violin," I said, once I felt secure in our steps, "he looks familiar, but I cannot place his name. Do you know him?"

"That's Charles Ingalls," he said, a new, hard set to his jaw.

"That's right." I remembered him then, a man quite prominent in De Smet. My mouth seemed determined to outrun my mind, and I heard myself saying, "His daughter was my teacher."

He gave me a weak smile that barely lifted the corner of his moustache. "Seems I remember hearing something about that." Then he moved his gaze above my head, not up into the stars, but beyond and beneath them.

"I'm sorry." I dipped my head to escape his scrutiny and felt my brow brush against his shirt. I left it there one step longer than I should have before pulling back. "I didn't mean to bring up bad memories again on such a joyous occasion."

If he sensed any irony in my statement, he gave no sign. "That's all right. I have plenty of good memories too."

"Did you love her?"

Oscar's steps were measured perfection, but at that moment we were jostled by another couple, tipsier and less talented. By the time we'd laughed and apologized and found our steps again, I hoped my question got lost in the tangle.

It hadn't.

"I thought I maybe did," he said, smoothing over our interruption. "But not enough to put up a fight for her. Almanzo was my friend. That mattered more. Besides, I take responsibility that they started courting in the first place. I dared him to ask to walk her home, and he did."

"You *dared* him?"

"Actually, I had it in mind for him to ask another girl, but fate would have it he got it wrong. Anyway, they both seemed inclined to marry, so they were better off with each other, I reckon."

"And you are not so inclined? To marry?"

He smiled, big enough to rival the brightness of the moon. "No woman's been able to catch me yet."

I was about to ask how many had tried, but Laura's father trailed out the final note of the waltz and we stepped apart to join our fellow dancers in applause. When the clapping died down, we heard the first sound of the far-off train, and the crowd erupted in *whoops* of joy. As Katrina rushed off to change out of her wedding dress and into something better suited for travel, the musicians declared enough time for one last song. I looked to Oscar but then felt another's touch on my arm.

"She's all yours, my friend," Oscar said, and I turned to see the achingly familiar face of my brother.

We danced, well-matched in our artlessness, and for the first time that day, I felt tears pooling in my eyes before streaming—unchecked—down my face.

"Oh Sister," he said, wiping them with the cuff of his sleeve. His suit, rumpled as it was and bearing the stains of everything from gravy to frosting, was apparently perfect for a night's journey on a train.

"I've never said goodbye to you. Ever."

"I'm coming back, you know. We're only staying away a week. And then I'll be home."

"It won't be the same."

"No, it won't."

And there we gave up every pretense of dancing, and he folded us up together while I sobbed into his shoulder. I missed him so much already, as if the closeness of the moment made me realize how far away he'd be not just in the week to come but forever. In a night, the entirety of my family was being ripped away, like the agonizing moment of pulling a leech from your flesh.

"I don't want to go to the train," I said, swallowing great sobs between my words. "I can't stand around waving and cheering and sending you off."

"That's fine," he said, patting my back as if I were a child stepping out of a tantrum. "It's a longer walk home from the station anyway. Should I ask Merrill to walk you?"

"No." I pushed myself away, hoping he didn't notice the tiny wobble to my step. "I've walked myself home from church more than once. I think I know the way."

"Never at night. Never this late at night and never after a few glasses of champagne. I'd feel better if someone walked with you."

Before I could answer, the crowd rushed away from us, their commotion stirred by Katrina's arrival on the church steps.

I nudged Charles. "Go. I think you're supposed to be there with her."

He hesitated before kissing my cheek—a rare show of affection that said everything I needed to hear—and rushing to the church steps at a gallop. The crowd gathered, then parted, making a pathway lit by lanterns held aloft. With absolutely no attention turned my way, I stepped back, away from the light, feeling for the moment the church lawn gave way to a pebbled path. At this point, my brother and his wife, their entourage and guests would turn left to make their way to the train station. I turned right and began my journey home.

The thoughts of the looming, empty house bothered me far more than the summer night darkness that swallowed me. In my mind, I knew I faced a few turns and the town would appear around a bend, nestled in a shallow prairie valley. I would smell the livery first, then—if anybody had bothered to light them—the towering streetlights would beckon and guide me to my front door.

At the first sound of footsteps behind me, I reasoned that somebody else, like me, realized their attendance in the crowd would not be missed and had decided to cut out for home. I did not turn to greet them, nor did I slow my step. My thoughts remained mired in my own self-pity until I heard them increase in rapidity, eventually a full-out run. Then I heard my name.

"Miss Patterson! Mariah!"

Still, I did not stop, and in no time Oscar Garland fell in step beside me, barely winded from his run.

"Did my brother send you?"

"Charles? No. But I thought I should tell you that you missed the bouquet toss."

"That's fine." I held out my tattered silk roses. "I'll have this one forever as a souvenir."

"Since I'm here, I may as well see you home."

His tone barely met the requirements of a gentlemanly offer, but I allowed my silence to masquerade as acceptance. Our steps were well matched, and we assumed a comfortable stroll.

"You didn't want to see them to the station?" I asked.

"I've seen people get on trains before."

"Charles and I said our goodbyes," I said, feeling obligated to explain my exit. "You know, this is the first wedding I've ever been to."

"Really? I've been to a few. They aren't always this grand."

"*Grand.* That's a good word for it. I had a grand time."

"I was watching you. That didn't always seem to be the case."

"There were isolated moments of grand," I said, while my mind fizzed with the idea of him watching me.

We came to the final bend that led into the first of our town's three streets. It was dark and quiet but familiar, and I told him I'd be fine to walk unaccompanied from here.

"Your brother would never forgive me," Oscar said. He touched my elbow as if to guide me but did not take another step. I knew instinctively that he would only do so at my express invitation. An uninvited but not unfamiliar desire rose up, managing to snake its way up my spine, gliding along my sweat-slicked flesh.

"Are you staying in town?" I asked, feeling my way through uncharted conversation. "Surely you're not heading back to De Smet this late?"

"I didn't give it a lot of thought." He wasn't gripping my arm, merely cupped my elbow in his palm, but even through the voluminous sleeve, I felt the stroke of his thumb. "I have my horse boarding at the livery. Figured I know enough people to find a bed for the night. Or a barn."

"You can stay with me." I said it before thinking, unless I'd been thinking it all along, dreading this night—this first night—all alone.

"I don't know that it would be a good idea, Mariah. People might think—"

"People wouldn't think anything. I'm not the sort of person people think about."

He stepped back, dropped his touch, and cocked his head, bemused. "You know, I once had a lady friend of mine tell me that all the girls in town had a saying. Two things every woman knows: *Don't walk out in a snowstorm, and don't catch yourself alone with Cap Garland.*"

I thought back to our conversation about his heroic feat. "Is that something you claim?"

He turned shy. "Let's just say I'm no more a scoundrel than I am a hero."

"Well, I've never had a group of lady friends to tell me anything," I said, amazed at the strength behind my words. "And the only time I've ever walked out into a snowstorm is when Laura Ingalls told me to."

"You ought to forget her."

"Why? You haven't."

"I bear no grudge."

"Don't you?"

I wasn't trying to achieve a note of finality, but I suppose I did, because Oscar said nothing. I walked, and he followed. We walked, turned a corner, walked, turned another, encountering no one in the street, and if anyone spied us from behind their candle-lit windows, they called nothing out in greeting.

"You can stay in Charles's room," I said when we got to the shop. "I made him clean it this morning." I was tall enough to reach the spare key in its hiding place above the door if I stood on my toes but availed myself of Oscar's shoulder for balance. Flat-footed, I opened the door with a steady hand and led him inside, where total darkness engulfed us. The familiar jingle of the closing door—Charles had finally fixed it as a parting gift to me—was the only sound other than our breathing. One step, and we were as close as we'd been when we danced. Now our bodies moved together in a decidedly different way as I felt the touch of his lips to mine, the silk of his moustache grazing my cheek. I offered no resistance, but my inexperience was an obstacle to overcome. He nudged me closer, pulled away and began again, and by the time I fully understood what it meant to kiss a man, I gave myself over until he consumed every bit of the woman I'd been until that moment.

Finally, I pulled away, my hands gripping his suspenders to keep me upright. By then, my eyes had adjusted to the darkness, and I could no longer bear to be here in the middle of my brother's workshop with nothing more than a window shade to hide my intent.

"Come upstairs with me," I said in a voice I hardly recognized as my own.

"Mariah, you don't know what you're asking."

He was right. I didn't. Not completely, anyway. But I knew I did not want to be alone in that house that night, and I knew that whatever feeling of shame awaited in the morning couldn't be worse than the sadness that gripped me in the night. I didn't answer. Instead, I made my way to Charles's work counter, drew a match from the box he kept on the top shelf behind it, and struck it. So much light from such a small flame, and Oscar came to life within it. I had no candle nearby, nor lamp, but the matchstick was long, and I knew from countless other nights that with my hand cupped round to guard it, the flame would last until I reached my room. I hadn't taken three steps before I felt him following me, and when I finally touched the flame to the lamp beside my bed, I turned to find him standing in my doorway.

I think he might have stood there all night, and I too immobile, if I hadn't asked him in, saying, "I need your help with my dress."

"You—what?"

I went to him and turned my back. "All the buttons. I can't reach them."

I don't know how long we stood there. He remained on the other side of the door, so not even his shadow stretched across my wall. He didn't step across the threshold, but neither did he turn away, though Charles's room was across the hall, its door open and inviting. Finally, I reached back and slipped the loop of string from the top button, the one entangled in the strands of hair that escaped the confines of my crown. I unfastened the second, then the third, and then I felt his fingers rough against my own. One by one, each button released, down to the point at the small of my back. While he worked, I took the pins from my hair and felt the single plait fall between my shoulder blades. He took it, moved it aside, and planted a kiss in the curve of my neck.

All day long I'd imagined I was melting—under Katrina's scrutiny, under the sun, under the soaring rafters of the church. Not until this moment did I know what it truly meant to lose all form and function of mind and body. I felt the fabric of my dress slip from my shoulders as he turned me.

"I said I wasn't a scoundrel, but I'm no saint, either."

"I don't want either."

"What do you want?"

I hooked my fingers under his suspenders and backed into my room. "Something for myself. Just once."

He followed. "I don't want you to think"—he closed his eyes, opened them, and started again. "I've no intentions of marrying you."

"I know."

"You're a fine woman, and you'll find a man of your own someday. But it won't be me. I don't love you."

I touched his face, placing my fingers against his lips. "I know." All my life I'd been living on scraps and donations and things that other people left behind. Somehow it was easier knowing he loved someone else, knowing he was capable of love, at least. It gave me an ugly hope.

Stepping back, I held out my hands in a gesture that, under any other circumstances, would look like some sort of supplication. I indicated the row of tiny buttons on my sleeves. "These too. Please?"

And with his lips pressed to my pulse, he obliged.

CHAPTER 9

TRIXIE

$\mathcal{T}$rixie tucked the book under one of the window seat's pillows, and after a quick check to see that GG was still sleeping, ran down the stairs and out the front door, meeting her mother at the foot of the front steps.

"Where's my car?"

"See?" Eugenie said, "I told you she'd have a fit straight off."

"I'm not having a fit," Trixie said. "Why should I be having a fit?"

"Calm down," her mother said. "Think about the child." This she said out of the corner of her mouth.

Samantha poked half of her body through the open car window. "Is she having a fit?"

"Everything's going to be fine, darling," Alma said, though Trixie couldn't tell if the reassurance was meant for her or the six-year-old.

"What's going to be fine, Mom?"

"Justus McCready said it happens all the time and wasn't anybody's fault."

"Justus McCready?"

"Mechanic," Grandma said. She walked up the steps, straight past Alma and Trixie. "Said it was the starter. Just went out." She punctuated her statement with the closing of the screen door, never looking back.

Her head still floating with disjointed pieces, Trixie once again focused on her mother.

Alma sighed. "We got in the car after church, and it wouldn't start. Dead. Not even a click. Mr. McCready was right there. He gave it a look over and—whatever Mother said. He's being kind enough to order the part today but won't be able to start work until tomorrow. Which is still incredibly generous of him. He's not even charging for the tow."

Listening to her mother, Trixie could only imagine the flirtatious edge of the conversation in the church parking lot. Still, "My car got towed?"

"Well, it couldn't very well sit in the church parking lot overnight, could it?"

She closed her eyes and bit back a retort as her mother too walked past her into the house. Up to this moment, Cam's engine had been running, but he cut it and stepped out of the car, admonishing Samantha to sit back down and wait, just for a minute.

Trixie stepped off the porch and met him halfway in the yard. "Thanks for bringing them home."

"It's not a problem."

"It's a twenty-minute drive."

"Which is not a problem."

She looked over his shoulder to see Samantha bouncing on the car seat. "I guess this means I won't be able to join you for your picnic."

Cam opened his arms in broad invitation. "Come with us now."

"I really shouldn't." She didn't have the heart to tell him that she hadn't given the idea a second thought since the moment he left. "I've learned something new about GG. Something about her past, and I'm hoping she'll tell me more. If she has a few good hours, if she's lucid and wants to talk, I want to be here."

"I understand completely," he said, and she knew that he did.

"But my offer still stands if you want to have lunch here. We're roasting a chicken, but if Samantha has her heart set on pimiento cheese sandwiches, I can make those too. And I know it's not exactly a park, but"—she gestured broadly—"we can sort of find a spot here to hang out. Spread a blanket, enjoy the afternoon."

"I don't want to impose."

"Please, if my mother thought I let you drive away *without* an invitation to stay for Sunday dinner, she'd kick me out and make me walk back to Minneapolis."

"Let me check with Sam."

He returned to his car and leaned in to talk to his daughter, giving Trixie a moment to fully appreciate the fit of his slacks. Good grief, the man was gorgeous from every angle. A minute later he opened the back door, and Samantha tumbled out. She was wearing a denim sundress and sandals, her hair fastened at each temple with pretty sunflower barrettes. *He's a good father*, she thought to herself, thinking of the stories she'd heard about herself at that age, resistant to having her own hair brushed and her flair for mismatched outfits.

Samantha ran straight for her and asked, "Can I go exploring?"

The Gowan house, not visible from the main road, sat half encircled by a copse of trees and a wheat field that grew right up to the property line.

Trixie looked down dubiously at Samantha's little toes. "I'm afraid your shoes won't be the best for running around."

"That's why I have these." Cam approached, dangling a pair of ratty Keds from his fingers. "The emergency car shoes."

"Better," Trixie said as Samantha took them, holding them out with a slightly wrinkled nose. "Go on inside and see if one of the nice old ladies in there will help you tie them. Or can you tie them yourself?" She had no idea what life skills such a small toothless girl might have mastered.

"I can tie them myself," Samantha said with an attitude of indignation mixed with pride.

"Can you? Good, then run inside and tell them that I have invited you and your father to stay for Sunday dinner. And tell them I'll be in shortly to help."

Like a shot, Samantha was off, running with a sense of purpose.

"She's thrilled," Cam said once the screen door slammed behind her.

"Is she?"

"This is better than any park."

"I used to have a tire swing from that tree." She pointed. "But the rope frayed, and Mom took it down. Too bad. It would have been fun for her."

"She'll be happy with a walk in the wheat field. Just to touch it. And to go into the woods."

Trixie laughed. "These are hardly woods."

"To a little girl, where two or more trees are gathered together, there are the woods. She's obsessed with Laura Ingalls, and I'm terrified that she's going to ask me to build her a cabin or dig a well or hunt a bear or something. None of which I am qualified to do. She's been begging me to let her use an outhouse. She wants a sunbonnet."

Trixie started walking back toward the house, leading him. "It's a phase. All little girls go through it. Like wanting a pony or being a mermaid. I remember it."

"And you grew out of it. I don't remember you ever having a pioneer vibe."

"Tell that to my coworkers." She felt a tiny tug of nostalgia, which was ridiculous since she'd been in the office forty-eight hours ago and would be back as soon as her car was fixed. "If you'll excuse me for a minute? I have to make a phone call."

"Okay, I'll just. . ."

She heard Samantha's excited voice coming from the kitchen. "Go on in there—they'll be thrilled."

She went upstairs to the landing where the telephone sat on a small table and the corner provided some protection from all the ears in the house. Nobody had a telephone in her own room, as none of their conversations required privacy. That was, of course, until Trixie herself was in high school dating Cam and had to cup her hand around the phone's mouthpiece to whisper her good nights to him. Now she dialed her own phone number and was about to hang up on the fourth ring when Ron's voice boomed across the line.

"Hello! Hello, Trixie Gowan residence."

"What took you so long?"

"Trixie?"

"Of course. Is everything all right? You took forever to get to the phone."

"Forever?"

"Long enough. It's a tiny apartment."

"How well I know that."

"I can usually answer my phone on the second ring."

"Haven't you ever heard of the Sunday afternoon nap?"

"Oh." She wound the phone cord around her finger. "You were sleeping."

"I *was*. And do you have any idea how uncomfortable your bed is?"

"What? No, it isn't."

"It is. You're a grown woman, Trixie. Why does a grown woman have a twin bed with a swirly iron headboard and footboard? You know I got my foot tangled in that stupid footboard last night and lost circulation. I woke up, panicked, because I couldn't feel my foot, and the only reasonable explanation I had was that your cat chewed it off while I was sleeping."

She giggled. "I've seen your feet. It would take House three days to chew one off."

"But you're almost as tall as me. Don't your feet stick out?"

They did, in fact. "I curl up."

"I'm too big. If I curl up, I'll hang over the edge."

"Can we please stop talking about how well you fit in my bed?"

At that moment, Cam poked his head around the corner. "Sorry. Just thought I'd pop in on Ms. Mariah while I'm here."

Trixie covered the mouthpiece. "Oh, cool. Yeah—I mean, yes. Great. You should." As he climbed the second flight of stairs, she closed her eyes and banged the earpiece against her forehead. Three times. "That was the doctor," she said, returning to the conversation. "Checking on GG."

"How is she?"

"She's good, actually," Trixie said, shoving aside the tiny lump that formed in her throat at Ron's tone of genuine care. "Better than I thought I'd find. We talked for quite a bit last night and. . .I learned something. Something fascinating."

"Really?"

"You've heard of Laura Ingalls Wilder."

"I'm from Wisconsin, so, no. Never. Who is this person?"

"Shut up. My great-grandmother knew her. Not *heard* of her or knew *about* her but *knew* her."

"That's really not so hard to believe. They lived in the same area around the same time, right?"

"Right. But do you remember me telling you how I grew up with my great-grandmother's all-consuming antipathy for Laura Ingalls?"

"I don't recall that coming up at any of the staff meetings, but we can try to work it into the next agenda."

"Don't be such a brat." In truth, though, she rather appreciated his comments. He took her off guard, kept her from getting all twizzled up in her own tension. "Anyway, it's a huge revelation. Like, this big family secret that, frankly, I don't know why she kept it a secret all these years. All these *Happy Golden Years*." She grinned at her own joke. "Get it?"

"No."

"Anyway, it's too complicated for a phone call. I'm hoping she tells me more today. Or tomorrow."

"So you won't be back?"

"I told you I might not be. It's okay. I'm caught up. You probably won't miss me until Wednesday at the earliest."

"You'd be wrong." There was nothing light or teasing in his voice, and for a moment neither said anything. She pictured him gripping her pretty white princess phone in his massive hand and wondered how in the world either of them would start up a conversation again.

Then she remembered her car.

"Besides, I'm having a bit of trouble with my car. The starter. Just died in the church parking lot. The guy says it might be a few days before it gets fixed."

"Oh? Well, if that's what the guy says."

"So, are you okay? Staying at my place a little longer?"

"I'm fine."

"You can always sleep at your place and kind of. . .check on House. How are you two getting along?"

"We are each other's soul mate."

The twinge of jealousy took her by surprise. "Good. Then everything is working out exactly as I planned."

His laughter rumbled through the line, and she felt it. She could have stayed in that moment for the rest of the afternoon, bantering until she came up with the perfect quip to make him laugh again, when Cam's shoes appeared on the first step.

"Look, Ron. I should go. Mom and Grandma are fixing dinner."

"Is it a roast? I picture them making a Sunday roast."

"Chicken, actually. But yes, roasted. And I should go help get everything together."

"Okay, well, keep me posted, Prairie Girl."

"I will. Bye, Ron." She was hanging up the phone when his voice beckoned her back. "Yes?"

"I'm glad to hear you're getting more time. You know, with your grandmother."

"Great-grandmother, but, yeah, me too. I'll tell you everything soon."

An hour later, after much nudging and winking from Alma and Eugenie, Trixie and Cam found themselves sharing a blanket on a small patch of green lawn, a platter of chicken and roasted potato wedges between them.

"So you draw the pictures in the newspapers?" Samantha asked with the solemnity of a lifelong subscriber.

"Not all the pictures. Just the advertisements. And sometimes I draw or use photos or find pictures in a big book and paste them."

"I guess I never realized it was an actual person doing that," Cam said, peeling a shred of meat from the chicken bone.

"There's an actual person behind almost everything," Trixie said, trying hard not to feel trivialized. She wondered what he would think of her burgeoning career with *Lost Laura*. If he realized that behind every comic strip, every panel of *Peanuts* and *Beetle Bailey* was a beating heart and a hand grasping a pencil.

Samantha had scarfed down a cheese-and-ketchup sandwich, only after Cam convinced the Gowan women that, yes, she ate such a thing on a regular basis and considered it the height of culinary satisfaction. Rather than being disappointed at not going to the park in De Smet, she was—as Cam predicted—entranced. Already she had collected nine different leaves and eleven different rocks and was sure she would find an arrowhead before the end of the day. Trixie felt a little guilty for that one, having planted the idea in the girl's head to keep her occupied so she and Cam could eat in peace. No such artifact had ever been found on this land or anywhere surrounding as far as she knew.

Cam had restricted Samantha to bringing home exactly three rocks, so she zoomed about, trading them out when she found something bigger, shinier, swirlier, or smoother. He and Trixie spackled conversation between each exchange.

"I'm so sorry you weren't blessed with an energetic, inquisitive child," Trixie said after promising to hold on to two rocks in case Samantha changed her mind.

Cam laughed. "I am exhausted all the time. But she's the best thing that's ever happened to me."

"You haven't told me anything about her mom," Trixie said, and followed quickly with, "and that's fine. If you don't want to. It's not really my business."

"It's okay. We haven't had a chance to talk about it, really. Her mom is in Chicago."

"So, you're divorced?"

"No."

"So. . .you're married?"

"No."

His answer sat between them for a moment while Samantha displayed a shiny brown pebble and debated its value against a slightly larger shiny brown pebble.

"Tell you what," Trixie said, "I know your dad said you could only take three home, but maybe you could go inside and ask Miss Alma or Miss Eugenie if they have a box or a tin and you can keep as many as you like here." She looked at Cam. "Is that okay with you?"

"Genius," he said, and Samantha was off, running with the thrill of the new challenge.

"Want to change the subject?" Trixie asked as soon as Samantha was out of earshot.

"Not at all." Cam switched positions, stretching out his legs and resting on his elbows. "Simple story. Boy meets girl—Cassandra, by the way—boy and girl lose themselves in all the free love happening around college campuses, girl gets pregnant."

"You didn't want to get married?"

"No. We talked about it once, but we'd actually broken up before Cassandra knew she was pregnant. I mean, she was beautiful—*is* beautiful—and smart and kind. She was a stewardess, but now she works as a ticket agent because it's too hard to be a single mother flying all over the country."

This was a moment when Trixie should have spoken some innocuous response. *Oh, I'm sure.* Or *How great that she has that option.* Instead, she indulged in a tiny twinge of. . .jealousy? Competition? Loss? Whatever it was, the silence lasted long enough to catch Cam's attention and bring him sitting up again.

"What is it, Trix?"

"Nothing." Another pause. "Only, I'm having a hard time seeing you as this free-loving guy having a passionate affair with a stewardess. Especially because, when we were dating, you were such a. . .gentleman, you know? You never, never even *tried* anything. With me."

"That's because I was a good kid and *you* were a good kid and we were—kids. Do you have any idea what I'd give to be that kid again? That's why I came here. After I got back from the war. I needed that peace and innocence again."

Trixie reached over instinctively and rested her hand on his knee. "I'm so sorry. I know it must have been—well, I don't *know*. We say that when we have no idea. Do you want to talk about it?"

He'd been staring at the space of blanket between them, but when he lifted his eyes, she saw that familiar guarded emptiness that came across any man with the war in his shadow.

"I'd rather talk about Samantha."

"I'd rather hear about her. And, I mean, it's a little weird that I'm just now hearing about her. For a while, my mother called me every time you popped your head into town. You'd think she'd tell me you had a daughter."

"She might not have known."

"Are you kidding? This town? People know when you switch toothpaste."

"Let me just say. . .my mother wasn't exactly eager to spread the news."

"Oh."

"And not to brand my daughter as some secret love child, but if we lived in a different time and place, my mother would have had both of them whisked away to some sort of home for wayward girls and their natural daughters."

"Your own little Fantine *et* Cossette," I said, wondering if he remembered how I tutored him through *Les Misérables* when he was three grades ahead of me in high school.

"Yes. Without the misery. I knew Mom was worried enough about the war. So at first I didn't want to add to that burden. Samantha was born while I was over there, actually. I didn't get to meet her until she was almost three. But she saved my life, Trix. Whenever I thought I might not live another minute or might not want to live another day, I'd think about meeting my daughter. And I'd pray for God to give me that. In a sense, she brought me back to God too. Because before that I hadn't prayed in a long, long time."

At some point, he'd taken her hand, and their fingers had entwined. "You don't know how much I've always wanted that to be my story," Trixie said. "All my life, knowing I had a father out there somewhere. Fighting. And never even knowing about me. Not knowing to come home and find me. Not even knowing if he came home at all."

Cam brought their joined hands to his lips and placed a kiss. It felt soft and familiar.

"I know. When Cassandra first told me—well, she wasn't planning to tell me at all. We lived near each other, and I ran into her at one of our old places, and she—I could tell she'd been crying. And she just blurted it out. And was saying that she didn't know if she even wanted it." He looked up, straight up into the trees, and they both said nothing for as long as it took for the awful truth to manifest. What might have silenced the beautiful voice streaming through the open window. "So, I told her your story. About you and your mom. And how you were this amazing girl and how your mom did such a great job with you. Alone. Without a father, I mean. And I promised her there in that diner that I would be this kid's father in every way."

"And you are."

"I try. And for good or for ill, Samantha isn't going to grow up with the same sort of stigma that you must have felt sometimes."

"Sometimes." She remembered the taunts whenever kids decided to end a truce and be cruel for a season. The awkward offers of church deacons to take her to father-daughter dances. The biggest blessing was that Father's Day was in June, during the school summer break, so she didn't have to be the only one not making a card or an ash tray. "You know that's why my mother overcompensates, right? Why she dresses like Donna Reed in a time warp—a good, stereotypical mother. So nobody would question. It's why she gave me this ridiculous name. *Trixie*. It sounds like a dog's name."

"I like your name."

"It's what my mother thought a nice, middle-class couple would name their daughter. She poured herself into inventing this persona, and my name was the final prop."

"All Cassandra worried about was losing her figure."

Trixie stopped herself from saying *Did she?*

"Anyway," he continued, "the whole world, you know, was such a mess. Still is, and there was this big question looming. We didn't feel much for each other in the first place, right? We didn't have a love for each other that would have lasted through the war. What if I came back and we were even more distant? Neither of us ever said it out loud, but we had this unspoken condition that if we wanted to, we could marry after my tour."

"And you didn't want to?"

He chuckled, shaking his head. "Not by a long shot. What matters is, we both love Samantha. We're dedicated to her. I was in her life every moment I could be while I was doing my residency, but this summer is the first time I've had her to myself for any length of time. This works for us, and it works for Samantha too, I think."

"She seems happy," Trixie said, her wistfulness unchecked.

"I wish she could grow up here. Like we did. Small town and all. But I guess if her mom and I do it right, she'll get the best of both."

"It sounds like you're doing it right."

They'd been holding hands throughout the conversation and reached a point where there was nothing to say, no reason to remain entwined, but no reason not to. He glanced over at the house. "Seems like she's taking forever."

"It's hard to find a good box."

"Should I go in there? Give the ladies some peace?"

"That house was designed for little girls. Trust me, they're having a blast. I'd be shocked if my mother lets you take her home."

"Well, then—" He dropped her hands long enough to stand himself up, then reached down to help her to her feet. "Walk with me?"

She looked up. If she were looking through her book of stock photographs for an ad, he would be labeled as Handsome Man. Classic. Perfect. Everything behind him green, everything above him blue. His expression was more hopeful than expectant, and the moment she stretched out her arm, let him grasp her, she knew where the walk would end.

They dropped their touch, each making a show of stretching, laughing at exaggerated stiffness in their limbs, soreness in their backs. Cam took her hand again, but with a loose, open grip—his fingers laid against her palm, signaling that she didn't have to hold his hand if she didn't want to, and she didn't want to, but she did anyway. He led, she followed, and neither made any attempt at conversation. Soon their steps took them into the shadow of the old silo that sat—empty now—at the corner of the Gowans' property. A few more steps, and they'd be behind it, invisible to anybody looking through the windows of the house but well within earshot of a slamming screen door.

"Trix," he said, exactly as she knew he would. His voice deeper, so the syllable rested in his throat. He touched her face the way he had a thousand times, revealing his intent, what she always thought of as the kiss before the kiss. The first time, on an iron-cold afternoon, sitting on an empty bleacher seat because neither wanted to go home after a football game, his touch was meant to give her time. Time to decide whether or not she would follow through. In the old days, she would have taken off her glasses, her signal that she wanted, welcomed his kiss. But today her face was bare, hard bits of plastic of her contact lenses keeping the world in focus while her thoughts blurred.

She laid her palms against his chest and said, "We shouldn't —" which was the exactly wrong combination of words and touch, because when he ignored her and brought her close, brought her lips to his with agonizing patience, her arms snaked right around his neck, and she felt the unyielding brick of the silo against her back.

They kissed like they were in high school—the way she hadn't kissed anybody *since* high school. Back then, their kisses bore a tremendous responsibility. They were the full expression of their desire, the gatekeeper of their adolescent virtue. What could be more thrilling than this communion? What other taste could satisfy a hunger too ominous to name? They would venture—trailing the lengths of each other's neck or behind an ear—but always returning to that wellspring of delight, kissing until their lips were sore and swollen. Until she would have to avert her face and cover her mouth with some sort of story when she was finally torn away by the calling of her name. Cam would always have the drive home to cool off and recover, but Trixie had to bound up the stairs, yelling, "Good night!" to her mother and grandmother and GG, while she still burned from Cam's touch. From the want of his touch. From the delicious guilt of his touch.

But nobody was calling her name this afternoon.

She both wanted to push him away and draw him closer—though there was little enough space between them.

"Is this okay?" he asked, freeing her mouth to answer.

"No," she said, without giving herself time to consider any other response.

Immediately, Cam dropped his touch and stepped away. "I'm sorry, you walked away with me—"

"I know."

"And I felt like we—"

"I know. We did. But Cam, it's not like we've been pining away for each other all these years. I never heard a word from you after you left. Not a letter, not a phone call."

"We broke up for good reasons. You were a junior in high school and I was in college and probably heading for war. But look at us now. All grown up. And grown up so nicely. . ."

Cam moved to plant a new kiss on her neck, but she dodged him and—this time—put a single hand on his shoulder. A true, resistant brace. "You didn't call me to tell me you were moving back to De Smet."

"I didn't have your number."

"My mother does. Trust me. She uses it every day. She would have told me if you'd approached her. She would have made me build an ad that said: 'Your ex-boyfriend THE DOCTOR is back in town.'" She emphasized *the doctor* and mimed it in capital letters.

"We didn't see each other."

"Not even at church?"

"I set up my practice in April and—I admit—didn't get back to church until Samantha got here. I know Cassandra won't take her, and it's important. Plus"—and here true pain flickered across his face—"it took a bit for my mother to. . .accept her. To even *want* to take her to church. She was ashamed."

"Oh Cam." Every instinct within her wanted to lean in, wrap her arms around him, and infuse whatever comfort he needed. She'd always known his mother to be a kind woman, one who blended in with all the other mothers lurking at the edges of her friends' lives. And yet this new glimpse of her was not the least surprising. It was more than their adolescent self-control that confined their passion to what could be explored above the neck. Sex was a forbidden subject, forbidden act, forbidden thought. Samantha was living proof that it had only taken a few steps away from the prairie grasses for Cam to forget it all.

"So," she said, turning the conversation, "you didn't reconnect with my family until. . ."

"Your mother called my office about your great-grandmother. She couldn't get anyone in town who would come out here for a house call, and one of the other practices in town recommended me."

He looked sheepish. She'd heard the term before and always wondered about the connection between the idiom and the animal, but there it was, right in front of her. Head downcast, eyes darting a bit. The expression of somebody who'd been caught but not exactly knowing they should have tried to hide. Trapped in a wide, open field.

"I'm sorry," he said.

"It's okay—"

"I couldn't call you and say, 'Hey, Trix! What have you been up to since finishing high school geometry? I've been to college, and war, and medical school, and I fathered a child with a woman I barely knew and didn't really like."

"But that doesn't mean we can skip all that and go straight for the silo."

"Some of the best moments of my life were with you behind this silo."

She waggled her eyebrows. *"Moments?"*

He waggled back. "Remember that time it was so cold, and you had a hole in your mitten—"

"And my fingers got frostbite and it was the most pain I've ever experienced?"

"I was thinking about the time you had a hole in your mitten so you put your hands up my shirt so my body temperature could keep them warm."

"Now you know why I never mended that mitten." For punctuation, she gave a bump of her hip against his.

Just then came the screech of the screen door—the familiar sound that had brought an end to many moments of passion, only this time the voice calling was not her mother's or her grandmother's or GG's. It was Samantha calling for her daddy, repeating the word over and over, alternating between whining and enthusiasm. For a moment, and for no other reason than to win some one-sided challenge, Trixie wanted to grab Cam by his church-shirt lapels and bring him against her once again and kiss him until the little girl's call was drowned out by their soft moans against each other. Instead, he touched her cheek and kissed it, softly, his lips against the corner of hers, where he muttered, "I don't think I'm ready to walk away from this yet."

"You have to," she said, feeling her words on his skin. "Your daughter is calling you."

She let him go, remaining in the shadow of the silo until he rounded the corner and disappeared from view. A strange, unwelcome ache spread through the pit of her stomach when his voice transformed an octave as he called his daughter's name. She edged around the curve and approached them at the edge of the blanket, Cam down on one knee, Samantha showing him an old cardboard box that Trixie once used to hold all of her crayons.

"So the rocks won't make as much noise," Samantha was explaining. Cam reached down and put a few of his daughter's treasures in the box and rattled it, holding it closed with his thumb. As Cam praised his daughter for her choice, Trixie couldn't help wondering what happened to the crayons in the box. Had she thrown them out years ago when she graduated to ink pens and paint with specialized brushes? Had they been lingering there, forgotten, for twenty years until her mother—this very afternoon—tipped them into a trash can? In any case, they were Trixie's no more, nor was the box. She closed her eyes and chided herself for yet another spark of jealousy. She'd never been one for sharing—anything. As the only child, grandchild, and great-grandchild of an indulgent cascade of mothers, she'd never had to. The recent interlude had been pleasant—more than pleasant—but she would have to share Cam. With his daughter, with his daughter's mother, with his patients, and with the lingering memories of war.

The moment Samantha took notice of Trixie, she tore away from Cam and went running toward her, calling, "See? See? Your mom said it was your crayon box, but you don't use crayons anymore because you're a grown-up artist, and I could have it and keep it." She lifted the lid, and Trixie saw the stray marks of hundreds of colors streaking the interior. She didn't need to see the bottom to know that her name was written on it. Her mother had wanted to write her name on the top—far more practical—but all the kids knew that Trixie had the best colors, and she was afraid her name would make her a target for theft. At least, she thought, her mother hadn't given Samantha the Crayola tin that held her sweet sixteen birthday gift of the coveted seventy-two-pack of crayons. It had been a lovely gift, given to her by GG as an attempt to heal her broken, abandoned heart.

Now, part of her was honored to think that little Samantha, daughter of her high school sweetheart, would have this treasure, and part of her wanted to snatch it back, dump the rocks, and rehome it to its forgotten spot. But *all* of her knew there was only one approved reaction.

"That's really cool," she said, giving the box a small shake.

"It is," Samantha said, her voice filled with awe. "So, so cool." Then, with the gasp of a remembered task, she looked up. "I was supposed to tell you. Your GG is awake, and she wants to talk to you."

CHAPTER 10

MARIAH

$\mathcal{A}$ny delusions that Oscar would become a lover to fill my nights while Charles and Katrina honeymooned were dispelled the next morning when he crept away in the predawn light, leaving a trail of apologies behind him. I stayed in bed most of the morning, replaying the night, waiting for regret and shame to overwhelm me, but neither appeared. I got up only when the heat of the afternoon made the room unbearable and went straight to the kitchen for a cool drink of water and a meal made of whatever didn't need to be heated on the stove.

I took a tepid bath, letting the cool water refresh my skin, raising gooseflesh as it evaporated, taking with it the memory of Oscar's touch. And it seemed memory was all I would have. I'd hoped against hope that he might call on me the following evening. Or the next. Certainly a courtship could arise from consummation. I'd heard enough whispered gossip to know I wasn't the first woman in the world to take a man to bed before meeting him at an altar. I would only put money on Katrina's chastity because I was that confident in Charles's inherent laziness. Still, I feared no rumors. I don't know that I ever crossed anyone's mind. Least of all Oscar's.

In the weeks that followed, I worked feverishly, erasing myself. As mine was the larger of the two rooms upstairs, I moved myself out and into the tiny room off the kitchen, giving Charles and Katrina the entirety of the second floor. I bought three wooden crates from the grocer (a nickel apiece) and used them to store my books, clearing the parlor shelves for all of her ridiculous knick-knacks. I filled the cupboards with her china and put her tea set on the table atop the lace tablecloth that had adorned our table at the wedding. I beat the rugs and sponged the furniture. A new bed ordered from Sears and Roebuck arrived, and I stared gape-mouthed at the size of it. I'd never seen such a behemoth of a bed and had to walk all the way around it to fit the sheets.

I couldn't help imagining myself and Oscar on that bed, doing all that we did in mine, only with the sanctity that comes with a marriage like Charles and Katrina had. But Oscar would never marry me, not after that night. His eyes were haunted by his love for another woman, and that love gripped him in a way I could never break. Still, the way he held me, the way he spoke, telling me I was a lovely girl, a fine woman—perhaps I'd chipped away a tiny piece of his resolve.

When Charles and Katrina returned, my place as the spinster sister in residence was firmly established. Sleeping in such proximity to the kitchen made it all the easier for me to start a pot of coffee each morning and have breakfast ready while Katrina lazed abed before coming downstairs fully dressed and coiffed.

I tried to teach her about a few of Charles's favorites—how he liked his bacon just under crispy and his mush sweetened with maple syrup, but she always seemed so helpless whenever she found herself with a spoon in her hand that I'd end up shooing her away from the stove to go do something less taxing.

Harvesttime was always a busy time for Charles, as every farmer within twenty miles seemed to have one piece of equipment or another in need of repair. When work wasn't brought in, he was called out, often coming home after dark, especially with the darkness coming earlier and earlier. Some evenings Katrina and I held dinner for him but then fell into a habit of setting a plate aside and spending a pleasant evening sewing or reading. Being deprived of both a mother and a sister, I never knew the pleasantness of female companionship, and while Katrina and I approached each other with the unease of hedgehogs, we got along well enough. We exchanged knowing smiles behind Charles's back as he complained about the farmers' use of well water in their giant harvesting machines.

"Gonna turn all that equipment into a locked-down broken mess," he said one supper through a mouthful of stew. "Or worse. I keep tellin' them. Ya gotta boil it. Refine it, or you're gonna have trouble. But they don't listen."

I smiled and reached across the table to pat his hand. "Nobody cares about a machine more than you do, Brother."

"So true," Katrina said. "That's why your talents are wasted here."

Charles shot her a warning look made all the more menacing in the candlelight. "Not now."

"I was only—"

"I said, *not now.*"

Rarely had I ever heard Charles assert any kind of authority. He and I mostly agreed on everything, and even when we didn't, he always preferred to bow to my opinion in exchange for avoiding conflict. But here he'd raised his voice, and even that little bit of a show set up the hairs on the back of my neck and caused Katrina's pretty mouth to pout.

I looked from one to the other. "What is it? What *not now?*"

"We have to tell her sometime," Katrina said.

Charles shoveled a forkful of food in reply.

I gave up on learning anything from my brother and spoke straight to his wife. "Tell me what?"

She cast a cautionary glance his way, took a deep breath, and set down her fork. "When we were in Minneapolis, we had a chance to tour the most interesting factory. Furniture, they make. The loveliest things. One of Papa's old schoolmates is an engineer there. Well, we came upon this whole gaggle of men standing around, staring at this piece of machinery. It was a—what was it, Charles?"

Charles muttered a multisyllabic response that sent Katrina into a giggling fit of admiration. "Do you hear that? How smart he is? All of those men standing and staring and not one of them with a clue how to fix that"—she gestured deferentially to Charles—"thing-amajig. But my Charlie? He steps right up and says, 'Why don't you give this a try?' And wham-a-bam, next thing everything's cranking again." She patted his hand. "You're a genius, sweetie. And you're wasting away here."

"I am not wasting away."

"You know what I mean," she said and turned to me. "They offered him a job. Right there. On the spot."

"Mechanic," Charles said with a hint of pride I'd never heard before, not even when he announced his upcoming marriage.

Katrina beamed. "And there's the most adorable little neighborhood close by where a lot of the workers live. We took a streetcar over and strolled around. Modest homes, not more than two or three bedrooms. But perfect for a little family. A *small* family, I mean."

I knew exactly what she meant.

"But I didn't take it," Charles said. "Not right off. Said I had to think about it. Harvesttime, you know. I'm always busy. Everybody's got their equipment for me to see to."

"And the foreman said, 'No problem. Come back the first of the year.'" Katrina said this with the impersonation of a rotund man whose lips clamped down an enormous cigar.

"So, you're leaving," I said, though Charles wouldn't face me. I felt the night's supper roiling in my stomach. "When were you going to tell me, Brother? In a note underneath the Christmas tree?"

"Don't be so hateful," Katrina admonished. "I can't believe you would want to keep him from such an opportunity. Why, he'd be getting a salary, not scraping a few coins over the counter."

"Those coins have kept us well," Charles said, equally admonishing.

"Maybe when it was just the two of you, content to be poor as church mice. But you have a wife now, Charlie. And soon, I hope, children. You have to think of the future."

The cooing tone of the last sentence provoked a nauseous response within me, and I clenched my teeth against the bile. Charles must have mistaken my reaction as an attempt to hold back tears, because he reached across the table and came very close to touching my hand in comfort before I snatched it away.

"Don't worry, Sister," he said, "maybe we can find someone to rent out the shop. That would be a good bit of income for you."

"Of course, dear," Katrina said, suddenly sweet again. "Why, we'd let you keep over half."

"You'll keep it all," Charles said. "And you're welcome to live here as long as you like."

My tongue, though thick, loosened. "Oh, may I? May I please continue to live in my home?"

"I believe the deed is in *both* of your names." She turned to Charles. "Isn't it, sweetie?"

That's when I knew they'd played out this conversation before. This scenario. All the low whispers and secretive looks I'd been attributing to the mystical ways of marriage had been nothing more than treachery and escape. I didn't begrudge my brother the opportunity. I would have gladly packed his bags and sent him— *and* his wife, I suppose— off to pursue such an honor. But to have it withheld from me. . . To think of all the weeks since their return (for it was now nearly the end of September) without a word. How I would have loved to have heard the story in my brother's voice, each word undergirded with his special brand of bashful pride. It was Katrina's place to beam beside him in silence, not to grab his thunder and throw it on the table. Did the two of them think my love so inferior to hers that I could not share in the joy? But then, the news being unfolded in such a manner, trailing its dreadful secrecy, I could not.

"The two of you," I said, teeth clenched, "you make me sick."

I removed myself from the table and went out into the yard behind the kitchen. Normally the cool night air of early autumn would bring welcome refreshment, but when I opened my mouth to take a gulp of it, the roiling in my stomach overwhelmed me and I bent over, vomiting my supper into the grass. I prayed that the two of them didn't have their noses pressed against the window watching. I heaved long after my stomach was empty and finally wiped my eyes, then nose, then mouth with the dinner napkin I'd had the presence of mind to bring. I don't know how long I stood outside, but eventually their movement caught my attention as they got up from the table and began to clear it. I'd taken a few steps away from where I'd been sick and waited, caught between wanting to be left alone and wishing one or the other would care enough to open the door and call to me.

Neither did.

I could not bear to walk back into that kitchen, so I made my way to the front of the building and let myself through the shop door, praying—now—that the conspirators in the kitchen would ignore the bell.

They did.

I wanted nothing more than to steal up to my room, but then I remembered. I had no room upstairs. I'd relegated myself to the oversized closet behind the kitchen, where Charles and Katrina were murmuring between the clinking of dishes and scrubbing of pots. I remained, trapped by circumstance in the shadows of Charles's shop. I thought about the hours he stood behind that counter fixing clocks and oiling anything with a gear. Repairing everything from toy trains to rabbit traps. How he worked by lamplight long into the dark in order to keep a promise. His tenacity and talent brought both of us favor when the owner took us in and left us everything. And now what could it be? A bookshop, maybe. Or library, if I could secure the funds. It would take work and time to rid the place of its distinctive smell of grease and metal shavings, though now they brought more comfort than the lingering smell of supper coming from the kitchen.

I assessed my body. Breathing? Normal. Skin? Cool to the touch. Tears? Dry and gone, with no hint of a return. I longed, however, for a drink of water to chase the sourness from my mouth, and there was only one place where I could go for that. As of now and always, this building belonged to me, and I had no reason to cower in the darkness any longer. Instead of stealing to my room, I strode into the kitchen. Katrina, drying the last dish, looked over her shoulder at my entrance.

"Mariah, dear. Are you all right?"

"I'm fine," I said, walking straight for the shelf where I kept the empty jars that once held Merrill Gowan's cousin's preserves. I filled it with water from the crock, knowing it would be cool to my burning throat, and walked past my brother who stood, looking dejected, with a dish towel draped over his shoulder. Mindful of my breath, I placed a soft, swift kiss on his cheek and whispered, "I'm so proud of you, Brother."

We tiptoed around each other for the next few days, barely conversing at the meals that brought us to the table together. I'd all but lost my appetite, running my spoon around the edges of my porridge bowl in the morning and nibbling bread and butter while pushing food around on my plate in the evening. For as many times as Charles said, "We need to talk about this, Sister," I had a retort ready to push the conversation off to another time. My head ached, my stomach was in a constant state of turmoil, and I found I barely had the energy to complete a simple chore before becoming overwhelmed with a depressing fatigue that took me to my little room, where I would lay, arm flung across my eyes, and give over to sleep. Charles made avoidance all the easier as he was gone most days, either working on farm equipment he'd been hired to repair or hiring himself out to work a day's harvest.

"Every little bit helps," Katrina said as she handed him a burlap sack of dinner and a kiss on his cheek. "We've a whole house to set up in Chicago." In these moments, I tried to make myself invisible, and I might as well have been for all the mind they paid me.

One day when Charles was out working for none other than Merrill Gowan, I came upon Katrina softly crying in the kitchen. The sound is what drew me, as I initially thought there might have been a nest of kittens born in the warmth of the cabinet by the oven. But, no, it was she, standing at the stove, stirring something with a wooden dowel. The part of my spirit that was mean wanted to turn on my heel and leave her to whatever invented drama she was experiencing, but the part of me that saw her as a sister—both literally and in spirit—wouldn't allow my escape. I remained in the safety of the doorway and merely said her name as a question. "Katrina?"

She looked up, sniffed, gave a wry smile, and lifted the dowel from the pot, showing the rag draped over it.

I found myself smiling too. On this detestable chore, at least, we stood on common ground. "I know it's not the most convenient, but it's never made me so upset. Or is the soap too strong? The steam burning your eyes?"

She shook her head, the ribbons in her hair oddly incongruous with her face. "I suppose this chore will always make me a little sad for a while."

"Sad?"

"It means I'm not with child. I was so hoping to become pregnant right away. But maybe it's best, considering the move." She resumed stirring. "I suppose I should have asked you how you wash and where you dry your"—she inclined her head to the pot. "My mother and I got our time practically on the same day every month. I shouldn't wonder that you and I will do the same. At least for as long as I'm here."

"Yes," I said, filling a bucket with cool water so the freshly washed rags could be cooled, rinsed, and wrung out.

"You must have perfected the art of hiding this bit of womanhood from your brother. I haven't noticed at all that you've had your time since I got here."

"Charles never was one to observe such details," I said, but my mind was far, far away from this conversation as I calculated. I hadn't had my monthly since Katrina arrived. And not while they were on their honeymoon, either, though I vaguely remembered expecting it during their time away.

"Mariah? Darling?" Katrina's voice seemed to come from a great distance as the room spun me away from her.

Perhaps if I'd grown up with a mother or a sister or any other woman who cared two bits about my health and well-being, I might have been quicker to give a name to my symptoms. I might have known to be more cautious before feeding that monstrous desire for Oscar on the night of my brother's wedding. I clutched at the edge of the table and fell into a chair, weighted with shame. I wasn't a child, for heaven's sake. I was a grown woman—however inexperienced in the ways of courtship and love. What happened with Oscar was neither, yet here I was, carrying the consequences.

Pregnant.

I could barely allow my mind to form the word. I dared not whisper it to myself, let alone give it as an answer to Katrina's constant repetition of questions.

"What is wrong? Mariah? Are you ill?"

"I'm fine. Just a bit dizzy all of a sudden."

"It's because you haven't been eating."

"Right. Yes, it must be that."

"I know you're upset about Charles and me leaving, but can't you be even a little bit happy for him? You're making him miserable, you know. He feels guilty. And now, if he thinks you'll be struck down sick, I'm worried he won't go at all."

She talked. Oh, how she talked, but her words created a wall for me to hide behind while my mind raced. She set a glass of water in front of me without taking so much as a breath in her diatribe against my existence. I thanked her, listening to her chatter on about their future children and needing to make their *own* family. And I thought—of course. Oscar. I had to tell him. He was a good man, an honorable man for all his flirtatiousness. He had to have known the risk—more so than I, for he'd clearly come to my bed with the experience of others. I hadn't seen him since that night and had no idea where to find him, but Charles would know. That would mean telling Charles, and the thought of that caused a fist-sized knot in my stomach. No, not my stomach. That was where a tiny baby might be growing. The fist was in my heart, protecting it from the way every person I knew and loved would think of me from this moment on.

Katrina was midsentence when I stood. Maybe even asking me a question. I don't know, didn't care.

"I'm going for a walk," I said, taking an apple from a basket on the sideboard and the heel of the day's bread.

It was more than an hour's walk to Merrill Gowan's place, but the day couldn't have been better crafted for the journey. The air was crisp, and I truly *felt* the descriptor, almost as if I could feel it framing my face. The sunlight held a golden tone that tinted everything in sight. Biting into the apple felt like tasting the day, and I thought—*everything in its season*. A few weeks ago, this apple would have been green, bitter, small, and hard. So had I—mere weeks ago—been lonely and utterly without a future. At least, not a future to be shared. But now. . .

Each step, each breath proved restorative.

I was carrying new life.

Merrill's crop grew right up to the edge of the road, tall and golden-proud. I ran my hand along it, dislodging some of the grain. This too was life. My father had never known success as a farmer; our claim had been his last-ditch effort to support our family off the fruit of the land. How he would have marveled at the expanse of red winter wheat stretched out as far as my eyes could see. And then, beyond its horizon, I saw the house. The top of it, anyway. Two solid stories, finished windows that looked over the bounty—and all of it painted a shade of blue that made it a peacock among the dull, wind-worn shade of white that adorned any other dwelling.

This is what he had offered. This—all of this—could have been mine. I gave the notion exactly three heartbeats to take hold, but even these riches paled in comparison to the tiny treasure within me. Strange how I'd woken up that very morning ignorant of my condition, and now it drove me—though exactly where, I wasn't sure. It was a temporary secret, something hidden away from the entire world, but for how long? Katrina's shrewdness would discover it soon enough.

I'd apparently arrived at the workers' dinner hour, for I heard no sound of machinery. Looking out to the place where the wheat lay flat on the ground, I saw the giant harvester at a standstill, a dozen or so men gathered around it. Merrill spotted me first. He stood to his feet and began striding toward me, a look of purposeful concern on his face. He shouted something over his shoulder, and Charles popped up to follow close behind at first, then overtaking Merrill at a run. He stopped breathless before me.

"What is it? Is it Katrina? Is anything wrong?"

His peppering questions took me off guard. I hadn't taken the time to think how it must look, my coming out to visit in the middle of the day. Outside of church obligations with sick congregants, I'd never embarked on an afternoon visit of any kind in my entire life. Yet here I was, and within seconds, Merrill was there too at Charles's elbow, echoing his concerns.

I laughed and held up my hands in surrender. "Everything is fine, Brother. Mr. Gowan. I'm sorry for the unwelcome surprise."

"Not unwelcome," Charles said, not sounding a bit relieved, "but, yes, a surprise."

"I need to talk to you," I said in a way that left no margin to include Merrill in the conversation.

"Right now?"

"Would I have walked the hour if it didn't need to be right now?"

"I'll just be a bit," Charles said to Merrill before taking my arm (more aggressively than the occasion called for) and steering me to a fledgling copse of trees that looked like a gathering of gangly boys in a field. "Now, what is it?" he said once we were safely under their lacy shade.

"I need you to find Oscar Garland."

"*Find* him?"

"Find him and talk to him on my behalf." I knew I sounded like a character from one of my frivolous novels, and the expression of incredulity on my brother's face confirmed it.

"Talk to him on your behalf?"

"Stop repeating everything I say, please."

"Then say something that makes some sense."

I took a deep breath and focused my thoughts. "It is very important, Charles, that you find Oscar Garland and talk to him."

He took a matching deep breath. "About what?"

"About me. You need to tell him—" And suddenly my bravado came to an end. Tears I'd been too proud to shed pooled in my eyes, and I could not speak for the quivering of my chin. Thinking it was my dear brother's earnest face in front of me, I looked away, into the sparse treetops behind him, their brave leaves fluttering valiantly in the wind.

"Sister." He drew me to him, and I buried my face in his shoulder. The rough fabric of his shirt abraded my skin, but it carried the scent of soap and starch, despite his morning's labor. That was Katrina's doing, no doubt, making sure his clothes were clean and pressed; I never attended to his laundry with such detail. He drew back. "Did Oscar—did he. . .hurt you?"

The full weight of his question was not lost to me. I wiped my nose on my sleeve, saying, "No. No. He—no. Not in the way you mean. He didn't hurt me. He didn't. . .he didn't *force* me."

"My God," he said, not in vain but in prayer. Charles had never been a religious man nor one to use the name of God in any casual sense. "What did he do?"

"Nothing I didn't invite." I would not make him a villain.

Charles took a full step back and stood utterly still. "Why do I need to talk to him, Mariah?"

"Because—" I pondered and swallowed every phrasing and decided to speak it plain. "I am pregnant."

He closed his eyes, shutting me away. "Are you sure?"

"As sure as a woman who knows nothing about these things can be." If his eyes had been open, he'd have seen my smile, my little attempt to lighten the moment. But it was gone by the time he opened them.

"What do you want me to do?" His question took me by surprise. Somehow, I'd expected him to be more gallant. "Don't you know what kind of man he is? Everybody within ten miles says he's a. . .a. . .well, I don't know the word."

I offered up no defense of his character nor mine.

"Am I supposed to go fight a duel or something?" he continued. "Defend your honor?"

"Of course not."

"Because honestly, Mariah, how do I know that your honor is worth defending?"

His question struck a blow. I staggered in my place, as if he'd taken a branch from one of the fledgling trees and struck me across my back. Immediately, regret formed on his face, and he dropped his voice to something more akin to comfort.

"Really, Sister, what do you want me to do?"

"Nothing. Don't do anything. I'm sorry I bothered—" Tears choked my words, and I wanted nothing more than the ground to swallow me whole, like some tragic Greek figure. What if my brother, who had loved me all of his life, was a preview of Oscar's reaction to the same news? I imagined myself, standing in dappled sunlight, telling Oscar Garland I was carrying his child, and his reaction.

What do you want me to do?

Out in the field, the harvester roared to life, calling Charles's attention.

"Go," I said. "There's nothing to do now. But, please"—I thought of Merrill Gowan—"please don't tell anyone."

"Of course I won't. But, you know," he glanced down at my stomach and back up at me in a blink, "it's not a secret you'll be able to keep forever."

"No, but I can keep it for now. *We* can keep it for now. Don't even tell Katrina. She'd be. . ."

"I know." Already my brother had become a man capable of knowing a woman's thoughts.

I felt his reassuring squeeze to my arm before he ran back to the work. He passed Merrill on the way, who stayed his ground while allowing his gaze to bridge the distance between us. My hand came up in a small, involuntary, weak wave, and he responded in kind. Then, before I could give myself over to a most tempting collapse, I turned my back on his peacock-blue house and began the long trek home.

CHAPTER 11

TRIXIE

*T*rixie ran up the stairs, feeling every bit the guilty teenager as Cam's kiss lingered on her lips. She stopped outside of GG's door, giving herself a moment to catch her breath and gather her thoughts. Her goodbye to Cam had sounded like something akin to a dismissal, and for all she knew, he'd gathered the remains of their lunch and walked them to the kitchen himself. Unforgivable rudeness on her part—something for which her mother would surely chide her—but GG's waking, coherent hours were as elusive and impermanent as dandelion spores, and she didn't want to miss a bit.

"That little girl," GG said the moment Trixie entered the room, "I keep thinking I've woken up back in time and it's you. Although you never made so much noise."

"She is a little noisemaker, isn't she?"

"She is."

Trixie scrutinized the old woman's face, amused at the unspoken rejoinder. Even as a little girl, Trixie knew, somehow, that while her great-grandmother unquestioningly loved her, she'd never been one to indulge or dote.

"Your mother," GG continued, "used to bribe you to sing. And to tell stories and play make-believe. You never did like to pretend, did you?"

Trixie shook her head. "I didn't. The real world has always been interesting enough."

"You seem interested in that doctor."

"It's Cam, GG. You remember him?"

GG's thin, dry lips spread into a tight smile. "I do. And you were plenty interested in him back then, as I recall."

Trixie felt her cheeks blush. "I was."

"But not so much now?"

"Not so much, no." She pulled a chair close to the bedside and sat, propping one elbow on the mattress and resting her chin in her palm. "But I don't want to talk about me, GG. I'm not that interesting."

"And you think I am, all of a sudden?"

Trixie chafed at the slight rebuke. "I—I didn't know who you were."

GG made a chuffing sound and lifted her thin hand dismissively. "I'm the same old woman you've always known. I haven't become a new person. The story of who I am hasn't changed."

"But that's just it. I don't know your story. At all, apparently."

"I spent a few weeks trapped in a cabin with that young woman playing school. That is all."

"That isn't all, GG. I can tell. I can see it in your eyes."

GG had been averting her gaze but now looked straight at her. Age had not brought a single cloud across the pale blue of her iris, though her vision had dulled after a lifetime of reading by pre-electric light. A pair of thick-lensed glasses sat on the bedside table. Mom had said she rarely wore them anymore, the weight more cumbersome than the correction merited.

"We were nearly the same age, Miss Ingalls—Laura and I."

"I gathered that from the book."

"I've wondered, since, why God couldn't divvy things up a little more evenly. She had everything."

"But wasn't she poor too?" Trixie had grown up on the stories of GG's poverty, romanticizing the tales of such a spartan existence. She'd imagined it a thrill to live so close to death at the hands of hunger or disease or the very blizzards that never brought anything more exciting than a day home from school. "I mean, wasn't Pa always losing the crop or getting kicked off his land or something?"

"She had a father. And a mother. A roof built for their family. A man who loved her."

Here her weak voice tapered, and she managed a faint request for water. Trixie obliged, filling a glass at the bathroom sink, not wanting to risk breaking the story connection with a trip downstairs to the kitchen. She came back and waited patiently for GG to take a series of slow, careful sips, wondering if she should nudge with a question or wait for a new memory to flow. The silence was interrupted by the roar of a car engine—Cam leaving, apparently. For a moment, she considered getting up, going to the window, and waving goodbye, but GG's silence anchored her, and the wait paid.

"I used to watch them," GG said, her gaze fixed on the window, perhaps drawn by the sound.

"Watch who?"

"All of them. The young people. On Sunday afternoons like this—in the winter. They would get in their little cutters and drive up and down Joliet Street. I would be working if I could find it—mending and sewing and such. Or reading. And if Charles didn't hire himself out, he'd be napping. Always said a morning at church made him more tired than a full day's labor."

"Your brother, Charles. Right?"

She made a small, affirmative sound. "The house where we rented a room would let us sit in the front parlor on Sunday afternoons, and it was warmer there most times, but I liked to save up to buy coal for our own little stove. We were up on the second floor, and I could see the whole street. Hear the jingle of the bells and the laughter. And the singing. Such a sound. There's never been a movie I liked better than watching them fly."

GG's face lit up as she spoke, and Trixie knew her great-grandmother had transported herself to that time and place she vividly remembered reading about in the book.

"You never wanted to join them?"

"Who would ask me? Who would know to ask me? Charles and I never went to school when we moved to De Smet. We were invisible. I know it seems like a small town compared to your big city, but things weren't so different. Like ran with like. Two penniless orphans? We weren't like the other people our age. We didn't go to socials and singing schools. I was an old woman before I was twenty."

"Did you recognize her? Miss Ingalls—Laura—when you were watching the sledding party on the street?"

"You couldn't miss her. She had a laugh that rang out above the bells and the most beautiful brown curls that poked out beneath her cap." As she spoke, GG absently fingered the soft, white tendrils that floated near her brow. "She had twice the beauty that I would ever have, a double portion of everything I lacked. Joy and youth. Courtship. Love." She brought a trembling hand to her mouth as if to catch the last word and somehow put it back.

"But you found love too, eventually?" Even as Trixie asked the question, a looming dread wrapped itself around the answer. "You married. Did my great-grandfather not love you?"

"He did," she said behind her fingers, not looking Trixie in the eye.

The companion question was, of course, did *she* love *him*, but Trixie couldn't bring herself to ask it. Instead, she moved to safer ground. "Did he not court you?"

GG dropped her hand. "There was no call for such a frivolous waste of time. We weren't young when we got married. Either of us."

"How old were you?" She searched her brain for this bit of trivia but found it nowhere.

"Twenty-six."

"Ouch," Trixie said with a lighthearted guffaw, pleased to see GG's commiserative smile.

"Things were different then. You can have any sort of life you want now, can't you?" She lifted a defiant, shaking fist. "Women's lib!"

"Yes!" Trixie said, mirroring the gesture.

"Burn your brassiere!"

"Or don't wear one!" This, she mock-shouted in a whisper.

GG's face grew serious. "I don't know if I ever would have married if circumstances were different."

This ushered in an entire new series of questions to race through Trixie's mind like blades on a snow-packed Sunday street, but she kept them to herself. For now. GG's voice had grown soft again, and she showed little inclination to elaborate. Her lids seemed to be drooping, and Trixie was about to take her leave when the old woman's feather-light grip stopped her.

"Will you be here tomorrow?"

"I will, yes."

"Will you take me somewhere?"

Trixie's first thought was of her car, hidden away with some mechanic. After that, she considered her great-grandmother's health. Her frailty. "I don't know, GG, if that would be the best idea."

"You think I'm too weak."

"No, no," Trixie said, trying to sound reassuring. "It's just that I don't have my car. It's in the shop. Something to do with the starter."

"Then I'll have to hold on another day. Or one more. There's someplace I need to see before I die."

Trixie redoubled her attempt to sound soothing and confident. "You aren't dying anytime soon, GG."

"I am, and I've made most of my peace."

"Most?"

"We can only make true peace with the living. The rest we leave to God to reconcile."

GG settled back into her pillow and closed her eyes as if exhausted from the conversation. Trixie felt the opposite, invigorated by questions and a driving desire to clean out everything left in her great-grandmother's long-held cache of secret memories. But when her softly spoken questions—GG? *What peace do you need to make?*—were answered with even softer snores, Trixie brought the light quilt up to cover those familiar, age-spotted arms and slipped out of the room.

The house was quiet, holding with the Sunday tradition wherein each woman retired to her room for an afternoon of napping or reading (or an alternating series of both). Growing up, Trixie had been trained to roam quietly—if roam she must—and any television or radio was strictly forbidden. She grabbed a handful of pencils and her sketchbook from her room, but before heading downstairs, she ducked into GG's room to snatch her copy of *These Happy Golden Years*. That is, GG's copy, the one not-so-artfully disguised in the bedside detritus of a bedridden woman. In the kitchen, Trixie grabbed a pop from the fridge and a half-empty bag of Fritos before heading outside to the back porch.

It was her favorite time of a summer's day, late afternoon when long shadows seemed to be reaching, ready to pull a blanket of darkness and tuck the world in for the night. She'd only have an hour or so of good light left. And a little more than that of silence before her mother and grandmother would descend, refreshed and ready to make a soup or sandwiches from the leftovers of the Sunday dinner.

Trixie opened her pop and, after carefully drying her fingers on a napkin, opened GG's book. The pages were soft, the paper thin. The copyright page had a notice at the bottom that the book had been manufactured in accordance with government regulations for saving paper. *Of course,* she thought. It was printed while the country was at war. Everything rationed. How marvelous to think, really, that any priority at all would be given to the publication of children's literature.

But then she thought of Samantha, longing for a taste of the world Laura Ingalls brought to life. Simple times full of simple pleasures, where every hardship created an opportunity for adventure. Darkness, disease, hunger—every threat met defeat under Wilder's prose. She and her family triumphed in every book if not in their actual lives.

She turned to the page depicting those first students, her great-grandmother among them. The Sewell and Boyle illustrations were typical of the time—curved, rounded features lacking shading and detail. Trixie could not shake the fact that her own drawing style, at least for the *Lost Laura* comics, seemed to be a derivative of these depictions.

For a while, her eyes and mind cut a repeating path between

the pages of the novel, the sketch pad on the table, and the place in the yard where she, Cam, and Samantha had shared their picnic. Slowly, a story formed—a five-day arc of Lost Laura in search of a picnic place in the city. Being chased off the front lawn of a massive suburban home. Kicked out of a busy nursery. A city park experience ruined by stray dogs and Frisbees. Finally, success. Her own back porch. In the rough sketch, she's leaning against the enormous basket she's been lugging around. In the final drawing, the window will be open with the drapes fluttering outside along with music notes from a distant radio.

Trixie jotted dialogue for all the strips along the margin of the page—quips that would disappear in the next breath if she didn't write them down. In thinking of the last, Lost Laura would say something like *All you need for a picnic is a good sandwich and fresh air.* Then a longing look at the empty spot on the other side of the basket.

The readers would get it. Lost Laura's growing fan base came with letters demanding a boyfriend. Up to now, Trixie had been against the idea. The whole point of the character was to bring out a budding spirit of independence. She was supposed to be this metaphor of womanhood, bewildered by all the changes in the world, equally confused and delighted by them. She was a female Rip Van Winkle, going to sleep as one of the March sisters and waking up as *That Girl*.

But even *That Girl* had a boyfriend.

Upstairs her great-grandmother, having lived the entirety of the century between Lost Laura's worlds, had spoken of romantic regret. She'd had nothing to say about the wars she'd witnessed or the Great Depression she'd survived or the man she'd watched walk on the moon or the miracle of bread that came from the grocery store perfectly sliced and bagged. GG had the experience of flushing a toilet for the first time, of heating a stove with a twist of a knob, of pulling clean clothes from a machine and tossing them into a dryer (though she still preferred a clothesline in summer). She was a time machine. The young woman illustrated in the novel would not recognize the woman sleeping upstairs, would not be able to survive in this world if not for the slow, day-to-day progression of life. The chapters in this novel were a few of those days and may have been forgotten if they hadn't been recorded. For anyone else, living in the pages of a national treasure would be an honor. A blessing even. But for GG Mariah, it seemed only to have unearthed everything she'd been denied over the course of her long, long life.

"Where did you get that?" Eugenie's smoky voice interrupted Trixie's reverie. *Smoky* was the best adjective to describe her voice, as her throat had been subjected to decades' worth of cigarette smoke. She had stopped smoking only after a doctor's warning that she would never see a woman in the White House if she continued with the habit. She had a glass of milky iced coffee made from what was left in the pot from this morning. The glass was one procured from a restaurant promotion; cubes of ice danced behind Porky Pig when she set it down on the table. She held out her hand for the book. "Did Mariah give this to you?"

"Sort of," Trixie said, closing her sketchbook. She never liked to share works in progress. "I mean, she made me aware of its existence, then left it out in the open."

Eugenie turned the book over and over in her hands. "She bought this the night you were born."

"Yeah. She told me."

"When the books first came out, she would brag on and on about how she knew Laura Ingalls. How she'd been one of her students when Laura was a teacher. How they were almost friends and ate their noon dinner together sometimes."

"It's cool, though, isn't it? Knowing this famous person."

"But always with an edge. She never bought *any* of the books. And this is a woman who bought every book she could get her hands on. Some of her favorites, like *Jane Eyre*? She had at least two copies—one for upstairs and one for downstairs. Just in case. Remember when we all went to Sioux Falls so she could get Jackie Collins to sign one of her books?"

"And Jackie Collins said, 'Now, *you*, my dear, look like one of my readers.'"

Trixie and Eugenie delivered this line in perfect unison and laughed.

"She told that story every night at dinner for a year," Eugenie said. "But she actually *appeared* in a Laura Ingalls Wilder book and never said a word about it."

"But you knew?"

Eugenie set the book down and took a sip of her coffee. "Everybody in the hospital knew. And they knew exactly how she felt about it. She apparently stormed out of the waiting room, shouting at the top of her lungs, and I finally found her on the hospital lawn." Eugenie's countenance, pleasantly unattractive, took on an expression of actual fear. "It was freezing cold, you know, one of those cold summer nights, and she hadn't even taken her coat. She was howling and hunched over like an animal. And when I ask her what's wrong, thinking it might be that Alma's up there with a baby and no husband, she thrusts the book out at me like this." Eugenie gave a demonstration so forceful, Trixie jumped back in her seat. "And she says, 'We don't ever talk of this again. I don't want to hear her name.'"

This line was familiar, as Trixie had heard it more than once growing up.

"I'd seen her like that once before," Eugenie continued, running a finger through the condensation on her glass. "When Mark died."

"Understandable," Trixie said. "He was her only son, right?"

Eugenie nodded, keeping her eyes on her glass after a quick glance over her shoulder at the door. "I never told you this, and it's my great shame. But I wasn't here when Mark died."

"Like, here? On the farm?" Trixie's grandfather had died from an infection that set in after injuring his hand in a piece of harvesting machinery.

"Not here at all. Before I married Mark, I worked as a researcher at 3M."

Trixie, who had been midsip, spluttered her pop and wiped her chin. "What? I always knew you worked there, but I assumed it was some sort of—"

"Factory position? Nope. I was a real-life lady scientist. Went to college and everything."

The pride beaming from her grandmother's time-worn face broke Trixie's heart. "Why did you leave?"

"I met Mark Gowan. I was visiting a friend here for their harvest festival, and he was the most handsome man I'd ever seen. I'll never know what he saw in me. But he was good and true, so we married and I lived here as a farmer's wife."

"And daughter-in-law."

"We always got along, Mariah and me. And she was a better mother to Alma than I was. But after a few years—Alma wasn't but two—I couldn't take it anymore. I was so. . .*bored*. And I left."

Never, in all of her years of listening to the grown-ups' after-dinner conversations, had Trixie heard any of this. "Where did you go?"

"Back to Minneapolis. Back to 3M. Back to the same little apartment I had before I met your grandfather. I asked God to forgive the thought, but I was so happy." Tears filled her eyes, and the ice rattled in her glass as she raised her hand to wipe them away. "I told Mariah how to reach me but asked her not to tell Mark because he'd come charging in and drag me right out of the laboratory, I was sure. So she calls one day and says Mark has been hurt. Then a week later and says that he died."

"A week later?" Trixie immediately regretted the accusatory tone.

"I didn't know what I could have done. And I think I might have stayed away. Like I said, she was so good with the baby, but when she called to say Mark died—I could hardly understand her. I came home, and she was like a walking ghost. Little Alma hadn't been washed or anything for days. Maybe not even fed."

"She was in mourning."

"True. But I *was* there when Merrill died. Her husband. And she didn't even skip breakfast. Anyhoo, I couldn't leave my daughter there, and I wasn't sure I could leave Mariah alone. So I stayed." Eugenie punctuated her story with a little shrug. "And you know the rest."

"But I don't know the rest," Trixie said. "So she and my great-grandfather had a tepid marriage. What does that have to do with her hating Laura Ingalls Wilder? What did the woman ever do to her?"

Another shrug. Another beat of silence to allow the question to go unanswered. "I used to worry about you, our little Trixie. Growing up in this house. None of us set a very good example of how to be a wife or mother. Almost like each of us could do one but not the other."

"Mom was a good mother," Trixie said, more from defensiveness than affection. She'd always known that Alma's maternal instincts were drawn from what she wanted the world to see, not for the sweet, private hours at home.

Eugenie made a *tsking* sound. "She carried so much shame—and none of it heaped by Mariah and me. Was there sin? Yes, but sin can be forgiven. Shame you drag around with you. And she dragged it, thinking she'd never find a man willing to forgive her. So you never had a father. I tried always to tell her to seek out love for herself, but she covers it all up. Anyway, all's to say I think you missed out, growing up with just the three of us."

"I love the three of you."

"Oh, I don't doubt that. But—"

"But nothing."

A light turned on in the kitchen, meaning Alma was up and around, ready to prepare a light supper. Eugenie started to hoist herself up from her chair, but Trixie detained her.

"Wait. There's something I want to tell you. I think Cam wants to start up again."

Eugenie chuckled. "Well, that's hardly a secret. How he looks at you."

"But I don't want to."

"No more feelings for him?"

"More than that. I just—Samantha's a sweet kid, right? But I don't want to be a mother. At least not right now. I don't want the responsibility when—" She swallowed back the details, thinking that even a career-defining moment with national syndication seemed a paltry detail in the light of motherhood. "I have opportunities for myself. Things I want to do and explore. Does that make me a horrible person?"

"I think I'm the last person alive who could make that call," Eugenie said. "But let me tell you this: if you loved Cam the way a woman needs to love a man in order to wrap her life around him, you wouldn't have a doubt in your mind."

The screen door creaked, and Alma stepped outside, saying, "What's up with the two of you? You look like you're sharing secrets."

"Just telling some old family stories," Eugenie said. "Nothing you haven't lived through."

"Well then, do you think you could give me a hand with supper? It's a warm night, so I thought I'd make a nice chicken salad. And fruit. They're showing *Carousel* on the Sunday Night Movie, and you know how I love Shirley Jones. So maybe a pan of Jiffy Pop too?"

"Sounds great," Trixie said. Most Sundays, her mother called to inform her of the Sunday Night Movie, as Trixie had yet to subscribe to *TV Guide*. Often she watched for the sole purpose of having that feeling of connectedness—two identical television screens separated by miles. "Do you think GG would feel up to coming downstairs to join us?"

"We can see," Eugenie said. "But she's never been much for musicals. Calls them frivolous."

"I love frivolous," Alma said, holding the door open.

Trixie stopped on the way in and kissed the top of her mother's head. "And I love you, Mom."

It was itself a frivolous gesture and a sentiment too rarely spoken.

The three women spent the next hour chopping, mixing, and serving up the chicken salad in a big scoop balanced atop a leaf of lettuce, with slices of buttered toast on the side. Trixie was put in charge of the popcorn, as the technology of the Jiffy Pop contraption confounded her mother and grandmother. She dumped two pans' worth in the giant Tupperware mixing bowl, its sides scarred with a million spoon swipes.

GG was awake and alert and wanting to join in the watching, though Trixie resented every uneasy step as she led her down the stairs. This could be precious time, better spent delving into what remained hidden in her past, but the conviviality of a light supper on TV trays with cans of pop and popcorn brought another kind of sweetness altogether.

The overstuffed living room was bathed in blue light as they ate during the overture, giving the screen all the attention they would give were they sitting in a grand theater and not on a mismatched collection of prewar furniture. Their silence deepened as Shirley Jones's Julie delivered the line about never getting married and needing to be all the pickier about who she courted because of that resolve.

Should have stuck to that, Trixie thought, wondering if the generations watching with her would agree.

Seconds into the first commercial, the phone rang, much to Alma's consternation. "Who in the world would call somebody at eight o'clock on a Sunday evening?"

"I'll get it," Trixie said, knowing she'd be the quickest to sprint into the kitchen and back before the movie resumed. Plus, she had a feeling about just who would be irreverent enough to call this late. Maybe not irreverent but unschooled in the ways of polite society. She picked up the phone and, taking a risk on sounding ridiculous, said, "Hello, Ron."

"How'd you know?" he said as a return greeting.

"Lucky guess."

"I figured it was safe to call during the commercial, right?"

Now it was her turn to be impressed. She mirrored his tone. "How'd you know?"

"Sunday Night Movie, right? *Carousel.* They spent half an hour singing about how much they don't love each other."

"How did you know I was watching the Sunday Night Movie?"

"You always watch the Sunday Night Movie."

"Yes, but how do you know?"

"Because every Monday morning you come in, make coffee, ask who watched the Sunday Night Movie, and then tell everybody who didn't watch it what they missed."

Trixie didn't know whether to be flattered that Ron paid such close attention or self-conscious about her predictability. "Yes, well. Is everything okay?" She couldn't imagine what would prompt a Sunday night phone call.

"I was thinking that you won't be there for the Monday morning staff meeting and wanted to see if there was anything I should know about. . .whatever it is that you usually contribute to the Monday morning staff meeting."

She smiled, coiled the phone cord around her finger, and leaned against the wall, tucking her chin down as if about to tell a secret. "Umm. . .usually it's a matter of Mack telling me what ads to build, and then after the meeting I go build them. I'm caught up for this issue unless something new comes in."

"So, I'll call you if something new comes in?"

"Yes. But, really, Mack could probably manage with my clip art catalog. It's in my bottom desk drawer." He knew all this—*all* of this. She'd told him before she left. Typed it up in a note that she left on the kitchen counter. Plus, he *ran* the paper and still had all of the ad staff he'd had before hiring her in the first place. But he called. Having spoken to her not more than four hours ago, he called, and if he was feeling the same delightful awkwardness on his end of the line as she was feeling on hers, the phone lines stretched between this rambling house and her bachelorette apartment must be crackling up a storm.

"Okay, well," he said, his voice once again its booming self, "looks like the commercial is about over, so back to the movie, right?"

"Right."

"And, I'm assuming, these two crooners are going to fall madly in love and go singing into the sunset?"

Trixie laughed. "Have you seen *Carousel*?"

"Don't judge, but no. I have not. I'm a sucker for a happy ending."

"Then you might be better off switching the channel to *Kojak*."

"How about if I turn the TV off and find a good book?"

"That'll work too."

"Or snuggle up with your cat and let him purr me to sleep?"

She wanted to laugh again, but the first inhalation stopped at a soft gasp, and for a second she couldn't breathe at all until she finally stammered, "I—I should go. It sounds like '*June is bustin' out all over*' in there."

"What is. . . What?" She pictured the quirk of his eyebrow.

"It's the next song. So I have to go, or else my mother is going to yell at me." Trixie knew she sounded like a kid, but she felt like one too, thinking she'd as soon stay here in the dark kitchen, clutching the phone, ping-ponging nonsense with Ron until one of them finally hung up. The song floated into the silence as the two of them held the line. She cringed at the lyrics, interpreting each bit of sexual innuendo, and hoped Ron had the volume turned down. "I guess I should go."

"Yeah." The word rumbled against her cheek.

"But call me tomorrow if you need to."

"I will."

"And say good night to House for me."

"He's right here."

"Oh, well in that case, don't mention me at all. Or he won't come near you."

"I think he likes hearing your voice."

"I think he likes knowing I'm disembodied and far away."

"Well, then, maybe I'm the one who likes hearing your voice."

Before Trixie could reply, her mother screeched from the living room, "Trixie! The number's almost over! You're missing it!"

She covered the mouthpiece. "On my way, Mom. It's work stuff." Then, to Ron, "I have to go. But seriously, turn this movie off. It's terrible." And before another thread of conversation could pop up, she rushed, "Good night, Ron."

"Good night, Prairie Girl."

And even then there was a space of a few breaths, a few beats. The phone was warm against her face—or maybe her face was warm against the phone. She reached up and used her finger to depress the cradle, cutting the call before actually hanging up, and walked into the darkened living room.

"Who was that?" Eugenie asked, distracted by the musical number on the screen.

"Work," Trixie said before curling herself into her corner of the couch.

"On a Sunday night?"

"Yeah."

The sad, sad story of Julie Jordan and Billy Bigelow unfolded in the dark room, and Trixie might have been tempted to lecture her mother and grandmother about the misogynistic, anti-feminist, abuse-apologetic themes of the film but confined herself to irritable comments laced with snark that earned an equally irritated *Shhh* from her mother and grandmother.

But not GG.

The old woman may have appeared to be dozing in her chair, but when Trixie quietly cheered as Billy Bigelow succumbed to his knife wound, a smile crept at the corner of her thin lips and a soft chortle made its way into the room.

When the movie ended, Trixie's mother stood, stretched, and crossed the room to turn off the television before the first story on the ten o'clock news. Eugenie gently helped GG from her chair, and the trio took careful, coordinated steps in the dark.

"Good night, girls," Trixie said, not moving an inch.

"Are you not going to bed?" Eugenie asked, the last one to head up the stairs.

"Not yet. I don't often get to sleep in on a Monday morning, so I might stay up and find a book to read. Stay up late, like the disobedient child that I am." She craned her neck, watching and listening until doors had been opened and shut, lights turned on and off, before stepping into the kitchen and taking the phone from its hook. Her fingers maneuvered the dial in the dark—so strange to dial one's own number.

He answered on the first ring.

"What *was* that?"

She giggled, quietly. "I told you. I told you it was a terrible movie."

"I know, but for real. What *was* that? How did women stand for that?"

The illogical fear that his voice would carry to the second floor prompted Trixie to drop her own to a whisper. "I learned tonight that my great-grandmother likely didn't love her husband. Like, at all."

The regret in his tone was immediate. "Oh geez. I'm sorry. I shouldn't make light—"

"No, it's okay. I don't think he was mean or abusive or anything. Just. . .I don't know what it was, but it wasn't love."

"She told you that?"

"No. My grandmother—her daughter-in-law did. I don't know why the idea seems so unsettling. I mean, romance was a luxury a lot of people couldn't afford back then, right? Especially women."

"That's why they ended up marrying abusive carnies with ill-fitting pants."

"The movie really got to you, didn't it?"

"Seriously. Can we talk? Do you have anything you have to go do right now?"

Trixie sank down, sitting on the floor, her knees bent to her chest. "Nothing. Because I don't have a Monday morning meeting tomorrow."

"Well," Ron said, "I'm the boss, so they can't get far without me."

"True enough. So, *Carousel*. Where to begin?"

"At the beginning," he said.

And they did. They talked about *Carousel*, then about Shirley Jones and *The Partridge Family*, and other favorite TV shows of their childhood, and favorite TV shows now, and the ones they hated, and the commercials that made them laugh, and products they'd been enticed to buy, and their favorite foods, and their favorite songs, and songs of their childhood, and books until—with her throat dry from talking and eyes sandy with sleep, she glanced at the clock and realized. . .it was Monday morning.

CHAPTER 12

MARIAH

$\mathcal{K}$atrina knew. She'd pieced together evidence and intuition and figured it out by the time I came home that afternoon, and she was not one bit happy.

"How could you?" Her pretty face pinched in distaste. "And with whom? With that farmer? Mr. Gowan?"

I didn't give her the benefit of a reply, let alone the truth. I stood in the kitchen—formerly *my* kitchen—and held a hand protectively over my stomach, as if Katrina could wield harm with her dismissive sneer.

"It's none of your affair," I said.

"Of course it's my affair. What are people going to say about us?"

"Why would they say anything?" But I knew. From this moment on, I would see the world through a mutual veil of shame. I'd seen it in Charles's eyes—the brother who shared every meaningful moment of my life. We'd once been each other's protectors, but he'd shut a door in my face and left me outside, alone.

I could only pray that Oscar would open his own to me.

"I hope you don't see this as your ticket to move to Chicago with Charlie and me," Katrina said. She was cutting biscuits for supper, giving each an angry little twist with the cutter, even though I'd told her time and again not to, as that sealed off the dough and made the edges hard. "Bad enough we can't start our marriage off alone in our own home. We don't need someone else's child running wild through it."

The coldness of her tone froze me in place, and I wondered if she'd be so unkind if Charles were here to witness.

"I've no intention of following you," I said. "I have a home here and have been taking care of myself longer than you've been alive. I suppose I'm capable of taking care of a child."

Katrina gave a snort and tossed a biscuit onto the pan. "So you're not going to tell me who the father is? If it's Mr. Gowan, there was no need to sully yourself this way. He was keen to marry you all summer. No need to trick him into it."

I suppose I should have corrected her, to save Merrill's reputation as mine was already ruined, but I had so little that was truly mine, I wasn't prepared to share. "I'm not tricking anybody."

"It's a woman's gamble, my mother always says. Doesn't take much to get a man to play along, but there's no guarantee he'll pay up when the time comes."

I thought about Oscar, gone in the morning before dawn even stretched light across the room and how he hadn't shown his face since. Silently, grudgingly, I envied her having a mother to dispense such advice.

"I'm going to lie down," I said, ready to take advantage of having another woman in the house. "I'm tired."

In that moment, a change came over Katrina, as if she realized the expected sisterhood that came from being not only a sister of sorts, but a general ally by the circumstance of our sex. She'd cut the last biscuit and was scattering the scraps of dough on the pan to bake into irregularly shaped snacks when they came out of the oven.

She heaved a sigh that bordered on sympathy. "Can I bring you a cup of tea?"

I pondered before answering. A cup of tea sounded restorative, but I'd managed to keep the wall of tears dammed up for the last twenty minutes of walking, and I could feel it threatening to burst. I welcomed her comfort but not her pity. I don't suppose any woman has ever dithered so long over the decision of whether or not to have a cup of tea, because she finally said for me to go in and lie down and she'd bring it in directly. Relieved, I followed her command and went into my little room behind the kitchen. It was warm, so I opened the window before sitting on the edge of my bed. I took off my shoes, my stockings, and finally my dress; I unpinned my hair and lay back upon my pillow, thinking how my life had changed a hundredfold since last I touched it.

The next I knew, it was dark, and I woke with the disorientation of having slept a day away into the evening. The room had turned cold, but I was covered by a warm, unfamiliar quilt. I sat up, drawing it to my chin, and willed my eyes to adjust to the shadows of the room while my mind dropped the moments of the day into place. As the darkness faded to shades of gray, I noticed the cup on the table by my bed and reached for it. Tea, long cold, but sweetened with sugar—I drank it down in three thirsty gulps and would have given anything for more. The smell of supper wafted in along with the voices of Katrina and Charles, too low for me to make out exactly what they were saying. Despite an overwhelming desire to never, ever leave this room, I wrapped my robe over my underclothes and left my hair undone as I stepped barefoot into the warm kitchen. Katrina was at the stove stirring, and Charles waited at the table with his empty, expectant plate. I had the distinct feeling that their conversation came to a stop midword at my arrival.

"Well, look who's awake," Katrina said, her voice as sweet as her tea, no doubt because of my brother's presence. "Let me set a place for you."

"I'll get it." Charles rose and took a bowl from the shelf.

I sat, tucking my hair behind my ears, and waited for Katrina to bring the pot to the table. It was a soup of white beans and ham, which I suspected came from her mother's kitchen, as there'd been no beans set to soak overnight and cook during the day. I'd keep her secret, though, because once I took a spoonful after Charles said the blessing, I found it a perfect, welcoming taste of salt. We all ate in silence, save for the muttered compliments of the dish. The biscuits, wholly Katrina's, benefited from a swipe around the empty bowl and a soak of the broth at the bottom.

I felt full and warm, but neither uncomfortably so. For the first time in weeks, my stomach showed no signs of rejecting its food. The kettle hissed on the stove, and Katrina prepared a fresh pot of tea, producing with it a platter of gingerbread (also, I suspected, from her mother's kitchen). I nibbled a square, embracing the spices, and took a comforting sip of tea. All was fine—quiet and soothing—until Charles cleared his throat.

"I've started asking around to see if I could find out where Garland's working."

I dropped my gingerbread to the table and glared at him, summoning daggers for my eyes.

"He told me," Katrina said, as if the softness of her voice would give me comfort.

My gaze didn't waver. "You had no right."

"And you have no choice," Charles said, his authority blocking any retort. "I was forced into a bit of a fib, asking around to all the fellows working today on his behalf, saying I thought he might be looking for work, but nobody could give me a good answer. Tomorrow—"

He was interrupted not by words but by the tiniest shift of Katrina in her seat—a movement so small, it might have gone unnoticed if it hadn't commanded Charles's full attention.

"Trina," he warned.

"I don't think it's a good idea, bringing him into this."

"I think he brought himself into this when he took advantage of my sister."

"He did not take advantage of me," I said, not knowing if my hackles rose in defense of Oscar or myself.

"All I'm saying," Katrina inserted, "is that there's no need to hurry."

Charles gaped at her. "No need to hurry? People are going to notice—"

"A lot of time passes between now and when she'll be big enough for people to notice anything. And a lot can happen during that time, to where people wouldn't ever have to know at all."

Candlelight turned us all into a gathering of shadows and gave an exaggerated sinister cast to her face.

"Are you suggesting. . ." I couldn't bring myself to give words to my suspicion.

She held her hand to her breast, offended. "Good heavens, no. Why, that you could even *think* I would suggest—I mean, and God forbid it should happen—but not every scare turns into a baby. Sometimes late is. . .late. And some children aren't meant to be more than wishes and angels. If you'd grown up around women, you'd know—that's why most wives don't even tell their *husbands* until they are three or four months along."

"It's almost like you wish—"

"I wish nothing. Life is precious, and you know how I long for my own. But suppose he does the noble thing and marries you. Outright. You know he doesn't love you. And then something happens to that baby and you're stuck with a man who doesn't want—"

"Trina," Charles said, trying to bring some softness to the table, but his wife hammered on.

"Has he ever come courting?" She turned to Charles. "Has he ever asked you to give his best to your sister? Be honest. Has he?"

Charles was honest in his silence.

"Has he ever acknowledged her existence when polite company didn't insist?"

I felt a little more demoralized with each question but summoned the strength to answer this last one. "Maybe not, but that was—before. This is his child. He has a right to know of *its* existence."

"He doesn't have a right to anything," Katrina said in what seemed to be an approach to sorority. "But he does have a responsibility. Tell him too soon, and he'll bolt."

"He wouldn't," I said, hackles raised. "He's a good man."

"He's not a good man. Good men don't do this to women. At least not to *good* women."

Whatever hint of sisterhood she offered disappeared with that comment. I sat, stunned. Silent. She would have called me a good woman when I sat at this very table for breakfast, wouldn't she? Yes, there'd been a revelation of my past and a thorny path to my future, but I was the same woman in the middle of both.

"Just wait until after the harvest," Charles said with an air of authority that came from a month of marriage. His wife nodded in affirmation.

"After the harvest," I repeated. "That could be another six weeks."

"Making it all the more compelling for him to do the right thing," Katrina said, "before the entire town sees you in disgrace."

Charles shot her a look. "Please don't say such about my sister. There's nobody at this table with a right to throw stones."

I almost giggled at the shock on Katrina's face, but there are some fires you don't need to stoke.

When Benjamin Franklin said that three could keep a secret only if two are dead, he did not have our family in mind. Whatever I'd thought of Katrina's hoity-toity ways, she proved herself to be a friend in my time of trouble, always at the ready with a cup of tea or a perfect salty broth. I kept to one of the rooms upstairs when smell of the morning breakfast beckoned my nausea, and she was ever at my side with a pillow for my feet or a new skein of yarn for the afghan I'd set myself to crochet. It was a safe bet too that Charles kept our secret, as he could barely bring himself to look at me during those weeks in October that seemed like nothing more than a month-long vigil, though each of us kept watch for our own private reasons.

There was no change to my body other than my breasts, which swelled to something unrecognizable and so tender that even brushing my own arm against them in the daily machinations of life sent unwelcome jolts of pain. What I lacked in stamina I more than made up for in overwrought emotion, finding tears at the back of my throat at the least provocation. One day I would speak with fear-fueled determination to stare down anybody who might judge my character; the next I would spend in a tearful huddle, knowing I was doomed to a lifetime of shunning and gossip. No matter the tock of the pendulum, Katrina was at the ready with words of encouragement or succor, though I expected her hands experienced their fair share of wringing at my expense.

Poor Charles, though, bore the brunt of my mercurial disposition. When I wasn't at the window, forehead against the cool pane, muttering my regret at having allowed Oscar Garland to treat me so dishonorably, I was at my brother's elbow, nagging him to tell me what he knew and what he'd heard about Oscar's whereabouts. He worked the harvest like a traveling salesman peddling his labor here and there all over the county and even for a few days across the state line. Charles gleaned all of this from casual conversations at his work counter and at various barns and toolsheds. *"Any idea where Garland's working?"* he'd ask with practiced nonchalance. And always he'd just been at this place or just left another.

"Slippery, that one," Katrina said one afternoon at Sunday dinner. Often we would share this meal with her family, in their fancy dining room, eating a fine roast that had been left on the stovetop all morning. On this day, though, our invitation had been hastily rescinded. "Slippery like a rat."

"Man's got a right to earn a living," Charles said.

"Besides," I said, "he doesn't know he has anything to slip away from, does he?"

"Not yet," Charles said, "but if I keep asking and you start"—he gestured with his fork in my general direction, moving it in a wide, round arc—"I figure people will put it all together."

"My mother knows," Katrina said, throwing the comment out as quickly and calmly as if declaring the beef on our plates was overcooked, which it was, having been unmercifully seared in a skillet upon our arrival home. My knife clattered to the table and Charles looked far too calm to be hearing this revelation for the first time. Katrina immediately defended herself. "She guessed."

I glared at her across the table. "She *guessed?*"

"A while back, when I was so worried about you, so sick and fatigued. Today she asked if you were feeling better, and I said no, not really. And then after church she pulled me aside and. . .guessed."

"Nothing solves a mystery better than gossip," I said, "but I suppose that counts as keeping it in the family." Still, I couldn't stay another minute at the table. The sound of my chair scooting away was so loud

I almost missed my brother's words that followed. "What did you say?"

He looked up at me. "Merrill too."

"You told Merrill Gowan that I am pregnant with Oscar Garland's child?"

"N—not like that. Not all of it. Not about Garland. But that you are in—trouble, I guess. He was worried about you because you looked so distraught when you came out to his place to talk to me. And at church. He said—"

"Probably what Mother said," Katrina interrupted, "that you look pale and tired."

"Distraught," Charles repeated.

"And Mother noticed your. . ." She pointed to her own ample bosom. "That you seemed. . .enhanced."

"Merrill didn't say anything about that," Charles was quick to explain.

"That's because men don't notice women's figures," Katrina said dismissively.

"Oh, I assure you we do."

"Not the same way women do."

"Stop!" I was standing behind my chair, gripping it like a shield. "So you *told* him? Am I to have no privacy at all?"

"Come January you sure won't," Katrina said. "This is nothing but a big mass of trouble that I'm glad to have no part in. We'll be long gone to the city before it's here."

She began to clear the table, a chore I would normally join in beside her, but instead I stood and watched, feeling completely invisible in the room, already abandoned.

"If it helps at all," Charles said, his voice calm in the aftermath of our dustup, "I know where he's working."

"Right now?" I felt my knees close to buckling.

"Fellow named Augusterson. Met him when I was over to De Smet last Thursday. He was in getting some tools and said he was looking to hire about ten men next week. Someone mentioned Garland's name, best harvester engineer in the county they said, and told him where to find him."

"Why are you just now telling me this?"

"Because I wanted a peaceful Sunday. And to make sure there was time for Augusterson to hire him on. He'll be there a week at least, Sister. I'll find him and talk to him before he leaves again."

Katrina made a *humph* sound that drew Charles's displeasure, sending her back to the sink.

"A few more days," he said in the same voice he had always used when we were on the brink of being without food or heat or a home.

I almost acquiesced. Almost agreed. Almost ready to bow my head to him and take my place far and away from the most important moment in my life. But what had I always done on those cold, lean, hungry days when Charles was ready to hope for things to get better? I'd gone out to find work. I'd scraped enough flour and lard together to create food. I'd rummaged for paper and sticks to burn in our tiny stove.

So, no, I would not wait until after the harvest to speak to Oscar. I would not live with a secret already revealed to people who had no business knowing it. Over the course of a Sunday morning, the chances of Oscar learning from someone other than myself had grown exponentially. No doubt every woman in church would have a fortuitous run-in with Mrs. Rose, who never had a single good thing to say about myself or my brother. Merrill might have told his entire work crew over their stew and corn bread supper. I walked around the table, leaned down, and spoke beneath the sound of the clattering dishes.

"I want to find and tell him tomorrow. Will you go with me?"

"I don't think—"

"I'm not asking what you think. I'm asking if you'll help."

He'd been twisting his napkin in his hand and finally tossed it on the table. "What kind of a brother would I be if I didn't?"

In the morning, I learned he was the kind of brother who would do anything to spare his sister, because when I awoke in the pre-dawn darkness, he was already gone.

"We talked about it last night after you went to bed," Katrina said, eyes bleary with sleep. It was cold enough in the house to warrant two pairs of socks, which she wore with a pretty pink quilted dressing gown, her golden hair loose around her shoulders as she put on a pot of coffee. "We decided that it would be best for him to talk to Oscar first in case his initial reaction isn't. . .favorable."

"Nobody thought to ask me what was best?" My words were argumentative, but deep down, I could not deny a sense of relief.

"We didn't want another scene. Charles left so early, he'll probably get to Augusterson's farm before the crew gets assembled."

Katrina and I settled on a truce for the day, stepping wide circles around each other in the silence of the house. We took turns minding the workbench, taking in small repair jobs over the counter and sending the larger ones away with the promise of Charles's return the next day. Katrina did some fine needlework, and I settled myself in for an afternoon of reading *Silas Marner*.

I suppose my reading choice came as a bit of self-loathing. Punishment, maybe, thinking about the conversation Charles may have already had with Oscar concerning the child we created out of such reckless behavior. In the novel's opening scene, a desperate, opium-addicted mother struggles through the snow, her illegitimate daughter abandoned to the storm. She—the mother—dies within pages, and I supposed I'd always held her in harsh judgment until now. But wasn't she merely trying to do the best for her child? Wasn't she merely trying to assure her daughter a life better than her own?

I couldn't begin to plan beyond this day, let alone months from now. By crude calculations and limited knowledge, I figured the baby would be born in the spring. April, maybe, and where would I be then? The answer to that question hinged on what Charles would say to Oscar today. I thought about my conversation with Katrina earlier: *We talked about it last night. . .We decided. . .We didn't want. . .* She and Charles so joined together that they spoke in a single voice. They would make wonderful parents—Katrina such a pretty mother, Charles so capable.

A new thought dawned. Did Katrina argue so vehemently against the idea of Oscar coming into my life because she wanted to take this baby for herself? After all, what did I have to offer? I didn't know how to be a mother; I'd never even had a doll. Yet here I was, too stunned to be afraid, willing to face the consequences of my actions but not willing to face them alone. I cannot honestly say that in those early, pre-fluttering months, I felt love for the child. What I did feel was pure protection. Throughout the day, I caught Katrina looking at me with a kind of hunger that made me want to keep this tiny life shielded. I splayed my open book across my stomach and turned my body from her gaze.

I spent the rest of that day and the next reading, losing myself in the happy moments and the tragic, weeping at both. When darkness fell on that second evening and Charles still hadn't returned, Katrina and I warmed up the previous night's supper and ate in near silence made up of questions and mutterings.

"Maybe he stayed on to work?"

"Mmm-hmm."

"Could be there was a problem with the harvester?"

"Hmmm."

We said nothing about Oscar, as if he wasn't the sole reason for Charles to be away from home at all.

Oscar.

I went to bed imagining the two of them, Oscar and my brother, staying up late after a long day's work, filling glass after foaming glass from a tapped keg, commiserating the end of their bachelorhood. Charles offering reassurance, Oscar feigning protest. These were the only two men I loved in the world, and surely Charles could broker a future that would bring a few tendrils of love my way.

With every fiber of my being—*both* of my beings—I hoped to wake up in the morning, put on coffee, and see the two of them walk through the kitchen door looking all the worse for wear. I did not dare envision Oscar taking me in his arms or any such romantic display. We were, in so many ways, only two travelers whose paths crossed one night, and now we were beholden to each other to continue on together.

At some point, I knelt by my bedside and prayed—wordy, rambling whispers, confessing the sin that was no secret to God and asking for His mercy. Not for myself but for the child. No child should have to pay for the sins of its mother.

"It will need a father," I said, speaking into my clasped hands. "You are a Father; You gave Your Son a Father on earth. Let my child have the same."

I don't know exactly when I fell asleep. I only know that my window was full of morning light when I opened my eyes. At some point, I had crawled beneath my covers, but at the faint sound of my brother's voice, I flung them to the floor, grabbed my dressing gown, and peeked into the kitchen.

Charles sat at the table, head cradled in his hands. Katrina stood behind him, her arms wrapped around his shoulders. She saw me and whispered, "Charles," before stepping away.

"Oh Sister." Charles raised his head, freezing me in place with his red-rimmed eyes. I needn't ask a single question. The anguish on his face made clear: there had been no night of rollicking banter. All that I envisioned disappeared like vapor, washed away by tears like I'd never seen on his freckled cheeks. Those castles I built in my late-night dreams would have no foundation.

When Charles reached out his hand, I padded barefoot across the kitchen to take it. And when he bade me, "Sit down," I obeyed.

CHAPTER 13

TRIXIE

*T*he next morning, Trixie woke up to the *flip* on her clock radio when 9:26 turned to 9:27. She looked at the time, stretched, turned over, cuddled her pillow, and closed her eyes again. This kind of luxurious sleep-in was a rare treat for a Monday morning when, on any other Monday, she would already be making the second pot of coffee for Ron's Monday Round-Up Meeting. Instead, she stretched her leg to find a cool spot between the sheets and let her mind wander to thoughts of Ron that had nothing to do with cups of coffee or a conference table.

Yes, from her first day at the *Newz*, she'd had a certifiable crush. He was so tall and big and warm. Manly. He filled the room with humor and comfort. And, yes, they'd cultivated a semi-flirtatious rapport, but did he ever show her any favor over any of the other women in the office? And how did that work, anyway? What makes years of professional interaction flip a switch to something more?

Flip. 9:28.

But last night was definitely something *more*. She couldn't even begin to replay their conversation as it had wandered from one topic to the next like a peg-legged drunk (a favorite saying of her grandmother's that had Ron laughing for a full two minutes). So while they racked up a long-distance bill that Eugenie would surely make her pay, they hadn't solved any world problems or even scratched the surface of each other's intimate secrets. Yet his very voice had imprinted on her like grooves in a record album.

By the time they'd finally said good night (then laughed because it was technically morning), her throat was dry and her words were coming out like the scratch when you first drop the needle on that album. And everything after—every thought and memory—was nothing but smooth, perfect music.

Flip. 9:29.

Flip. 9:30.

Flip. 9:31.

Then a chipper, five-raps knock at the door. "Trixie? Honey? Are you awake?"

"No," she said, answering her mother's question exactly as she would have on a school holiday Monday morning.

"There's coffee. And breakfast. Bacon chip pancakes."

Trixie burrowed deeper. "Give me twenty minutes?"

"Exactly that," her mother said. "And then it's cold cereal and toast."

She knew her mother meant it. There was an unwritten rule to have all of breakfast cleared away and the kitchen clean before nine o'clock on any given morning, so she was already snoozing on borrowed time, but nothing about the day stretched in front of her seemed appealing. GG may or may not be lucid and talkative. Her mother may or may not be bearable. Her grandmother may or may not be a reliable source of entertainment and support. The only prediction she could make with certainty involved episodes of *Ryan's Hope* and a string of game shows. She could sketch out ideas for future *Lost Laura* cartoons or, better yet, think of how she would respond to The Guy.

Without leaving the bed, she stretched across and rifled through her bag, finding the letter typed on the impressive stamped stationery.

Dear Ms. Gowan it began. *Ms.* She once tried to convince her mother to take on that identifier and received a tongue-lashing in return about how women needed to accept who they are—married or not—and not hide behind some made-up feminist title. And so there were two Mrs. Gowans by marriage, one Miss Gowan by missing out on marriage, and now, representing the latest generation, Ms. Gowan, by choice. She thought of her signature in the corner of her cartoon, the *T* and *G* nestled together with the *owan* tucked inside. She'd spent time developing the perfect look, balancing an Old World sensibility with a modern, stylish twist. Reflective of the cartoon itself. And at some point, she'd decided she'd never change her name, married or not—which had nothing to do with an all-night conversation with Ron and the fact that, were that to develop, she'd be Trixie Tumble. The thought never entered her mind until now.

Flip 9:42.

Breakfast beckoned, and Trixie gave herself over to a tiny suspicion that had been niggling since her mother announced the treat of bacon-chip pancakes. These weren't chocolate chip pancakes, but pancake batter infused with cooked and crumbled bacon—a family delicacy that she'd never experienced outside of this kitchen. She'd told Ron about them last night, somewhere between their dissection of the Cuban Missile Crisis and the debate over which was the better Darren on *Bewitched*. He'd declared he'd never heard of anything so awesome and begged her to make them for him some morning for breakfast.

The statement had earned a moment of awkward silence, as if breakfast between the two of them would ever be a common occurrence. Trixie broke it by reminding him that breakfast makes the best suppers and promised him a *supper* some evening. But now she had a new suspicion: that her mother had conveniently overheard the discourse and this was her way of confession.

A more strident knock on her door and her grandmother's voice to match. "Trixie! Get up! Morning is wasting away."

She squinted at the clock. "Ten more minutes."

"Ten minutes, my eye. No good ever came from lazing past the sunrise."

Trixie flipped her pillow to the cool side. Her grandmother had no idea.

Strange, wasn't it? How this—this *thing* with Ron blasted off the moment they left each other's orbit. Like they'd been circling each other in a parallel path day in and day out until the time came for a true send-off, and he'd sent her off with a kiss. At least she thought he did. Somehow, that never came up in the anecdote marathon of last night. Still, it was such an opposite phenomenon of what happened with Cam. Years they'd been together—*years*—and formative ones at that. Young love, first love, physical longing, a life built from the same bricks, and yet once he left, that was it. If Ron was a rocket launch, Cam was a refrigerator light. A handsome, sexy, successful, great refrigerator light, but only alight when he was right in front of her. Close the door, and all goes dark.

Flip. 9:45.

Groaning, she slid her legs over the side of the bed and planted her feet on the floor. She had a roommate in college one semester who swore it was bad luck to start the day with your left foot on the floor and good luck with the right. Trixie had indulged the girl and given her the side of the room that would best suit her fortune. Though she had never been superstitious, she'd developed a self-consciousness about the habit and ever since had made it a point to put both feet on the floor at the same time. Every morning—another tidbit she'd shared with Ron sometime around 1:00 a.m. when they were trying to decide who was more of a morning person.

Flip. 9:46.

This time the knock on her door was so soft, she might have missed it if her head was still buried in her pillow with the blanket drawn up to her ears. More like a soft pawing, followed by an even softer "Trixie? Are you still here?"

GG!

Trixie tugged on a pair of jogging shorts to go with the T-shirt she slept in and opened the door to find her great-grandmother fully dressed, though her blouse was misbuttoned, her patterned shorts didn't quite match, and her Keds were untied. She shifted her eyes to the left and right before saying, "I need you to take me to town."

Trixie sighed. "I told you, I can't." She'd been hoping her

great-grandmother would forget this request, but apparently her mind was the same trap it had ever been. "I don't have my car."

"Eugenie has a car."

"Which only she can drive." It was a fact. Her ancient Oldsmobile seemed to have the supernatural ability to know when somebody other than Eugenie was gripping the gearshift and would refuse to obey. "But maybe she can take both of us?"

"No." GG's lips puckered toothlessly around the word. "This is for you. And me. They won't understand."

"Then maybe tomorrow?"

"I don't know how many tomorrows I have left." There was no sadness in the statement, nor resentment, nor anger. Nothing but the South Dakota prairie pragmatism that carried everything she said.

"Then let's hope you have at least one more. Now, this is too deep of a conversation to have before coffee. Have you had breakfast?"

"Course I have."

"Well, I haven't. Do you want to come downstairs with me?"

GG looked like she was calculating the cost and whether or not the trip would mean a depletion of what life might be left for the day. Finally, she muttered, "Better not," and turned to go back to her room, already deflated from the woman she'd been when Trixie opened the door.

"I'll phone about my car," Trixie called to her back. "If it's ready today. . ." But GG didn't turn around to hear anymore.

She finger-combed her hair and braided it into a single, loose plait as she descended the stairs and had a ready smile for the feast that awaited. Her coffee was already poured into a favorite mug, and Alma took a plate stacked with bacon-chip pancakes out of the oven where they'd been keeping warm.

"Careful," she said, putting the plate on the table, "hot plate. Don't touch it."

Which, of course, Trixie did and snapped her finger away. "And why am I getting such a treat for breakfast this morning?"

"Can't a mother make her daughter pancakes for no reason at all?"

"You made pancakes yesterday."

Alma sat across from her with a steaming cup of coffee. "I overheard you talking about them last night."

"*Overheard?*"

"When I came downstairs to get a glass of water."

"Why would you come all the way downstairs to the kitchen for a glass of water?" Trixie was lifting each pancake off the stack and placing a pat of butter between each one. "Besides, you never came in here."

"Because I heard you talking. And I wanted a little snack too. So now that you've thoroughly investigated my pancake motive, who were you talking to at all hours last night?"

Trixie drizzled syrup over the top of the stack and cut down through it, stuffing her mouth before saying, "Ron. My boss."

"Who talks to their *boss* all night?"

Trixie chewed, savoring the mix of the salty bacon and the sweet syrup. Not even her mother's inquisition would ruin this moment. "He's also house-sitting for me. And taking care of my cat."

"What about Cam?"

"What about Cam?" She dug in again.

"It seemed like you two were getting along well enough yesterday."

Trixie swallowed. "Don't tell me you were out getting a snack by the silo."

Alma wrinkled her nose in the way she did when she wanted to come off as a prude. "It's not good of you to lead one man on in the afternoon and spend the night talking with another man entirely."

"I didn't lead Cam on. There's nothing between us."

"It didn't look—"

"Appearances can be deceiving, Mom. We had a moment. And then a talk. And now it's done."

"But—"

"Done." Trixie punctuated by pointing her pancake-laden fork and took satisfaction in her mother's visible retreat.

"So, then, can we talk about this other man? Your boss?"

"Ron?"

"Yes."

"No."

Now Alma pouted like a child, her perfectly made-up face taking on the visage of a toddler. "Why not?"

"Because, Mom, there's nothing to talk about. Not yet, anyway. So let me enjoy my breakfast while we talk about something else. Anything else. Like how Great-Grandma seems to be doing really well."

"Isn't she? I hope you don't think we lured you here under false pretenses. She has these swings, you know. Where we think she might be cleaning her feet on heaven's welcome mat. We can't hardly stand to let her go to sleep for fear she won't wake up again. And then—boom—she's down here making oatmeal."

Trixie smiled at the familiar image. GG cooked a pot of oatmeal every day and had throughout two world wars and the Depression. "Quaker could make a fortune from her testimony."

"It's only lately that she's seemed. . .agitated."

Trixie almost choked on her coffee. "*Lately*? I've never known her *not* to be agitated."

"I mean in a preoccupied way. She's always been one to speak her mind, but these days it's like she's holding something back. Like she has unfinished business she doesn't want any of us to know about."

She chewed, thoughtfully, letting all the flavors fall into place, and washed them down with coffee. "Why did you call me to come here, Mom?"

"Grandma—"

"Truthfully."

Alma set her coffee down. "*Truthfully*. Because you great-grandmother seemed to be edging away, and I didn't want you to hate yourself for missing her final moments."

"You just told me she has a lot of *final moments*. You've never called me before."

"But this one seemed—"

"At first I thought it was to try to get me and Cam back together."

"Well, yes. That too."

"Aha!" Trixie pointed with her fork again—this time empty—and Alma jumped. "*That too*. What's the *too*, Mom? You know GG has a secret."

Alma took a deep breath and looked over as Eugenie came into the kitchen. "She was all about muttering, 'A first time and a last time.' And that she shouldn't have waited. But when your grandma or I would ask her, she'd clam up. Tell us it was the rambling of an old woman and not to pay her any mind. And," Alma added quietly, "she kept asking for you."

"So you lied to me?"

"The way we see it," Eugenie said, easing into a chair, "she just as much lied to us. Taking to her bed like she did. Laid there looking like death itself come to visit, but then I'd look close and see her eyes dancing whenever we said your name and that you were coming."

"You made Cam call me?"

"That was your mother's idea."

"Of course."

"Two birds," Alma said, shrugging.

"Has she said anything to you?" Eugenie asked. "Anything. . . important?"

Why did Trixie all of a sudden feel like she was in some film noir confession scene? Like Eugenie was two steps away from slapping the rest of her pancakes away from her while Alma tilted the Depression glass light fixture to try to burn out a confession. What did she know that they didn't? She thought of her conversation the previous night with Eugenie, her grandmother's verbal tiptoe. Was there anything about this visit that wasn't tinged with subterfuge?

"You could have asked me, you know," Trixie said. "You could have called and said that GG was acting odd and that you wanted me to come talk to her. Why couldn't you be honest about something so simple?"

"I don't think we were dishonest," Alma said.

"Of course you don't," Trixie said, her words laden with the subtext of the entirety of her mother's facade.

Alma steeled herself against the insult. "And now, knowing

what's brewing between you and—well, I don't know if we could have enticed you away for an afternoon, let alone a nice, long stay."

A new thought crept in, unbidden. One that threatened to sour every bite of breakfast. "My car. Did the starter really go out? Or was that a ruse to get me to stay?"

"You think we'd stoop to that?" Eugenie asked, eyes wide and swimming behind the thick lenses of her glasses.

"I think you look like those nuns on *The Sound of Music* caught with a handful of sparkplugs."

"We didn't do anything to your car," Eugenie said, sounding short of convincing and nowhere near innocent.

"We would never," Alma chimed in, sounding less of both.

"Well, you know what? I'm going to call him," Trixie said, rising. "That mechanic. I'm going to call and ask him exactly what's wrong and see if his story matches up with yours."

"Fine," Eugenie said.

"I mean it."

"Fine," Alma echoed.

Trixie got up and strode over to the phone where the Yellow Pages waited in a wood-scrolled rack bolted to the wall. "What's the name of his shop?"

Alma responded by reciting a phone number.

Trixie eyed her suspiciously. "You know the shop's number?"

"Justus and I are rather involved," Alma said.

"Of course you are," Trixie said, and asked her to repeat the number.

The line rang and rang and rang and rang, and as Trixie was about to hang up, a gruff voice spoke. "McCready Mechanics."

"Hi, this is Trixie Gowan, owner of the '68 Chevelle that was brought in yesterday? I wanted to check on the status. See what's wrong and when it will possibly be ready for me to pick up." She hated the fact that her side of the conversation was a mere series of questions, as if she needed permission to even make the phone call.

"Hold on."

By *hold on*, he obviously meant stay on the line while he set the phone down, because all she heard after that was the rumble of men's voices with the occasional clang of metal. She pressed the phone closer to her ear, as if that would do anything to make the conversation more distinct, listening for the make of her car or her mother's name. Soon enough, a man was back on the line.

"Sixty-eight Chevelle?"

"Yes," Trixie said, working authority into her voice.

"We'll get back to you." And then the phone went dead.

Trixie stared at the receiver in disbelief. "He hung up on me."

"Was it Justus?" Alma was leaning on her elbows, cup poised in front of her lips.

"I don't know. He didn't say." She hung up the phone, wanting nothing more than to crawl back into bed and start the day over again. "I'm going upstairs to shower."

She trudged upstairs thinking that if she were back at work, they'd all be gathered for the Monday Morning Meeting. Needing a distraction longer than a shower, she dug through her closet and found her old running shoes. They were crumpled in on each other from years of emptiness but fit around her foot as if she'd worn them yesterday. She shouted to the house at large that she had decided to go for a run but didn't wait for any acknowledgment of her change of plans. She took a slow jog until she was out of view of the house before stopping to stretch in a way that would make her high school track coach proud. Not until she turned onto the main road did she pick up her pace.

The morning was hot and close, bringing a trickle of sweat down her back and dampening the armpits of her T-shirt within minutes. The dirt in the shoulder that ran alongside the paved road was packed tight, and for long stretches of time the only sound was the rhythmic *thump thump* of her shoes keeping time with her steady, even breath. Occasionally she'd hear a car's engine behind her, and she turned her head long enough to gauge its distance before shifting to the right a bit as it blew by, trying not to equate the gust of wind against her with the power the vehicle had to send her into the open field.

GG used to tease her about this, about running. She knew what it meant to have no choice but to take to your feet to go from town to town. When she was Trixie's age, owning a horse—let alone something for it to draw—was a luxury.

"Imagine," she'd say, sipping coffee while watching Trixie stuff her gym bag, "running for the sake of running."

"It keeps us healthy and fit," Trixie said one time. "What did you do for exercise?"

GG had laughed. "Life was exercise. We never got to stop moving until we died."

Trixie thought about that conversation as she ran, just one of the scenarios that flitted through her mind, like scenes from previous episodes of her life. GG telling stories about footraces and baseball games she watched in her youth in De Smet and later when they moved to Silver Meadow, the town that folded in on itself as farms conglomerated and families moved away. There were no photos, but Trixie pictured the competitions in sepia-toned images—farmers in pants and shirts and suspenders, running in their heavy leather boots; groups of young men in old-timey baseball uniforms, wrinkled cotton, each face festooned with a moustache.

She always loved it when GG slipped away into the past, forgetting the harshness of her growing up and the mysterious bitterness that gripped her most of the time. She appreciated the fact that GG didn't exaggerate in her stories. She had been every bit as hungry, as cold, as frightened as she claimed to be, so when she allowed an occasional happy memory to slip in, Trixie wanted to share that too.

She'd asked once, "Didn't you ever participate, GG? Surely they let the girls run too."

"No," GG said, looking young and shy. "I was a watcher. Sometimes I took a book and got a glass of lemonade and enjoyed watching the others have their fun. Got teased about that, of course. Cap said, 'How are you going to watch the game with your nose buried in a book?'"

The bit of conversation rang as clearly as if GG were running beside her. Or speaking from the trees. Or chatting in the back seat of the car that honked, startling Trixie to a stumbling halt. She bent, putting her hands on her knees, and breathed heavily.

Cap.

Cap Garland.

If Trixie hadn't spent the previous day reading Wilder's *These Happy Golden Years,* the name buried in the recovered memory might never have drifted up to the surface. But she had. Cap Garland's place in the novel now ran alongside GG's reflections as closely as the two lines of paint running down the middle of the road. Cap Garland in a horse-drawn cutter, zipping down Joliet Street on a Sunday afternoon. Cap Garland among the gatherings of young people at socials and singings. Cap Garland daring Almanzo Wilder to take that treacherous ride in the dangerous cold to fetch his love home for the weekend.

Cap Garland had never been more than a tertiary character in an all-but-forgotten book. And yet this was the book that turned GG into a grieving shell the night Trixie was born. He was a vibrant point of color in a book where GG was nothing more than a single, unflattering sketch.

Last night her grandmother recalled GG boldly speaking of her friendship (if not friendship, then certainly connection) with Laura Ingalls Wilder, something she touted until the publication of Wilder's final novel. Something she'd been proud to share as an invisible accomplishment until the smallness of it, the perhaps *falseness* of it, came out in black and white. Young Mariah Patterson disappeared from the story, even though she'd taken up her life in De Smet during those years when Laura was finishing school and living the life of Little Bachelorette on the Prairie.

They were close to the same age, lived in the same town, yet GG had spent her youth watching. Not invited, not included. Perhaps seeing it played out in the pages had been a painful reminder of what she'd missed. No frivolous courtship. GG married a man she didn't love because. . .she was twenty-six, and time for a family was running out. Maybe her life would have been different if she'd been a part of the clique—Laura and Almanzo, Mary and Nellie and

Cap. The names, fresh from reading, listed themselves as Trixie's feet resumed their pace.

Laura, Almanzo, Mary and Nellie and Cap.

Laura, Almanzo, Mary and Nellie and Cap.

She glanced up at the cirrus clouds and thought of her great-grandmother's hair, how it fell around her face in wispy tendrils. She saw her standing in her bedroom doorway, mismatched and malbuttoned, saying she had somewhere to go. Someone she had to see.

Laura, Almanzo, Mary and Nellie and Cap.

And Cap.

GG wasn't bitter because she hadn't been invited to sleigh rides with the cool kids in town. She'd been living with a decades-old broken heart, and that heart had been broken by Cap Garland. Image after image dropped into her brain like slides on a carousel, those rare, unguarded moments when GG told her few happy stories—so few, in fact, that they were told over and over in rotation. Trixie could hear the text and the delivery; she could picture the dreamy expression on GG's face as it aged over time. A baseball game, and Cap looking dashing at third. A dinner, and Cap sopping gravy with his bread. A three-legged race at a Harvest Festival, and Cap dragging his partner across the line. Cap riding out in a blizzard to bring wheat to the town. Dancing with Cap at her brother's wedding.

Stringing the tales together like this, Trixie realized she'd heard more about Cap Garland than her great-grandfather. She listened to her feet trying to remember his name.

Melvin? Marvin? Merrill...

Merrill. Merrill Gowan.

And his son, Mark Gowan, who married Eugenie Post, who became Eugenie Gowan.

And their daughter, Alma Gowan.

Mother of Trixie Gowan.

Four generations, not a Garland in the bunch.

Trixie came to the county road sign that marked her turnaround to head back home. She resisted the urge to stop, fearing she'd never get the momentum back again to carry her all the way, but then she had a new motivation to be the wind at her back.

Questions.

If young Mariah loved Cap Garland, then why had she married Merrill Gowan? Did Cap love someone else? Did he *marry* someone else? Why wasn't his fate part of the common lore?

Why? Because Laura married Almanzo, and Cap dropped out of the story. At least in the Wilder books. Not in Mariah's memory.

Trixie's T-shirt hung heavy on her shoulders, drenched with sweat, as was the waistband of her jogging shorts. With no cars in sight, she lifted the hem of her shirt and wiped her face. She lifted the sodden braid off the back of her neck and created a breeze with her movement. Morning runs were meant for mornings, and figuring it was by now after eleven, well, morning was long gone. The sun beat down with the full force of noon, holding the air captive and still in its heat. Trixie's stomach and throat reminded her that she'd consumed bacon and pancakes and coffee—but not a drop of water. Sweat poured down her face, but her lips were dry and she worried that, motivation or not, she might be too soggy to keep up this pace for the rest of the run home.

Three cars passed her in quick succession, the first one startling her with a series of three quick honks, the second sending such a blast of black smoke from its muffler that she had to close her eyes and head deeper onto the shoulder so she wouldn't stagger into traffic. The third was coming upon her as her vision cleared, and she wasn't quite sure if she should trust her eyes. Midnight-blue. Mustang. Convertible. And a familiar set of wide shoulders behind the wheel. The driver glanced over his shoulder, put on the blinker, and the quiet of the morning filled with the crunch of tires on tiny pebbles.

She ran, not slowing her steps until she could make out the song coming from the radio—"Layla." Then she walked, finally stopping to lean her elbows on top of the passenger door.

"Hey, Prairie Girl," Ron said, as if running into each other on the side of the road leading into her family's property nearly two hundred miles away from Minneapolis was the most normal thing ever. His hair—that mass of wild brown curls—looked remarkably undisturbed by the journey, its tangle resistant to movement. He turned in his seat, one elbow up on the seat back, the other draped casually over the wheel. "Didn't know you were a jogger."

"Runner, actually." The distinction mattered. "High school track, and then whenever I get the chance." Obviously not often enough. "Wait—what are you doing here?"

"For one thing, if you're heading home, I'm really, really happy to know I'm not lost. Are you?"

"Am I lost?"

"Are you heading home? Because otherwise, I'm going in the totally wrong direction."

"Yes, I'm heading home."

"Great. Then get in, I'll drive you. Or does that defeat the purpose of running? And then someday maybe you can explain the actual purpose of running."

Resigned that there would be no answers here on the side of the road, Trixie opened the door and got in, mindful of her sweaty body against the car's leather seat. "Layla" still poured from the speakers as Ron brought the car back onto the road, the song easing into its coda. She raised herself up, her body and soul revived by the rush of air, knowing it would last a few minutes until she would instruct him to turn it off. Beside her, Ron was humming with the instrumentation, solidly on key, and the question of why he was here battled for supremacy with the question of why wouldn't he be. The momentum of the car brought out the sweetness in the air, turning the wheat fields into a blurred blanket of gold.

It wasn't until the Mustang was maneuvering the twists to her family's property that Trixie asked again, "Why are you here? Is everything okay?"

"That depends on your definition of *okay*, I suppose."

"You must have skipped out on Monday Morning Meeting to get here."

"Literally any person there is more than capable. Even Patrick, and he's seventeen years old. Is that the house?"

He had his eyes trained on the structure, heedless of the flanking trees or hard-packed drive below. Even in profile, the admiration on his face was clear, and she felt a flush of pride.

"That's it. Now, if you want to see inside, you have to tell me—what's up? Why are you here?"

Ron put the car in park and turned to her. "Got a message on your answering machine this morning as I was leaving your house. The Guy expressing some concern that they haven't heard back from you."

"Oh. What did you say?"

"Nothing. I let the machine get it. But then I got to the office, and there was *another* message from this fellow saying he has business in St. Paul, so he's wanting to come by and meet with you."

"They're coming to me?"

"They are." There was a certain beaming to the way he looked at her, making her suddenly self-conscious of her hair—tendrils plastered to her cheeks, the braid all but forgotten—and a shirt too soaked to show the stains of perspiration. She could picture the red blotches on her face, and she could only imagine her smell. And yet she found herself beaming too for a second, before the nerves hit.

"That's not the way things like this generally work, is it?"

"I don't know. I've never been the object of a syndication's desire. But *you* are."

"When?"

"Tomorrow. So go get yourself cleaned up. I'm taking you home."

He opened his door, and in the time it took for him to come around and open hers, she took a sweeping glance of the house and gained a new image of home. It wasn't this place where all her memories lived, stacked upon each other like every dish in the kitchen. Her home was a cozy bachelorette pad, carved out of a rambling house, with a dismissive cat and a waiting workplace. The sound of the word in Ron Tumble's voice gave him a place in it—not the little apartment, of course, but the life she lived there. Her hours, her mornings and nights. How else to explain her happiness but lack of surprise at seeing him on the side of the road out of the blue? Even in this fraction of a moment when he crossed from one side of the car to the next, she felt a tiny shot of reunion when her door swung open and she stepped into his space.

"Thank you," she said, pressing herself against the warmth of the car as he leaned in to close the door. "But there's one thing we have to do before heading back."

"Oh yeah?" His smile was boyish, expectant.

"Yeah. We're going to take my great-grandmother out on a date."

CHAPTER 14

MARIAH

*T*he details were whispered in the corners of the little church in Willow Lake. They passed along the wind-whipped talk as a train of mourners and family and farmers made their way to the cemetery. And the details were horrific.

"Heard the explosion from five miles out."

"One leg clean off. And his face. The burns. Pray his mother didn't have to see that."

"Pray his mother didn't see any of it, the poor woman."

Oscar's mother walked near the front of the procession, her steps mostly strong and resolute, though her daughter Florence's husband kept close for the occasional falter. This was the daughter who left home shortly before Charles and I came to live in the Garland boardinghouse, so I'd only met her on occasional visits. There was a little girl too, Oscar's niece, born to his older sister, Vena, who wove her way up and down the procession like a thin black ribbon, solemnly announcing to anyone who would listen, "My uncle Oscar got blown up."

The girl—Madge, I'd heard her called—said this to me as we gathered in the street to begin our procession. I could see Oscar in her face—all of the Garland siblings were attractive, though I'd never thought his sisters to be as pretty as he was handsome. She had flaxen blond hair, left loose save for a braid secured at her crown. The tips of her ears were pink in the cold, her lips red and chapped. I thought about the baby nestled inside of me and wondered if it would favor its father as successfully.

"You shouldn't say such things," I told her in what I hoped sounded both authoritative and kind.

"It's true, though."

"It is. But saying something sad, even if it's true, makes everyone else feel sadder."

Her large gray eyes filled with tears. "I can't imagine feeling sadder than I do right now."

And she was off, a voice to herald the passing of her uncle. Maybe it made her feel better, saying the words out loud. Maybe each speaking of the event took a bit of the horror and exhaled it, to where the child would eventually be left whole, her spirit knitting itself together within the gap. Her youth and innocence gave her the privilege to speak her grief. As I watched her flit from one person to another, it became clear that I was the only one to admonish her announcement. Everyone else adopted a sympathetic frown and patted her sweet head, saying, "I know. I know, dearie. But your uncle is in heaven now, and that must be our comfort."

Mrs. Garland didn't seem to be particularly comforted by the idea of her son being blown to heaven, though. She'd wept throughout the service, and occasionally the November wind brought the sound of her wailing all the way down to myself and my fellow stragglers who walked behind those more deserving of grief. Witnesses reported that she had been brought out to the field where her son lay dead, his body broken and twisted, his exposed skin the color of fiery pain. There she had fallen to her knees, begging God to heal him there beneath the late harvest sky.

Now, those who knew him and loved him envisioned their beloved Cap Garland dancing with the angels, playing baseball on true Elysian fields. His shattered body was healed and whole, his face wearing a perpetual smile.

"I'll wager he's even singing," one woman said with a wistful giggle. "Goodness knows he could never hold a note in singing school."

I had a faint acquaintance with the woman. Her name was Mary, and Oscar had brought her around often enough in the days after we moved in. I'd seen her tucked in beside him as they ran their sleighs up and down the snow-covered streets on Sunday afternoon. I'd also spied her in spring, climbing down from his buggy with her hair unpinned by a breezy afternoon ride. I assumed they would marry—that they were courting, at least. Perhaps Mary assumed so too. She must have guessed that Oscar's heart belonged to another. In any case, it didn't belong to her, for she had a husband walking behind her, allowing her to reminisce with the childhood friends who'd known Oscar as a companion.

I was not among them. Not in spirit and not in place, even as my steps matched theirs. In the days between his death and this procession, I'd been torn by the conflict of whether I should come to the funeral at all. Katrina argued that I should, of course, stay home. Not only did I not have an appropriate black dress, but I had no good, ready answer for those who would ask, *How did you know our Oscar?*

"His mother would remember me," I'd said. "Charles and I lived with her for over a year. She was quite kind and fond of us both."

"All the more reason not to bring up sad memories," Katrina replied. "Plus, the little one is bumping out a bit. You don't want to start rumors."

She was right about the little one. I woke up the day after learning of Oscar's death to find a small, hard mound spanning my otherwise flat stomach. "Surely no one will notice once I'm dressed and wearing a cloak."

"You don't have a place there, sweetie," she'd said with a little pat to my hand. "Not like Charles, who was his friend and who was. . .*there*. And I have to go to support Charles. It's hit him hard."

This too was true. For it was Charles who had inspected the thresher days before, leaving a warning with Augusterson that he mustn't use the ground water to fuel it. *Too alkaline*, he'd said, the admonition he gave to every farmer within a hundred miles who came to him for advice and repair. He'd been ignored, and three days later, two men were dead, more injured.

"Heard he was thrown thirty feet," someone behind me said.

There were, in fact, few people behind me, so I surmised this to be a man attending more for the meal than for mourning. "Straight up in the air, like he was shot from a cannon."

"Them boilers is tricky," a commiserative voice said.

I was glad Charles wasn't beside me to hear this conversation, as he would have been infuriated enough to turn around and set them straight. *Boilers ain't tricky*, I imagined him saying. *They can only do what they're meant to do, and they can only do that if they're maintained and treated right.* With the exceptions of Katrina and me, Charles only ever had a heart for the machines he encountered in life. I half-expected he would want to dig a grave for the ruined thresher with a hole blown three feet wide in its boiler.

It was Charles who insisted I come, telling me that I had as much reason to grieve Oscar's death as anyone else. Maybe more even.

"I should have told him sooner," I'd said. "If I'd realized. If I knew."

"And how would that have changed things, Sister?" Charles asked. "Do you think he would have skipped out on a day's work, knowing he had a child to provide for?"

In the end, Charles used the money Augusterson paid for his inspection of the machine to buy me a black blouse to wear with my black skirt, thereby cutting in half Katrina's argument that I should stay home. The two of them walked ahead of me, their heads bent together in the sort of whispering posture I'd grown accustomed to.

We assembled beside a gaping grave, fresh earth piled high beside it. The preacher stood alone at the top end, holding his Bible to his breast. He said all the things I've since learned are the custom to say at a funeral. That we should seek comfort knowing Oscar's eternal peace. That we are not to question God's will in such things. That there is a time for everything: to rejoice and to mourn, to sow and to reap. That we have a heavenly Father whose house has many rooms, and that each of us has a room waiting, giving us a place to live for our eternity. And, finally, that Oscar remains with us. His spirit lives on in our memories. His heart in the love we have for one another. His voice as we recall words he said.

God help me and forgive me, but at that moment those words rang truer than any others the preacher said. The chill that I felt in the afternoon breeze abated as I remembered what it felt like to be in Oscar's arms, his breath mingled with mine, our bodies entwined. I heard echoes of his promise that he didn't love me, and I cast it aside the way I did that night. I could taste his whiskey-tinged breath and feel the softness of the morning beard upon his cheek.

Eight men were chosen for the task of lowering the casket into the ground—most I recognized from playing on the De Smet baseball team, but the final two were more familiar: my brother, Charles, and Merrill Gowan. I'd seen him at the church, sitting in a center spot of a crowded pew in front of me. He'd walked in front of me too after allowing the smallest tip of his hat in greeting. He held the leather strap and walked with measured steps from the hearse to the grave, softly counting aloud to keep the other casket bearers in stride. He did the same as they lowered the casket into the grave, keeping the silk-finished box even in its descent. I know all of this not because I watched but because I listened, staring only at the scuffed toes of my boots peeking out from under my skirt, hearing only the rush of the wind and Merrill Gowan's soft-spoken cadence.

Then the time came for those so honored to throw a handful of earth atop the casket. The wind snapped our cloaks and skirts, even lifting Mrs. Garland's veil to reveal her grief-stricken face. Somehow all the seconds of time converged, and her eyes met mine where I stood on the opposite side, on the opposite end.

Part of him lives, I wanted to say and might have if I'd been close enough to whisper. *Not in our memories, not in our hearts. But here. Flesh and blood, alive.* I thought of the tiny beating heart, the body not yet knit together, the spirit waiting for its first breath.

The preacher led us in a recitation of the Lord's Prayer, but my mind was filled with Katrina's ominous warning—"*So much can happen in those first weeks and months. . .*" At the graveside of the child's father, I prayed fiercely, whispered aloud, "Holy Father, let it live." My prayer meshed in with those asking forgiveness for their trespasses, and in my heart I knew the living child would be a piece of God's mercy I could hold in my hands. I felt his love in a way I would never feel Oscar's. I swallowed his forgiveness along with my unshed tears. While the preacher prayed a final blessing over Oscar's family—his mother, his sisters, their husbands, their child—I took a physical step back and away from the crowd, knowing that I would never, ever share this new life with them. It was to be *my* comfort, a single drop of belonging in a world where everyone I loved seemed destined to leave me.

It was announced that we were all invited to the Garland home for a light supper provided by the church family in honor of Oscar, but I begged at Charles's arm not to go. I couldn't face the idea of walking into that house again, offering my condolences to his mother as she sat in the wing-backed chair by the window where I'd been allowed to sit and read on chilly afternoons. However, I kept this reason to myself and only claimed a near collapsing fatigue (which was real) and the logic that if we drove straight home from here we could be in our own cozy kitchen before dark. To my relief, Katrina agreed and offered to represent us in reassuring our prayers to the family—one of the sisters, perhaps—before heading home.

From the corner of my eye, I saw Merrill Gowan making a purposeful approach, meeting up with Charles and asking if he might accompany us home. "Times like this," he said, "it's good to have someone to talk to."

"Of course," Charles said, "if you don't mind riding in the back of the wagon." Our wagon seat could comfortably sit three abreast, and we'd ridden together with Katrina sitting stoically in the center.

Before Merrill could answer, I piped in saying *I* would ride in the back. I knew there was a layer of hay left in for those times when Charles needed it to cushion bits of machinery he hauled back and forth for repair as well as a stack of blankets for extra packing. "Let you men catch up and talk about whatever men need to talk about."

Charles gave me a long look. "Are you sure?"

I nodded, as eager for solitude as Merrill Gowan was for company. By the time Katrina was back from her social duty, I was settled in, warm and more comfortable than I'd been in half the beds of my life. Katrina sat between the two men, so I imagined her equally warm, and felt begrudgingly happy for her.

The day had been one tinged with the orange light of autumn, but I was chilly from the shadow cast by the wagon's wall. The wool blanket was itchy but tolerably so, and I pulled it up to my chin, taking in the familiar scent of iron and oil that made up my brother's livelihood. The deep, intermittent conversation between Charles and Merrill lulled me in and out of a shallow sleep, with Katrina's high-pitched bursts bringing me awake. They—Charles and Katrina—spoke of their future, the factory job awaiting Charles and the home they hoped to find in the outlying neighborhoods. Nothing fancy, of course, to start. Only manageable, so they could put money aside for something bigger. All of this talk came from Katrina, while Charles spoke of the machinery, the intricacies of the working parts, the ideas he had for further streamlining. This, I knew, bored Katrina to tears, and I thought I heard a few of her distinctive, frustrated harrumphs when the men talked over her attempts to change the subject. But I imagined her silence being folded up in my brother's words, and I could not picture a safer place to be.

I opened my eyes to a violet sky, the color that comes when there's not a trace of sunlight left but darkness hasn't yet settled its blanket. I heard Charles declaring he would return the wagon and team to the livery down the street and offered to take Merrill's horse too if he wanted to spend the night in the extra room upstairs.

"Thank you, no," Merrill said. "I've chores to get back to."

"Then stay for a bite to eat," Katrina said. "Mother said she'd bring over some supper for us to come home to."

I sat up, then stood, keeping a steadying hand while Merrill folded down the tailgate, where he made no effort to help me as I sat on its edge and dropped safely to the ground before Charles drove away. "Would you mind," he asked as I brushed stray bits of straw from my skirt, "Miss Mariah, if I stayed for supper?"

"You are most welcome to stay," I said, fully realizing it was not my place to say who was welcome and who wasn't. "I know I am famished."

"Then come in and help," Katrina said over her shoulder.

Charles had brought the wagon around the back of the building by the kitchen door. I took one step to follow her when Merrill's hand caught mine. Neither of us said anything, and I made no attempt to take my hand away. The evening grew darker with every breath, but soon enough Katrina lit a lamp in the kitchen and we found ourselves standing in the window's amber square of light.

"I know I said I'd never ask you again," Merrill said, "but this will be the first and last promise I ever break."

I looked up into his broad face, made leaner—as was the rest of his body—after months of harvest labor. His features were just as soft, cheeks just as round, hair just as thin, though longer and left messy by the wind. His eyes held nothing but kindness and hope. "I'm asking you again to be my wife. To let me give you and the child a home. I'll take care of you all of your life, Mariah. And I'll give the child my name. Boy or girl, it will inherit all I have. I promise to love it as my own and to love you as much as you will allow."

This last declaration made summoned my first smile in recent memory, and I offered a closed, guarded sniff of a laugh. "I don't have any promises to offer in return."

"I only ask that you accept mine."

"I cannot promise to love you."

"I know."

"Or to obey you."

"I won't ask."

Having said all of that, there seemed nothing left. But then I thought about Merrill's big blue house with its fledgling copse of trees sitting at the edge of a field so fertile he had to hire out help to harvest it. I remembered the preacher speaking the promise of Oscar's home—a big house with many rooms—and wondered why Oscar's child should have to wait to live a life and die before knowing such a thing. With Merrill as its father, this child would never suffer the hunger and cold as I had. There were two hearts beating within me, but I answered only for one.

"I will honor you," I said. "And never speak to you or another soul about this child's father."

He smiled, kissed my hand, then—with my face raised in permission—placed a soft kiss on my lips. "How soon, do you think?"

I glanced through the window and saw that Charles had returned, having come through the shop. He glanced out the window and raised a hand in salute before walking out of frame, presumably to help Katrina with the supper.

"Tomorrow," I said without hesitation.

"Are you worried you will change your mind?"

"Maybe. But there's no reason to wait. We aren't promised a tomorrow, are we? The congregation will be gathered. We can ask the reverend to perform a quick ceremony after the sermon."

"And you aren't worried that people will suspect?"

I shrugged. "They'll suspect what they suspect when we have a child in seven months' time. Then they'll remember that you came to dinner every week all summer and they'll come to their conclusions."

"Tomorrow, then," he said, his voice tinged with a hint of disbelief. "Tomorrow my home will be your home."

"I want to bring my books. And my table. And chairs. They are mine."

"I will build you shelves in the front parlor."

He kissed me again, holding me a bit longer but releasing me before I could pull away. After having spoken all the vows that would bind us, I took his hand and led him into the warm, bright kitchen where my brother's blessing waited.

CHAPTER 15

TRIXIE

*T*rixie made the introductions all around, ignoring the bemused quality of her mother's and grandmother's reception.

"GG is upstairs, resting," she explained. "Maybe we'll bring her downstairs later to meet you."

"That would be nice," Ron said, but with a slight lift in his voice, as if questioning.

She tried to imagine what the Gowan house looked like through his eyes—bookshelves crammed with modern paperbacks and antique editions, all set at different angles, some page-facing, others with covers torn straight down the spine. Spindly Victorian end tables cozied up against overstuffed recliners. Knickknacks strewn across every horizontal surface—dog figurines, cut-glass ashtrays, milk-glass bowls filled with antique candy. A few Christmas cards remained clipped to a string draped across the doorway to the dining room, and Trixie's graduation portrait hung above the fireplace as if the skinny girl in the track uniform and letterman jacket was the presiding lady who laid the cornerstone.

"Cute," Ron said, looking at the picture. Then, at her, where he waggled his eyebrows in obvious appreciation.

"Well, I'm a mess right now," she said, aware of every sticky, sweaty inch of herself not because of Ron's scrutiny but her mother's.

"Why don't you go upstairs and get cleaned up," Alma said, her hands clasped loosely in front of her as if delivering a proper directive, "and Mother can take your young man on a tour of the property. The petunias in the garden are blooming like crazy."

Ron rocked back on his heels. "I love petunias."

Eugenie leaned into him. "That's code for let's not have a gentleman in the house when one of us is in the shower." She inclined to Trixie. "At least I hope you're planning a shower."

Trixie should have blushed or demurred in some other ladylike way, but she'd long been used to her grandmother's boldness. In response, she lifted her arms and gave a sniff under each. "Maybe a quick one. I have petunias to compete with."

She bounded up the stairs, the word *quick* setting her pace. A peek into GG's room showed the woman sitting in her rocking chair, looking out the window.

"GG?"

She turned. "Oh Trixie. That car! Did you see it?"

Trixie laughed. "I saw it, and I rode in it. And you are too, as soon as I get myself cleaned up to take you."

"They'd never let me go in something like that." GG pouted, taking a hundred years off her face.

"*They* don't have to know. It can be our little secret. Sit tight."

There was no time for a proper shampoo—much less time for a proper drying. After her shower, Trixie rubbed a towel through her damp tresses and pinned them in a loose twist. She kept her makeup light—just a bit of lip gloss and mascara. Finally, she double-knotted the halter top on her sundress, spurred by the unlikely scenario of the wind catching the strings and untying them.

Back in GG's room, she performed a final check, straightening the buttons on the strawberry blouse and exchanging her bedroom slippers for a soft pair of worn Keds. "Wait right up here," Trixie said, tying the laces, "and I'll be back for you. We'll take you wherever you want to go."

"*We?*" GG questioned. "I don't want the girls to go."

Trixie smiled, thinking of her mother and grandmother as *the girls*. "Not the girls, GG. A guy. A friend. A guy. . .friend." It was an easy enough label for the moment.

She slipped her feet into her favorite clogs and was coming

downstairs just as Ron and Eugenie were coming in, both laughing at some shared joke.

"This place is great," Ron said, closing the screen door behind him. "Have you seen the barn?"

"I have," Trixie said. "Antiquers paradise, isn't it?"

"I think it's cleaner than my house," he said. Then, at the shocked look on Alma's face, "Of course that's all on my roommate. I'm kind of a neat freak myself."

Trixie, thinking of his cluttered office, the bulletin board jammed with yellowed, curled clippings, and the desk riddled with empty (and half-empty) pop cans, sent him a wry smile. Here they were, sharing a secret while he tried to impress her mother.

"Hey, Mom," Trixie said, sidling close enough to Ron that the fabric of his T-shirt sleeve brushed against her arm, "Ron's too shy to ask for himself, but he's heard so much about your amazing grilled cheese sandwiches, and I know he's a little hungry from the road. . ." Losing herself in the moment, she brought her hand across to pat his belly, as if they were so familiar with each other's bodies that such a gesture was instinctive. Normal. Then, in the same vein, Ron put his arm around her, tucking her up to his side where—to her pleasant surprise—she fit perfectly.

"Yep," he said. "Says they're the best."

He delivered the line with a little bit of a squeeze that sent a thrill through her not only because of its warm physicality but because he'd fallen so quickly into her improvisation.

"Well," Alma said, obviously thrilled too for the accolade, "I can't tell you the whole secret, but it's a *miracle* that I learned to *whip* up a few years ago."

"Mmm," Ron said appreciatively. Trixie felt the rumble.

"So, would you mind? Making him a sandwich? I know it's early for lunch—"

"Of course," Alma said. "You two come on in and tell us more about"—she made a gesture encapsulating their cozy stance—"this."

Trixie stood straight but did not take herself away. "I'm still super full from breakfast, and I never have much of an appetite after a run." That last bit was a lie she hoped to get away with. "But maybe he could watch? So he could replicate it for himself? You know how hopeless I am in the kitchen."

"She really is," Ron said, and for that he got a bit of a jab.

"This is the first we've heard of her cooking for anybody," Eugenie said, sending Trixie a sidelong look.

"I haven't—" Trixie said.

"She doesn't—" Ron said at the same time.

"You two," Alma said with a wink. "Let's go get this boy a snack."

Alma took herself off to the kitchen, and Eugenie, after another long look, followed, leaving Ron and Trixie entwined and alone.

He leaned down and whispered, "What's happening right now?"

"I need you to keep them busy while I sneak my GG down to your car."

"Sneak?"

"I don't know that they'd be one hundred percent on board with our little outing. And I know for sure that GG doesn't want them to go along."

"So I get to be a spy *and* get the world's best grilled cheese sandwich? Which, by the way, you've *never* mentioned before, so you've been holding out on me. Or you're wildly overselling."

She stepped away and gave him a little push. "Go. And trust. Your life is about to change. Tell them I'm up visiting GG, and keep them in the kitchen. When you're done, come straight out to your car. We'll be waiting."

There it was again, that inexplicable frisson that came with planning an escapade together, and its effervescence carried her up the stairs.

GG was waiting, perched on the edge of her bed. In the time that Trixie had been downstairs, she'd brushed and braided her hair into a plait that fell across her shoulder. Trixie paused, gripping the doorframe, mesmerized by the sight, unable to bring her great-grandmother into focus. She shimmered, seeming to appear every age she'd ever been all at once—a child, a girl, a woman. Youth and age passed intermittently across her face, defined by her wavering smile.

"Are we going now?"

"Yes," Trixie said, brought into the moment by the familiar voice.

"And the girls?"

"Are busy in the kitchen. Come on."

GG did the closest thing to hopping that a century-old woman could do and did not take Trixie's arm until they came to the stairs. They walked carefully, quietly together, easing the screen door past its squeaking and closing it silently behind.

"Look at that," GG said, accompanied by a low whistle.

"Have you ever ridden in a convertible before?"

"Does a buggy count?" She paused at the top of the front steps, then proceeded down them unaided. "Just kidding. Of course I have. I may have been born in a tar shack, but that don't mean I was raised in one. My husband was probably one of the first people to own a car around these parts."

As GG walked and talked, Trixie kept herself near, like a spotter, waiting for the woman's steps to falter, but they never did. The moment they got to the car, however, GG extended her hand and ran her fingers along the length of it while she walked. Trixie followed, curious about the near reverence with which her great-grandmother approached the car. Trixie moved around her and opened the door. Knowing the older woman would never be able to maneuver herself into the back seat, she settled her into the front, gently drawing the seat belt over her and clicking it in place.

GG clasped her arm. "Are you driving?"

Trixie laughed. "No, GG. This isn't my car."

"Does that matter?"

Trixie considered for a moment and concluded that, no, it didn't. She crossed to the driver's side and climbed in. The keys were on the dash where Ron left them (after she'd assured him there were no car thieves lurking in the wheat field). When the engine roared to life, she and GG exchanged a look of pure delight, as if both were experiencing the phenomenon for the first time. Led Zeppelin poured from the speakers—"Ramble On"—and Trixie thought to herself: *Just to the main road. To the main road and back, me and GG.*

She was adjusting the rearview mirror when the front door opened and Ron appeared, clutching what looked to be a grilled cheese sandwich in one hand and a can of pop in the other. Grape soda, she surmised, as he ran closer.

"Thief!" he shouted around a mouthful of sandwich. "You're the thief in the wheat field!"

Trixie opened the door, hopped out, and folded the front seat down, saying, "Get in—quick! Before they stop us."

"You're driving?"

"Yep. I drive, you eat." She held the can of pop while he settled in. Then she was back behind the wheel, and off they went. Even creeping along on the dirt-packed drive to the main road, she could feel the power of the engine waiting to spring to life. And when the road lay open before her, she whispered, "Let's go, kids."

The speedometer was nudged past 60 when she glanced over to see GG's arms raised high and a look of pure joy on her face the likes of which Trixie had never seen before. Unguarded, girlish. This is who she would have been on a Sunday afternoon ride with cutters racing on the snow-packed street. Trixie let out a *Whoop!* and Ron attempted to match Robert Plant's gritty falsetto.

They had a few miles of road behind them before it occurred to Trixie to ask exactly where they were going. She assumed *town*, which meant De Smet, but GG hadn't actually named a destination. She asked her now, pitching her voice above the wind and the radio, to which GG replied, "I don't care. Keep driving."

"I'm with Grandma," Ron said from the back.

"Town it is," Trixie said before slowing down to a reasonable speed.

When the prairie grasses gave way to the wide, shop-lined streets, Trixie turned down the radio, reasoning that the muscle car would attract enough attention on its own.

"I'm sorry, but did you turn my car into a time machine?" Ron was leaning forward, speaking straight into the curve of her neck, making it a bit difficult to drive even though there were few cars on the street.

"What are you talking about?"

"This place. It looks frozen in time. Like we could turn a corner and run into a gunfight or something."

"You've never been here?"

"Not unless it was a past life. Maybe I was a blacksmith or something."

"Well, it's perfectly modern. Drugstores, grocery stores, café." A thought snapped. "Car repair places. Think I'm going to check on my guy."

Failing to remember the name or address of the garage, Trixie pulled into a parking space along the street and asked the next passerby for information and directions. When she got back, Ron was standing by the open car door, clearly intending to take over the driving.

"So, this is like one of those small towns where people talk to each other? Strangers on the street?"

"Yep," Trixie said, climbing into the back seat. "As long as you don't think of them as strangers."

Now it was her turn to lean forward. She rested her hand on his shoulder and brought her lips close enough to his ear that she could give him directions in a low enough voice that GG could remain blissfully ignorant beside them. Repeating the directions—turn left, one block, then right—she glanced intermittently over at GG, who seemed perfectly content to take in the sights as if she didn't have the whole town memorized.

"Now, what are we doing here?" Ron asked. "Picking up your car?"

"No," Trixie said, ducking behind him. "I want to know if my car really had a problem with the starter or if my mother and grandmother used it as a ruse to keep me in town."

"Sounds perfectly reasonable."

He slowed the car to a snail's pace, and Trixie craned her neck. Half a dozen cars were parked in the lot next to the garage, and there her baby sat among them. She gasped.

"What?" Ron braked a little more aggressively than necessary, making Trixie brace herself to avoid tossing over the front of the seat. GG, thankfully, appeared nonplussed.

"See?" Trixie pointed. "It's not even in the garage. It's just. . .*parked* there."

"Didn't you say they had to order a part?"

"That's what they *said*."

"Well, if that's the case, then, yeah. They're not going to take up space in the bay if they don't have the part."

"The *bay*?"

"The bay. Yes. That's where they fix the cars."

"I've never been to a bay," GG said dreamily. "Or the ocean. Or a boardwalk. And never will."

Chagrinned, Trixie fell silent against the back of the seat. This was supposed to be GG's outing after all, and she'd hijacked it with paranoia. But before she could say, *Forget it, move on,* Ron was parking the Mustang and getting out of the car.

Trixie reached out a futile hand. "What are you doing?"

"Getting some answers."

He'd left the engine running and the radio station launched into a series of commercials, so Trixie stretched across the expanse of the front seat to turn it off.

"I like him," GG said, fully present in the moment. "That man of yours."

It was on the tip of Trixie's lips to say, *He's not my man,* but if GG liked him, what could be the harm of letting her hold the thought? It wasn't such an unpleasant thought, after all. "I like him too," she said, congratulating herself on speaking wholly appropriate truth.

"He seems like a good man."

"He is."

"I married a good man."

"I know you did, GG." The two couldn't look directly at each other, but maybe that would make the conversation flow a little more smoothly. "I'm sure you loved him."

GG shook her head, rolling it against the leather headrest. "I didn't. At first. And by the time I did, he didn't love me. And then it was too late for us to love each other."

Trixie leaned closer. "But you loved somebody, didn't you?"

GG pressed her lips together, holding back a response, closed her eyes, and shook her head again.

"It's all right if you did. That's the way it works. You love someone, and it doesn't work out. So you find someone else. Or—maybe someone finds you?"

"Why are we here?" GG's eyes fluttered open, and Trixie noticed a new agitation as she gripped at the hem of her shorts. "What are we doing? I don't know this place. I don't want to be here."

Her voice became higher and thinner, almost childlike, and Trixie felt her own anxiety rise. They had to leave, now. Just as she was about to climb out of the car, Ron appeared, a new confidence to his step.

"Everything's cool," he said, getting in.

"Oh, is it? It's cool? Groovy. Now, let's get out of here."

"To where, exactly?"

Trixie sighed. "I don't know yet, exactly. Can we just—drive? Like, up and down streets for a while?"

"Can I parade my Mustang up and down the grand old neighborhoods of De Smet, South Dakota, and spark envy in the hearts of all? Why, yes, Prairie Girl, I think I can."

Beside him, GG chuckled and muttered, "Prairie Girl. You have no idea what the prairie is, my girl. No idea."

It was a relief to have GG back, and Trixie gave Ron's shoulder a squeeze in gratitude. "What did they say about my car? Besides everything being *cool*."

"I walked in there, told them my girlfriend had some urgent business back home in Minneapolis, and that my girlfriend needed to know when the car would be done so my girlfriend could make arrangements to come get it."

"*Hmm.* Okay. And did you get a sense that they were on the up-and-up about the problem?"

"Yep. Laid it out the way you told me your grandmother told you."

"You're sure he wasn't yanking your chain?"

"My chain remains unyanked."

"And are you positive you used the word *girlfriend* three times?"

"At least."

"Because you know, I am not, in fact, your girlfriend."

"Well, I thought about calling you the ad builder for my neighborhood shopper newspaper, but that didn't have the same zip."

"So, you jumped straight to *girlfriend*?"

"I did."

"Does that mean when I go to pick it up, I'll have to call you my *boyfriend*?"

Ron signaled and executed a left-hand turn. "Maybe by then it will be true."

Trixie fell back against the seat, and the three drove through the residential streets lined with houses of varying degrees of sprawl. Some looked like cabins that had been expanded with ill-conceived additions; others were grand multistory homes that must have been the culmination of somebody's dream. Ancient trees stretched canopies of shade over trimmed lawns and proud front gardens. She watched as Ron pointed out interesting sights to GG—stained glass windows and flags and wrought iron works of art. She responded well and pointed out a few things on her own. On Third Street they drove by a simple, weather-worn white house with a sign posted in the yard. Trixie held her breath.

Ingalls Home & Museum

The House That Pa Built

Trixie watched GG's hand reach over and touch Ron gently on his arm. "I been there, once," she said. "Long time ago on a fool's errand."

"Oh yeah? Looks to be open to the public. Want to go in?"

"No," GG said, sounding almost amused. "There's nothing for me to see there now. There was nothing for me then either."

"Where *do* you want to go, GG?" Trixie leaned forward. "You seemed pretty determined to get somewhere."

"You won't want to go."

"Are you kidding? Would I miss a chance to go *anywhere* on a gorgeous summer day in a car like this?"

"Aw, thanks," Ron said, patting the dashboard affectionately. "The feeling is mutual."

"Tell me, GG," Trixie said. "Name the place, and we'll take you there. Like a magic carpet ride."

Ron immediately joined in with the Steppenwolf lyric. *"Close your eyes, girl."*

Trixie followed: *"Look inside, girl."*

And together they sang, *"Let the sound take you away."*

"Willow Lake," GG said, ignoring their concert.

"Willow Lake?" Trixie knew the town—tiny even by Little Town on the Prairie standards—but couldn't make a connection to the family. For all she knew, they didn't have any relatives anywhere, let alone in a town so close by. She herself had been to the lake a few times, teenage parties with bonfires and beer, but never with her family. "Who do you know in Willow Lake?"

"Nobody," GG said.

"Sounds like a good enough reason to go," Ron said. "Shall we find another stranger to ask directions?"

"Not a stranger, no." Trixie dug through her purse, found the business card, and talked Ron through the directions.

Cam's office was a small building with a neat, green lawn behind a white picket fence. If not for the Dr. Campbell Carter, Physician signboard hanging on the porch, it might have been a delightful honeymoon cottage. As Ron brought the Mustang to a stop, Trixie noticed Samantha lounging on a blanket in the shade of a willow tree in the side yard. She had a thick coloring book and a shoebox full of crayons, all of which she abandoned on sight.

"Trixie!" Her usual greeting, a full-body slam of a hug, made Trixie a little self-conscious under Ron's curious gaze.

"Hey, Samantha. What are you up to?"

"Daddy has patients to see this afternoon, but then he says we're going for ice cream, and then I get to go to the library to get books. And he's going to get books too. And then tonight's supper is burgers and books."

"Burgers and books are the best," Trixie said, working a respectable distance between them. "So, he's with someone right now?"

Sam shook her head. "A lady left a few minutes ago. And he says one more in about"—she pointed to her watch—"fifteen minutes."

If not for the overpowering lisp, Samantha could have been a front-desk receptionist. Trixie thanked her, turned to send Ron a *Just give me a minute* sign, and went inside. The actual front-desk receptionist was a beautiful girl—*yes, girl. Twenty tops.* Her strawberry-blond hair flipped in a soft frame around her face, which was round and shone with health and gloss. She flashed a welcoming, perfect smile and said, "Good afternoon. Do you have an appointment?"

"No," Trixie said. "I need to talk to Cam for a second?"

An immediate change came over the girl. Less welcoming, more predatory. "Is he expecting you?"

"No. But he'll see me. Can you tell him Trixie's here?"

"Trixie? Like the cereal?"

Trixie worked to keep her face pleasant, eyes blinking furiously. "Can you just—" She mimed picking up a phone, underestimating the tininess of the office, because Cam's voice was already coming down the hall.

"Trix? What are you doing here?" He wore a dress shirt, slacks, and tie underneath a pristine white coat, with a stethoscope slung around his neck like an appendage. He turned to the girl. "Nancy, if Mrs. Hudgens shows up, go ahead and take her back to exam room two." He took Trixie's hand, making her realize immediately how warm and sticky hers was after an hour in the car next to his cold, clean one. She took it away.

"No. I just—could you come outside for a second? GG's here—"

He immediately transformed to Dr. Carter, MD. "Oh, is everything all right?"

"Yeah. I mean, yes, I think so? She wants to go to Willow Lake."

His brow furrowed. "Willow Lake? Okay. So, what's the problem."

"She *seems* lucid. But, you're a better guess at that than I am. Could you—would you mind coming out and talking to her? A quick assessment? I'd feel better."

"Of course. Of course." He turned to Nancy. "If—"

"Mrs. Hudgens. Exam room two." Her smile didn't quite reach her blue-shadowed eyes. "Got it."

Cam kept his hand on the small of Trixie's back as they left the office. "Did you see Sam?"

"I did. She told me about books and burger night."

"You're welcome to join us if you like. Check out something on my library card."

They were at the car, where Sam had been regaling Ron with the details of her growing rock collection but was distracted by her father's invitation. "Yes! Yes! Yes!" She jumped up and down and grabbed Trixie's hand. "Come to burgers and books with us."

"That sounds great," Trixie said, gently disentangling herself, "but I can't. I have. . .plans." She met Ron's eyes and sent a silent plea for rescue, but his bemused expression gave little hope that any would soon be coming. Cam, meanwhile, had opened the passenger door of the Mustang and was crouched down, eye level with GG.

"Good afternoon, Mrs. Gowan. This is some snazzy ride you have here."

"It's like flying," she said, prompting a chuckle from all but Samantha, who declared she wanted to fly too. Thankfully, Cam ignored her.

"Trixie says you want to go out to Willow Lake?"

GG nodded.

"Any particular reason?"

"I'm not off in my mind, if that's what you're thinking. There's something I have to do."

"Okay." Cam's voice was soothing, almost to the point of mesmerizing. "Can you tell us more about that?"

"No." GG's entire face went firm. "I'll tell them as they need to know. I'd go on my own if I could, but I can't. Even an old woman is entitled to a little privacy."

"You're right," Cam said. "You're right. Mind if I do a quick check, though? Make sure you're up for this wild ride?" He took his stethoscope from his neck, to which GG offered a faint protest. Cam listened, smiling, and declared her in perfect shape for an afternoon outing. "And if you like," he said, directing his words at Trixie as he stood, "I'd be happy to call to the house and tell the ladies so."

"They called you?"

"Your mother did, yes. You caused a bit of a panic sneaking her out of the house like that. How long have you been out driving?"

Trixie calculated. "Maybe about an hour?" She looked to Ron to confirm.

"Maybe then," Cam said, "it would be a good idea to make sure she gets a good stretch of the legs?"

"Yes. Maybe a nice walk at the lake?"

"And watch that you don't overdo. Keep the speed down, get her home before dark." Cam's hand sat protectively on GG's shoulder, but his gaze never wavered from Ron, who stared straight back.

"She's in good hands," Ron said.

"Oh, sorry. I should have introduced—Cam, this is Ron, my boss, and Ron, this is Cam, an old friend from high school."

"They used to be boyfriend and girlfriend," Samantha sing-songed. "And they were kissing yesterday."

"Samantha," Cam warned.

"Really?" Ron said, though it wasn't clear if he sought confirmation from Cam, Sam, or Trixie, who wanted nothing more than the earth to swallow all of them in one gulp.

"We should go," she said, opening the driver's side door. "Thanks so much, Cam. And tell Mom and Grandma not to worry about anything. We'll be home in a couple of hours."

"Can I go too?" Samantha asked, to which all four adults—including GG—answered a resounding, "No." She pouted and attached herself to her father's side, sparking almost enough pity for Trixie to forgive her for the kissing outburst. Almost.

She climbed into the back seat of the Mustang with as much grace as she could muster but did not sit down until Ron was behind the wheel. He double-checked GG's seat belt, put on his own, and brought the engine to life. Cam and Samantha remained, waving them away like the last vestige of a family visit. They were still standing, though not waving, when Trixie turned in her seat and watched until Ron turned a corner and they disappeared.

It was a half-hour's drive to Willow Lake. Wheat stretched out in golden, rippling waves under the brutal afternoon sun. The three were silent in the car—GG turned in her seat with her cheek against the headrest, Ron and Trixie with the weight of open air between them. Once they were out of De Smet, Ron put an Eagles tape in the 8-track, and the music proved a perfect soundtrack to the drive—a soft, soothing groove, with lyrics too intricate to talk over. GG's hands seemed to be doing a kind of drifting dance with the music, and Ron's eyes frequently met Trixie's in the rearview mirror, then quickly returned to the road.

Stupid Samantha.

The final *oooohhhhs* of "Peaceful, Easy Feeling" were fading as they passed the sign with a welcome to Willow Lake.

"Where to from here?"

Trixie leaned forward. "GG?"

"I'm afraid it will fly away."

The words were nearly carried away on the wind, so Trixie nudged Ron's arm, telling him to pull over, stop the car, and turn off the music. Once he'd done all three, GG asked for her purse. It was an ancient thing of pale, ratty straw, and GG's fingers began to shake as she twisted the clasp.

"Do you need help, GG?" Trixie asked, inexplicably nervous.

"No." She focused on rifling through and took out a soft leather notebook, thumbing through the pages until a single sheet of yellowed paper fell out into her lap. This she picked up and handed to Ron, saying, "Men are better with these things."

Trixie suppressed her instinctive response and kept her eyes glued to the paper as Ron—with all the reverence of handling a treasured artifact—unfolded the paper. On it was a hand-drawn map, a sparse series of roads and numbers and arrows. It had obviously been folded and refolded hundreds of times, the creases pronounced.

GG stretched a finger to the upper corner. "Can you find this? And take me there?"

"Absolutely," Ron said, then shifted in his seat to give Trixie a better view. A shaky, unfamiliar hand had drawn a box of sorts and labeled it *Willow Lake Cemetery* and a narrow path straight to it.

She took the paper from him, glad they'd taken the precaution to stop the car, or it might have been blown to feathers in her hand. "Who do you want to visit there, GG?" Every person she knew to share her blood was buried in the fenced plot beside the house.

"Please," GG said. "I need to see him one more time."

Ron drove directly to the cemetery not because of the directions drawn on the ancient paper but, he said, because he had an aunt buried there and had been to the funeral a few years ago. When they arrived at the neat, well-maintained place, Trixie furrowed her brow, trying to place it in her memories. They drove down a narrow road, which became a narrow causeway with shallow swampland on either side. Then a hard-packed dirt path that dead-ended at a cornfield with the carpet of grass and tombstones stretched out on the right. Ron stopped the car and turned off the engine; the new silence fell like a blanket around them.

Trixie leaned over the seat. "Who are we here to see?" she asked, though she had a feeling she knew. "Is it Cap? Cap Garland?"

GG closed her eyes and nodded.

"Because you loved him?"

"Not just that," she said, her voice grown so low and whispery Trixie could barely hear. She pushed Ron's shoulder.

"Switch with me."

Without a word, he got out of the car and she clambered over the seat, maneuvering her body so she could look GG face-to-face.

"I promised I never would," GG said, tears gathered in the crepe-thin skin at the corners of her eyes.

"You don't have to tell me anything you don't want to," Trixie whispered, hiding her words from Ron and the souls at peace around them, "but if it would ease your burden, you can trust me. And tell me, and I'll keep whatever you say locked in my heart."

"Find him. Find my Oscar, take me to him, and I'll tell you everything."

Sighing, Trixie climbed out of the car and sidled up to Ron, who stood contemplating the grave of a woman buried with two infants listed on the stone. "Imagine all the stories here," he said, bending for a closer look.

"Yeah, well, we need to find one specifically."

"Any idea where?"

"None. The name is Garland. Cap—no, wait. Oscar. He's Cap in the books."

"So let's start walking," Ron said. "Do you think your great-grandmother will be all right in the car if we have to go far?"

"She's not a dog. She's in an open car. Think of it as a leather park bench with wheels. She'll be fine."

"As long as she doesn't try to drive."

Trixie explained to GG that they were going to walk to find the Garland grave and that she wasn't—under any circumstances—to leave the car. And that if she needed anything, to honk the horn, and they would be right back. With matters thus settled, Ron made the arbitrary decision to turn right, and she followed. For a while, the only sound was the rustle of the wind through the distant corn-field and the crunch of their steps on the tiny-pebbled path.

"Thank you for doing this," Trixie said after a time, her eyes skimming the names on the tombstones as they passed. "I'm sure this isn't where you thought you'd be when you woke up this morning."

"I didn't think I *wouldn't* be at a cemetery looking for my friend's great-grandmother's lost love."

Trixie had an arm looped loosely around his and almost dropped it, but held on. "So I've been demoted? At McCready's I was your girlfriend."

"That was before I met your boyfriend."

At *that*, she dropped his arm and her step. He stopped beside her. "He's not my boyfriend."

"So he's what? My competition?"

Trixie bristled. "No, because I'm not a prize. He is my great-grandmother's doctor and, yes, an ex-boyfriend of mine. Way ex. Like, high school."

"Who you kissed yesterday."

"Yes." She took up her steps again, and he fell in beside her. For a while, they filled the silence by reading the names on the stones out loud, their steps in easy sync.

"I don't know if you noticed or not," Ron said, "but that guy is super handsome."

She smiled. "I noticed."

"Like, Sears catalog pajama model handsome."

"I've never seen him in pajamas. But I'll take your word for it."

"He could be a stuntman for Robert Redford. Like, if Redford ever had a scene where he wasn't handsome enough for a close-up? They could use this guy."

Trixie laughed. "I don't think that's how stuntmen work."

They came to the end of the row and, faced with both choices, turned right, again. This time their steps led them closer and closer to Ron's car, GG's soft hair floating above the headrest like strands of cirrus clouds.

"Anyway," she said after they walked past three or four stones, "I think I kissed you too."

"You *think* you kissed me?"

"Before I left. In my driveway, Saturday. It happened so fast."

"That was weird," he said. "And I'm sorry. I'm not supposed to kiss you because I'm your boss."

"Oh." More steps, more crunches. "Is that why you're so invested in my finding syndication for *Lost Laura*? So I'll become a famous cartoonist and quit the *Newz* and you won't be my boss anymore?"

"Actually, I happen to think you are a talented artist with an engaging point of view, and I think your Laura might have some important things to say to the women of America and beyond."

"Good answer," she said with not-so-mock approval.

"And, yeah. Kissing you with impunity would be cool too." He draped an arm across her shoulder in a gesture that, by now, seemed comfortable and expected, and she leaned in, their hips bumping against each other intermittently.

"*With impunity.*"

"Among other things, yes."

They were halfway to the car, but soon her vision was filled with the expanse of Ron's blue shirt. She needed only to tilt her head a little to see his eyes boring straight into hers, the heat behind them like pools of the waning afternoon.

She spoke around the heartbeat that had lodged itself in her throat. "Like what?"

He brought his finger to the tip of her cheek. "Like intentionality. And purpose."

"And reciprocation?"

"Most of all."

A gust of wind took up an errant curl of his hair and lodged it beneath his brow. Trixie reached up and brushed it back, allowing her fingers to linger, to pull him closer. But in so doing, she caught a glimpse of the Mustang ahead, GG's arm raised, her hand playing with the breeze. "Just, maybe not. . .now."

"You mean not here. In a cemetery. In the middle of looking for your long-lost relative's tombstone."

"Exactly."

"But later, for sure, maybe? I'll take you back to your place. We can make something for dinner and then make out like teenagers for an hour on the couch?"

"If House won't mind sharing you."

"Good point. Let's have a quick practice in front of "—he looked to his left—"Norma Kramer 1842–1857. See what she thinks."

And then he kissed her, with everything he'd held back before, and she responded, feeling the approval of all the departed souls around them. In a place that marked the end of a life, here she felt something new beginning. Trixie might have been content to stay right here in this embrace forever if a new thought hadn't wiggled its way through the delicious appreciation of Ron's lips.

She pulled away. "Wait—what did you just say?"

His eyes were still closed. "Norma Kramer?"

"Before that."

"Making out like teenagers?"

"Before that."

"I have no recollection of any thoughts before that."

"You said we were looking for my long-lost relative. But Oscar Garland isn't a relative. He's just—"

"An ex-boyfriend?"

"Not an ex, though. She still loves him today. But the day I got here, she told me I look like him."

"Him, Oscar?"

Trixie grabbed Ron's hand and started a brisk walk toward the car. "She didn't say so, but I. . .I know. She said she didn't marry for love. What if she married out of. . .necessity? Survival."

"Sounds like you're taking quite a leap."

"Does it? I think—"

Before she finished the thought, the peace of the afternoon was shattered by the blaring of the car's horn. Trixie dropped Ron's hand and broke into a run, making up the distance back to the car in a fraction of the time it had taken to walk away. When she arrived, GG's shaking hand was pointing ahead, to the left.

"There," she said. "I think he would have something grand."

Trixie followed GG's gaze. "I'll go see," she said just as Ron arrived at her side.

She walked across a half dozen graves and then to the other side of the stone to read the inscription.

Oscar E. Garland

Died

Nov 3 1891

She could feel her heartbeat in her ears, and her feet felt inexplicably mired to the ground. She locked eyes with Ron's across the distance and gave a little nod, enough to spur him into action as he opened the car door and gently helped GG from it. He braced one arm behind her back and reached across himself to hold her hand, bending low as he walked to ensure that she had safety on all sides. The two took careful steps across the uneven terrain, and Trixie loved them both more and more with each one.

"Here, GG," she said when they arrived, stepping to the opposite side as they brought her around to read the stone. "It's him."

She would never be able to adequately describe the sound GG made at that moment. A strangled mixture of relief and pain, like a reunion not only with a loved one but with love itself. She cupped one hand to her mouth and reached the other out to touch the obelisk atop the stone.

"Oh Oscar, Oscar." She reached back for Trixie's hand, and Trixie knew.

EPILOGUE

𝒯he most difficult decision of Trixie Gowan's professional life was choosing the right color for Lost Laura's calico dress. Red seemed too garish, green too ambiguous, yellow too likely to bleed, blue too Holly Hobbie. In the end, she went with a purple, something between plum and mulberry, with tiny periwinkle dots and a white pinafore. In the first of her six-panel Sunday debut, she is sitting in a detailed, fussy Victorian chair, looking like the portrait of any nineteenth-century girl, with one braid properly behind her back and the other slightly elevated above her shoulder. In panel after panel, she stands up, moves away from the chair, looks out a window, opens a door, and steps outside. There is a progression of color throughout, until she is surrounded by the full-blown beauty of a summer day. Next, she is running on a grassy field, flying a kite emblazoned with an even more cartoonish image of herself. The final panel is only her face, in more close-up detail than Trixie had ever depicted. She spent forever on that portrait, trying to get the proportion of the neck and jawline just right, the long nose with its bulbous tip, the hair a shade that would be accurate yet easily replicable. She added a bit of curl to the wisps around the face and the slightest downturn of the eyes. The expression on Lost Laura's face was one of discovery and surprise, her braids snaking up to the corners of the panel.

"What do you think?" she'd said to Ron after the final stroke of her pen. She had replaced her little kitchen table with a substantial drafting desk and worked best in the mornings when the natural light poured in. When she finished the last panel, however, it was almost seven o'clock at night, and Ron was busy at her stove sautéing something that smelled delicious.

He came and looked over her shoulder. "Oh wow, Trixie. It's you."

"Is it?" She showed him the illustration torn from her third copy of *These Happy Golden Years*. "Look."

He regarded both with a barely perceptible move of his head. "It's her too."

"*Too?*"

"Your wit. Her wisdom."

She smiled and kissed him, getting a taste of the supper yet to come. "You always have the perfect thing to say."

Now, on a September evening, she looked at the strip, cut from the Sunday paper and secured to the refrigerator at the Gowan house with a Niagara Falls souvenir magnet. Trixie smiled at it as she shut the door, her arms full of a variety of cans of pop. Ron manned this stove too, flipping a series of grilled cheese sandwiches to be cut into triangles and stacked high on the family platter. The popper was full of fat, yellow bursts of popcorn ready for butter and salt. There were chocolate chip cookies and apple slices and a bowl of pickles—everything that constituted a Gowan family TV feast. Ron's first and Trixie's last, as a Gowan, anyway. That is if she decided to take Ron's name, which she hadn't yet.

"*I can't go through life as Trixie Tumble,*" she'd said the night he proposed. "*You have to be okay with that.*"

"It's starting," Eugenie called from the living room.

Trixie glanced at the clock. 7:45. "No, it's not."

"It almost is! We'll need time to make our plates."

"And don't forget to add the dash of Heinz 57 to the dipping sauce." This from Trixie's mother who breezed through the kitchen to grab the cans of pop. She stopped long enough to give Ron's stack of sandwiches a show of approval.

"Are you sure you want to marry into this clan?" Trixie asked, going back to the refrigerator to retrieve the condiments from the door.

"Maybe we should reserve all judgment until you meet my family at Thanksgiving," Ron said, retrieving a small bowl from the top shelf of the cabinet at Trixie's direction. "This platter of sandwiches? My brothers and I could tear it down ourselves during a commercial break at halftime."

"Well, that sounds manly."

He nuzzled the back of her neck, but she elbowed him away, putting him to work pouring catsup out of the bottle into the bowl over the small mound of mayonnaise. As instructed, she shook in a bit of Heinz 57 sauce and gave it all a stir, ready to be spooned onto plates for sandwich dipping. "GG would have a fit," she said, gathering as much as she could carry, "having a man over to supper and serving grilled cheese sandwiches and snacks."

"Not if the man is me," Ron said, taking the platter with the golden pyramid. "She loved me."

"I wish you could have known her more."

"I know you. I love you. In a way, that's just the same."

Trixie led the way into the front room, where Alma and Eugenie sat on their respective ends of the sofa, TV trays ready and waiting. The coffee table in the middle of the room had been cleared of magazines and mail and the piles of paperwork that came with death. Ron and Trixie soon filled it with plates and platters and bowls, and the four of them circled it like a miniature buffet. Ron stood, plate in hand, looking around the room a bit unsure.

"You can take Grandma's seat," Alma said, gesturing to the worn blue recliner.

"I'm over here," Trixie said, finding her familiar chair.

"If you want to sit together, do it at your own place," Eugenie said, plopping behind her tray. "We've all grown accustomed."

Trixie shot him an unapologetic look and shrugged her shoulders before settling in. "We can make up for it later by making out on the landing."

"Hush," Alma said. "It's starting."

The room was aglow with television light. The screen filled with a prairie blue sky, and four lonesome notes sounded from a French horn. Strings filled out a score that sounded like something watered down from a western film. Sparse trees on the horizon, a sloping plain scattered with wildflowers. *Little House on the Prairie.*

"*Whoop! Whoop!*" Ron said, raising his pop can in salute. Alma and Eugenie hushed him, but Trixie's heart swelled with love and pride and something that made her want to drop her dinner and drag him into the next room and kiss his beard off.

A wagon appeared in the distance, zooming in on a handsome, smiling couple—she tucking strands of hair into a sunbonnet, and he—

"Michael Landon," Alma said, her voice one long, appreciative sigh.

"Oh, he makes my cheese melt," Eugenie said, sandwich poised on the corner of her bottom lip.

"That is one handsome man," Ron confirmed before shoving a handful of popcorn in his mouth.

Trixie countered them all: "Did the producers ever even *see* a picture of Charles Ingalls?"

The camera panned to show three little girls running down the hillside. The first, obviously Laura, with an impish smile and bouncing braids. The second, Mary, with ash-blond locks flowing freely, unfettered. And finally, the littlest. Carrie? Yes, Carrie, who took a few steps, lost control of herself, and went tumbling boots-over-buttons down the hill. Trixie's mother and grandmother chuckled at the sight, but Ron sat forward, saying, "Man. I hope she's all right. Probably scraped up her little hands."

The show went to a commercial immediately after the opening scene.

"You know that tumbling girl would have been GG's favorite moment," Trixie said, nibbling an apple slice.

"You know we wouldn't be watching this at all if she was still with us," Eugenie said. "When that TV movie came on last spring, she said she'd chuck the set out the window if we watched it."

"Well," Alma said, "she's over all of that now. Probably chatting with the real Laura, catching up on old times."

"Somehow, I doubt that," Trixie said. The last words she ever heard from GG's mouth came late in the afternoon after the drive home from the cemetery at Willow Lake. The old woman had dozed on and off, an odd, sweet smile reaching through her sleep. When they got home, Ron carried her upstairs like a child, and Trixie put her to bed, fully dressed atop the covers, with a flannel sheet draped softly over her.

"Thank you," she'd said as Trixie was walking away.

"It was nice," Trixie said, making her way back.

"He always loved her, you know."

"Who?" Trixie was kneeling now, unwilling to miss a word.

"Laura." The utterance was little more than the whisper of a dry leaf against a stone. "He loved her, but he gave himself to me."

She'd closed her eyes, and Trixie kissed her weathered cheek, her smooth brow, and finally, her thin, contented lips. Downstairs, Ron had been waiting to take her home, and the next day—after meeting with The Guy, she'd gone back to her apartment to find a message on her answering machine from Cam.

She passed peacefully, sweetheart. Like walking away in a dream.

It seemed fitting that she'd heard the news from Cam, sparing her the histrionics of her mother or Eugenie's overt stoicism. When Trixie dialed the house, it was Cam who answered the phone, narrating GG's final moments.

"I was just checking in," he'd said, "and when I went upstairs, she'd passed. I don't think I've ever seen a face so at peace. Like her beauty had been waiting all this time to show through."

Trixie tasted the salt of her tears on the phone's mouthpiece. "You're not just telling me what I want to hear?"

Cam's chuckle was more comforting than it should have been. "No, Trix. Not at all. Call me if you need anything. To talk or—anything."

He gave her his home number, but she didn't write it down.

They spoke at the funeral, and afterward, back at the house, were herded toward one another by well-meaning cupids who didn't know what she and Cam knew: that sometimes first love exists as a foundation for new love. Trixie spent the day threading herself through small talk and stories, finding her way back to Ron's side, checking up. Checking in. Rescuing him from the ever-curious Samantha who seemed bent on conquering him with questions, trying to stump him.

"You can convince a kid of anything if you say it with confidence," Ron said after Trixie lured Samantha away with the promise of peanut butter cookies. "I just told her that penguins are actually aliens on earth, and she totally bought it."

She'd leaned into Ron as they watched Samantha tear through the crowd to deliver this revelation to Cam, who bent down to listen, nodded sagely, and sent a look of amused disapproval in their direction.

Now, as the credits rolled on the premiere episode of *Little House on the Prairie*, Trixie felt a strange little lump of affection, wondering if Samantha and her mother were curled up together somewhere in the big city, watching. Her own mother and grandmother were still recovering from the sight of Michael Landon, shirtless, his California-tanned torso wrapped in an ace bandage after a misfortune in a feedstore when Trixie turned off the television and declared she had no reason to ever watch another episode of *Little House on the Prairie*.

"Aw," Eugenie said, "I thought it was sweet."

"So sweet," Trixie said, "like I need to go to the dentist."

"That's the dozen cookies you ate," Alma said, gathering up the empty plates. "But thank you both for making the drive out here to enjoy the premiere with us."

"Thanks for inviting us," Ron said.

Eugenie gave him a strong pat on his cheek. "You're a good man, wanting to hang out with a couple of old ladies and watch TV."

"We're practically family now, right?" Ron said, sending Trixie a glance, pleading rescue.

"Family who sleeps in separate rooms," Alma said over her shoulder on her way into the kitchen.

"There's irony speaking," Trixie said out of the corner of her mouth. She took Ron's hand. "Come on, I'll take you to my old room."

"You know," Ron said, taking in a deep breath, "I think I might head back into town tonight."

"Now? It'll be after midnight before you get home."

"Want to come with me? Or are you staying?"

"Didn't you hear me? *Midnight*."

"And? You don't have an office to get to in the morning." Trixie's advance had allowed her to quit her position at the *Newz*, which she did with some reluctance.

"No, but you do."

"I'm the boss, remember? Nobody needs me. I'd be late in the morning anyway. This way I won't be late with a broken back from sleeping on a girly twin bed."

"Okay." She leaned in and gave him a kiss, enjoying the new familiarity of the act. "But be careful. It's dark on those country roads. Call me when you get there?"

"Did you forget that we came in your car?"

"I trust you."

"Now that, my girl, is love."

Trixie rifled through her purse and found her keys, then grabbed an afghan from the back of the couch and wrapped it around her shoulders for the walk outside. The stars were out in full force and the air sweet with the smell of harvest. At her car, she leaned her hip against the door. He followed suit, wrapping his arms around her as she lifted hers over his shoulders, encasing them both in GG's soft crochet. This time when he kissed her, there would be no mistake, no forgetting, no hiding of intent. His mouth was warm against the backdrop of the chilly night.

"Are you sure you don't want to come home with me?" he murmured against her cheek.

"I'm sure it's a good thing you're not sleeping across the hall," she said.

He made a growly sound and pulled her closer, something she would have thought impossible only moments ago. "I love you, Trixie Gowan."

"I love you, Ron Tumble."

"And you'll marry me?"

"Yes."

"Any idea when?"

"No. But soon, I promise. Will you check on House in the morning and give him breakfast? You know Mrs. Claxon will let him starve."

He kissed her again, inching her away from the door. "I will. Now get back inside. It's cold out here."

On a warmer evening, she might have put up a flirtatious fight, but the wind had picked up for the night. She tugged the afghan close and sprinted for the porch, reminding him to call her as soon as he was home. Inside, she shouted a good night to the house at large and ran upstairs to GG's room to watch from the window as her own headlights disappeared into the night.

She'd left her overnight bag in her old room (Ron had never taken his from the car), and when she crossed the hall and flipped the light switch, all the remnants of her past life here came into stark view. There was nothing shocking or unfamiliar; the room had remained largely unchanged for well over a decade, and she'd been here nearly every other weekend after GG died to help with arrangements and fill the new bit of emptiness in the house. Now, though, looking at the trophies and ribbons, the photographs and posters and dressers stuffed with jerseys and sweaters that belonged to another girl—another life—she could only look at the bed and think, *I don't want to dream here.* She grabbed her toothbrush and pajamas, her sketchbook and pen, and went back to the room that held much warmer memories.

They'd changed out the mattress and bedding since GG passed and had donated her clothes to a woman's charity in De Smet, knowing none of the women in the household could begin to fit into them. Crossing in the dark, Trixie lit the lamp by the bedside, bringing a perfect circle of warm light into the room. She left it to go into the bathroom where she washed up for the night, catching a glimpse of herself in the mirror as she ran a warm washcloth across her face. Her shoulders were broad, nearly filling the vanity mirror. Her mother always told her she had the shoulders of a teenage boy—something not meant to be flattering to a girl in a sundress. But maybe. . .

She put on her pajamas and climbed into GG's bed—no, the *new* bed. Never slept in, under sheets and blankets brand-new, never used. Angling it to the light, she opened her sketchbook and began a swift rendering of her own frame. Broad shoulders, narrow waist, long neck. In her left hand, she gripped an assortment of colored pencils and took one at a time, covering the frame with a pair of high-waisted brown pants, a dapper blue-and-yellow striped shirt with a flat collar buttoned to the top. Black suspenders, brown shoes. Flipping to a clean page, she worked the details of the face. Long nose, minus the bulb. Hooded eyes, which today would be called *bedroom*, but no one would have said that where he came from. A mixture of butter and gold for his hair and moustache. She absentmindedly touched the mole on the hinge of her jaw, just below her ear, and—with the stroke of a pencil—gave him one too. She flipped the page and drew him again, head to toe, features miniaturized, all black and white and shading. She flipped the page and drew him again, faster this time, moving his body, finding his stance, his posture. She flipped the page and drew him again, this time with her—with Laura, fitting them together.

But there was something missing. Something he needed for his final bit of personality. Something to capture his otherworldliness, to show that he felt more at home in sepia tones than in the color printed pages of a Sunday newspaper. She turned back to the first drawing, the mannequin sketch of a man, his head nothing more than a shape to bring proportion. Gripping a burgundy-lead pencil, she drew then shaded a perfectly angled newsboy cap. Then she went back, adding it to each rendition, perfecting the angle, realizing it could carry expression the same way Laura's braids did—lifted off his head in surprise, dropped low in consternation.

"Hello there. . ." Who? Not Oscar; he wasn't an Oscar. Not Cap, either.

Trixie tapped a pencil to her chin, thinking. Then stopped, remembering.

She climbed out of bed and crossed over to GG's tall dresser, taking the pristine first edition of *These Happy Golden Years* from its resting place in the top drawer. Opening the front cover, she found the photograph, a tall, white gravestone topped with a smooth white concrete ball. Ron had taken her back to the cemetery at Willow Lake sometime after GG's burial in their family plot.

"I feel like I should tell him," she'd said, knowing the idea was equally romantic and ridiculous.

Ron responded to the romance.

There she'd snapped a picture and had it developed by the guys at the *Newz*. Just one copy, slipped inside this book. She brought it over to the light and looked close, jogging her memory. Oscar Ed Garland.

She looked back through her sketches. "Hello, Eddie."

Trixie drew through the night. Drew them holding hands, eating pizza, dodging geese. She shaded blush to their cheeks, perfected their tension, created a secret, antique word for their unspoken attraction. She made notes on where they would meet, what they would say. A bar, of course, giving a nod to this modern world. But their order? Sarsaparilla, spoken in perfect unison. And when? *Thanksgiving*. The Sunday after meeting Ron's parents. She'd be ready then too to take a new step. And that morning, across the country, for everyone to see, Lost Laura was going to look up and find love.

FINAL NOTES

I have always had a crush on Cap Garland. Always. He seemed more fun than Almanzo—bolder, somewhat dangerous. Rereading the Wilder books in preparing to write this story, I have to wonder if Laura didn't feel that too. Just a bit.

The manner in which Oscar Garland dies in this story is true to his story. His reputation as a scoundrel is embellished by my imagination. I spent a summer afternoon looking for his grave, standing beside it when the air was thick with the scent of the Canadian fires, and the only sound, wind blowing through the cornfield. That journey wasn't necessary for the research—I had photos of the grave marker and knew the horrific details of his death. But I wanted to go, wanted to see it for myself. It was a lovely, peaceful few moments. The light of late afternoon hung somewhere between violet and gray. His marker stands for the tragedy of a life cut short but a legacy that lives beyond anything he could have imagined.

The characters of Charles and Mariah (Martha/Marthe) have also been given a story line bred purely from my imagination. My research shows that the two as described in both *These Happy Golden Years* and *Pioneer Girl* aren't found in any official records in the area. Perhaps they were cut from Wilder's imagination too. Or they may have been created from the personae of other Bouchie (Brewster in the novel) children. Since they are kind of free-floating in history, I snatched them up and planted them in my pages.

One thing I learned in writing this story is that it is just as challenging to research and represent history from fifty years ago as it is history from five hundred years ago and all the years-ago in between. As such, I beg readers to forgive a few story choices I made that might not particularly jive with history. First, I cannot say with certainty that *Carousel* aired as the Sunday Night Movie in June 1974. I also took liberty with the Dr Pepper slogan "Be a Pepper," describing Great-Grandmother Mariah as "a Pepper" before the slogan was coined. But, really, wasn't she a Pepper? Fans of the beverage will agree with me. Finally, as the family gathers to watch the premiere of *Little House on the Prairie*, I like to note that this was not actually the premiere of the series, as its true first airing was as a television movie the previous spring.

I have to say a huge thank-you to the lovely docents and hostesses and guides at the Laura Ingalls Wilder Historic Home and Museum in De Smet, South Dakota. They are so gracious and devoted to Laura and her family. I showed up with a million questions and left inspired to research a few more. Some of those questions turned into this book. Others will turn up in the next one. And—my husband, Mikey, will forever be my hero for letting me drag him through it all.

Finally, I have no scientific proof that a cat can accurately alphabetize anything. But as the owner of three, it wouldn't surprise me.

ALLISON PITTMAN is the author of more than a dozen critically acclaimed novels and a four-time Christy finalist—twice for her Sister Wife series, once for *All for a Story* from her take on the Roaring Twenties, and most recently for the critically acclaimed *The Seamstress*, which takes a cameo character from the Dickens classic *A Tale of Two Cities* and whisks her to life amid the French Revolution. Allison Pittman lives in San Antonio, Texas, blissfully sharing an empty nest with her husband, Mike. Connect with her on Facebook (Allison Pittman Author), Twitter (@allisonkpittman), or her website, allisonkpittman.com.

Doors to the Past

Visit historic American landmarks through the **Doors to the Past** series. History and today collide in stories full of mystery, intrigue, faith, and romance.

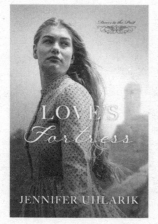

LOVE'S FORTRESS
By Jennifer Uhlarik

Upon receiving word that her long-estranged father has passed away, Dani Sango inherits the former art forger's entire estate. Among his many pieces of artwork are a series of Native American drawings and paintings, which lead her to research St. Augustine of 1875. Broken Bow is transported to Florida to join other Cheyenne braves already being held in Fort Marion. Sally Jo Harris is at the fort teaching the Indians. When a friendship develops between them and false accusations fly, it could cost them their lives. Can Dani discover how their story ends and how it shaped her own father's life?

Paperback / 978-1-63609-181-5 / $12.99

A PROMISE ENGRAVED
By Liz Tolsma

Young, spirited Josie Wilkins's life is about to take a turn when faced with political turmoil and forbidden love in San Antonio of 1836. Will she survive an epic battle to leave a legacy of love? Nearly two hundred years later, Kayleigh Hernandez takes breaks from her job as a refugee coordinator working with Mexican migrants to attend flea markets, where she has found a uniquely engraved ring. Enlisting the help of appraiser Brandon Shuman, they piece together a love story long forgotten. But will dangers linked to Kayleigh's work end her own hopes for leaving a legacy built on hope, faith, and love?

Paperback / 978-1-63609-249-2 / $12.99